Death's Intern

The Intern Diaries Series- Book 1

D. C. Gomez

Death's Intern Copyright © D. C. Gomez (2017).

All rights reserved. This book is a work of fiction. No part of this publication may be reproduced, stored in a retrieval system, or transmitted, in any form or by any means, without the prior written permission of the author, except for the use of brief quotations in a book review.

Cover design by Christine Gerardi Designs

ISBN-13: 9781977585349 for Paperback Editions

ISBN: 978-1-7333160-8-8 for Hardcover Editions

Published by Gomez Expeditions

Request to publish work from this book should be sent to: author@dcgomez-author.com

For Antonio and Kathleen:
thank you for being my own dream team.

Chapter One

Friday night, and I was living the dream. Yeah, right! I had cleaned the same three tables at least fifty times in the last three hours at Abuelita's. Abuelita's was a small—OK, more like a hole-in-the-wall—Tex-Mex restaurant in Texarkana, Texas. Of all the places I had ever dreamed of living and had moved to, staying there was beyond me. To make things even more confusing, Texarkana had a twin city, Texarkana, Arkansas. I guess the founders were not very creative with the name selection, but who was I to judge? Compared to most major cities, Texarkana was a tiny dot on the map. For the locals, it was the largest city within sixty miles in any direction. It was by accident that I'd found it. Located on the northeast tip of Texas, it was in the middle of everything and near nowhere.

I was sure my godmother would love this. I'd promised myself I would never follow in her footsteps of wandering like a nomad. Now here I was, in my fifth town in less than six months. The good news was that I had managed to stay here the longest, a whole three months. I was probably brain-dead—I had moved to Texas in the middle of summer. With the temperatures hitting over ninety degrees and with over 90 percent humidity, I was surprised I hadn't melted. My curiosity in learning everything about the King of Ragtime was now extinguished. I was sure I understood why Mr. Joplin had left. Why hadn't I just read *Wikipedia*? According to the calendar, fall was six days away, and the weather was still suffocating.

"Isis, are you listening to me?" Oops. I had blanked out Abuelita's voice from the kitchen.

Abuelita had named the place after herself. More accurately, she had used her nickname. In her words, the only thing she was after her husband and daughter died was a grandmother. She embraced it and became a grandmother to the world. Her place was open to everyone, and a wide diversity of people patronized the place. Abuelita was probably in her late sixties and tall, around five eleven, with a solid body. I was a couple of inches shorter, and it was odd to have a woman taller than me in this area. She was still strong and beautiful, with her silver hair. That shiny silver hair was the only indication of her age. She had been blessed with genes that aged in slow motion, like most Latinas.

"I'm sorry, Abuelita. I was distracted." I sucked at lying, so no need to even try.

"With what? We haven't had a soul in hours. Not even our regulars came in. Start getting the place ready for tomorrow. No need to waste time. Might as well close early today."

I was speechless. In the three months I had been working there, Abuelita had never closed early. Granted, it was already 9:00 p.m., and we normally closed at 11:00 p.m. So it wasn't that early, but without customers, the cleanup was done. Closing usually took us at least an hour. I was not planning to argue with Abuelita. She was a very eccentric woman. I was sure she and my godmother would have bonded instantly. I really needed to call her. She was the only family I had.

The dining area of Abuelita's had three tables, with four chairs each. Two of the tables were by the large window at the front of the restaurant. The register area doubled as a bar, with six stools on the dining side. I took a chair by the window with a stack of forks, knives, and spoons. I was not in any hurry. There was plenty of silverware wrapped in napkins already since nobody had come in. Abuelita's faced Highway 82, past Walmart and the other Mexican restaurant heading toward Nash. Normally, I saw the high school kids driving around. Tonight, even the highway was a ghost area. A bit creepy for my taste.

It was probably a blessing it was empty, because Angelito was missing. Angelito was Abuelita's grandson and the other staff member on weekends with me. The only thing angelic about that boy was his name. He went through more girls than most people went through underwear. In his mind, he was a ladies' man, and unfortunately for the ladies, he was hot. At twenty-one he was over six feet tall and weighed maybe around 180 pounds, with a great complexion and incredible hazel eyes. The one great thing about Angelito was that he lived with his grandmother. He was a spoiled boy, but he adored his grandma. If Abuelita told him she needed him, he would change his plans for her.

I could have passed for his older sister. Angelito and Abuelita were of Mexican descent but looked European. I could have passed for anything, from Italian to even Middle Eastern. My parents died when I was little, and my Gypsy godmother wasn't sure of their nationalities. I could be anything, with my long, thick black hair and mocha complexion that could place me anywhere in the world. For most of my life, I'd been described as exotic. I guess it was a better way of saying *outcast*. It didn't help that my parents had named me Isis—Isis Black. In the age of terrorists, I had the worst name on the planet.

At times, I wondered what kind of parents I had who would trust their only daughter to a woman like my godmother. Don't get me wrong; my godmother was a beautiful woman with an incredibly caring soul. She was also a little rebel with a complete disregard for authority. Maybe my subconscious was rebelling against my upbringing when I joined the military. I was sure my godmother would have been proud if I had joined a band or run away with the circus. I kind of did both by joining the Eighty-Second Airborne's band.

Oh, there it was again—that same weird Mustang. That was the fifth time that it had driven by tonight. Hard to miss a greenish-yellow car. It almost looked sick. Why would anyone buy a car like that? Instead of tinted windows, the car had an almost mirrorlike quality. Of course, I could hear its engines roaring from inside.

Around ten o'clock, just on cue, Bob showed up. Bob was a veteran. He was also homeless, as far as I knew. He had served in the first Gulf War. We joked that we had served in the same sandpit just decades apart. Bob was in his late forties, with sandy-blond hair and deep-green eyes. In his younger days, he had probably been very handsome. Now he rarely smiled, and most of the time, he was paranoid. Bob was also the one person I called a friend. My war stories made sense to him.

I ran behind the bar to the big window between the dining area and the kitchen. "Abuelita, Bob is here. May I take my break now?"

"Of course, Isis. We're still empty. Here's Bob's plate. At least I can count on Bob." Abuelita handed me a large plate of carnitas with rice and beans for Bob. According to Abuelita, Bob was a creature of habit. For the last three years, he had been coming in at exactly ten o'clock. Bob ate the same pork meal every Friday night and said very little.

Bob did odd jobs around the restaurant for Abuelita. He had once stopped a few kids from robbing Abuelita. Ever since, Bob was the unofficial night guard of the place. He made sure Abuelita locked up in peace. In return, Abuelita made sure he had a hot meal each night.

I took Bob his plate and brought quesadillas for myself. Unlike Bob, I would change my mind about dinner at least five times before ordering. Lucky for me, Abuelita's quesadillas were the best in town. It was pretty hard to mess up tortillas and cheese. I loved Abuelita's food, since she had a special menu for non-meat eaters.

"Hi, Bob. Are you ready for dinner?"

Bob was looking around the place with concern. I followed his gaze but couldn't see anything wrong. I took a seat on the picnic bench Abuelita had outside. After several long minutes, Bob joined me.

"Isis, any trouble tonight?" Bob sounded worried.

"It's been a cemetery around here all day," I replied between mouthfuls of food. How could I be hungry? I hadn't done a single thing all day.

"Don't joke about those things. Death walks the night." Bob was intense at times, but tonight, it was even more dramatic. *Death walks the night.* Was Bob drunk? OK, according to Bob, he had quit drinking years ago. But that was just odd.

"Bob, it was just a figure of speech. Nobody came in all night, including death." I was aiming for funny and clever.

Bob didn't even blink. "Isis, make sure you go directly home tonight. It's not right tonight." Bob was staring at me with those piercing sea-green eyes.

"It's going to be hard to clear my busy schedule, but for you, I'll do it."

I think he missed the sarcasm in my voice, because he visibly relaxed and started eating his food.

"Oh yeah, Angelito didn't come in today." Bob arched an eyebrow at me. I swallowed quickly and proceeded to explain before Bob decided to go full assault squad in search of Angelito. "Nothing major. Abuelita said he has a new girlfriend. He met her this week, I guess."

"Have you ever wondered where he finds all those girls? Texarkana has fewer than a hundred thousand people when you combine the Texas and Arkansas sides. Most people are either related by blood or marriage. How is he not dead from messing with the wrong family?"

Wow. That was the longest speech Bob had ever given all at once. Angelito's wild life must have really been puzzling Bob for him to say that much. I was nice and didn't point out how he had used death to describe Angelito's potential future. I didn't need another lecture.

"According to him, he doesn't lie, and he doesn't make any promises he can't keep, so nobody is ever mad at him. I'm twenty-five, and I haven't met a twenty-one-year-old boy who didn't lie about himself." I didn't have the best track record with men my age, so I was probably not a great judge of character.

"You sound a little jaded there." Bob was very talkative today. I didn't think Bob was that good at reading people. Or maybe I just needed to work on not being so transparent.

"Thank you, Captain Obvious." I added a glare for good measured.

"Anytime, Grasshopper." Bob actually smiled at me. Maybe my dad was a little like Bob—focused but not taking himself too seriously. Bob was suffering from terrible spells of PTSD, so he couldn't hold down a job. PTSD was the new term the government was using to describe what most returning vets were going through, post-traumatic stress disorder. According to Bob, it was hard to take yourself too seriously when you were struggling.

Bob finished his food and started to look around the place. At that same moment, the pale Mustang drove by. I was staring east on 82 after it when Bob turned to face me.

"What's wrong?" He had that worried tone again.

"Oh, nothing. Just been seeing a car driving around here tonight." I started yawning. Slow nights were painful. At the end of the day, you ended up tired and with nothing to show for it.

"Anything suspicious about it?" Now Bob was in full paranoid mode.

"Nothing really. Just an odd color. OK, we're closing early, so I need to hurry." I left with the empty plates before Bob could ask me more questions.

I walked directly to the kitchen with the plates. The kitchen area was immaculate. Abuelita ran a tight ship, and tonight, she was ready to go. I washed the plates and forks while Abuelita finished putting pots away.

"OK, Isis, you can take off." Abuelita didn't even turn around when she said it. I was ready for bed but didn't want to sound too excited. "Are you sure? I can help you lock up." I was really praying she would say no, but I would stay if she needed me.

"I'm good, child. Besides, Bob is doing his rounds. I'm sure I'll be OK." She smiled when she said that. Bob was very efficient.

"Thank you, Abuelita. Good night." I dried my hands and gave her a kiss on the cheek on my way out.

"Good night, Isis," she said as I ran out the door.

"Good night, Bob," I yelled at the night. There were no buildings near the little restaurant, so I knew sound would travel.

My minivan was parked in its usual place, the spot farthest from the restaurant. Abuelita liked her paying customers to have front-row parking.

The minivan was old and beaten up, and it had once been midnight blue. Now it was just a faded blue. My godmother had given it to me, and I had nicknamed it the Whale. I wasn't complaining; the Whale saved me on gas, and I could pack my whole life into it. On top of that, it was paid for. I opened the door and was blasted by the heat that was still trapped inside. How could it be in the high eighties in September?

This night, I was ready to go home to my small apartment on Summerhill Road. It was a seven-minute drive using the service roads next to 30, Highway 30, but I was exhausted all of a sudden.

Chapter Two

Did I mention that everything I owned fit into the Whale? That included everything in my one-bedroom apartment. It wasn't in one of the fancy complexes in town, but for $400 a month, I wasn't complaining. Compared to my last apartment in Washington Heights in New York, this was luxury.

I owned a small futon that doubled as my bed and sofa. A wicker table sat in the middle with my books and sheet music. The bedroom was actually my studio, where my sax hung out. Most of my clothes were in plastic storage containers from Walmart. The bathroom was next to the bedroom. A small hallway with appliances made the kitchen area. It was a good thing I didn't cook much, because there was barely any room in the kitchen to walk around. I loved cooking, but it's too much trouble to cook for just one person.

Most of my stuff had come from Walmart. I probably had an obsession with the supercenter—or, more accurately, I couldn't afford any other place. I spent way too much time wandering the store buying things I didn't need, like more books. The apartment had no curtains, or even pictures on the wall. I never bothered with that stuff. I was never in one place long enough to settle. I had piles of books all over the apartment; they were neat and organized. I just refused to buy bookshelves. Those things were hard to move. On the positive side, everything was paid for, and I had no debt. Keeps things simple when you need to move in a hurry.

There was a knock at my door. It was almost eleven, and I had no friends. All the people I knew, I'd left at Abuelita's. Texarkana was a relatively safe city by my standards, and I wasn't too excited to get killed there. When it comes to crime rates, most people have a hard time looking at the big picture. For the natives, Texarkana was becoming too big and dangerous. They wanted to keep the small-town feel. When people know your name at the restaurant you frequent, you live in a small town. No matter what the natives believe. With that in mind, I grabbed my bat and walked to the door.

"Who is it?" I tried to make my voice sound mean and menacing. Instead, I sounded as if I had swallowed a frog. Just my luck.

"I have a message from Brooklyn. Could we talk?" a female voice said. The voice had a slight accent, maybe European. She sounded friendly, but the Brooklyn part didn't make me feel better. I had left Brooklyn in a hurry. Besides my godmother, nobody from that life knew where I was.

"Isis, we can talk in private, or we can do it this way. It's up to you."

How did she know my name? I slowly opened the door with my left hand, keeping my right on the bat. I peered through the crack, trying to look mean.

I had heard stories that when Death comes for you, your life flashes before your eyes. Well, that was a lie. My life didn't flash. Instead, everything froze. As I stared at the woman on my threshold, I knew I was seeing Death. Don't get me wrong; I'm not talking about someone who was there to kill me. I was actually staring at Death herself, the Grim Reaper. Why Death was wearing a very expensive designer suit and four-inch heels was beyond me. For that matter, why was Death beautiful, with a curvaceous body and long, silky brown hair?

"Can I come in now, or do you just plan to stare at me?" There was mischief in her voice, and I couldn't help but feel a bit sheepish.

"Sure, why not?" If Death was at my door, there was no point in hiding.

"Do you know who I am?" She strolled into the apartment and did a quick scan. She was wearing a light jacket over her suit. I guess Death doesn't feel heat or cold, because it was still too warm for all those layers even in September.

"Death." The word came out harsh, even for me. That was all I was able to say. I was feeling nauseated.

"Not bad. May I?" She pointed at the futon. I nodded. She slowly took a seat with a grace I had seen only in Miss America pageants. I had a couple of folding chairs by a wall, but I was too shocked to move.

"Are you here to kill me?" I found the courage to ask.

Death raised an eyebrow and analyzed me. "Sorry, dear, I'm not in the killing business. I'm more in the delivery one. So, no, I'm here because we have some business to attend to."

I was totally lost. What did "delivery business" mean, and why did I have business with Death?

"Ma'am, I'm sorry, but I'm not following you." Nobody could accuse me of not being polite. I was feeling pretty brave. I had spoken a whole sentence to Death.

"Do you remember Brooklyn, March ninth?"

Was she serious? I was so dead. This was getting worse by the minute.

"Unfortunately, I can't forget it." There was no need to lie to this woman—or being, or whatever she was. I'd had an ongoing countdown in my head starting on that day. It had been six months and six days exactly.

"Good. Tell me what happened." She leaned back and waited. I wasn't sure she was breathing.

"Excuse me? What?" The horror on my face was probably showing, because Death smiled very gently at me.

"Relax, dear. I want to hear your side of the story. So, start from the moment you got to the party. And try not to leave anything out, OK?" The voice was soothing but firm. She was leaving no room for interpretation. She wanted the truth, and she wanted it now. I took a breath and then exhaled.

"My friend Tamara invited me to a party at one of her friend's. I was planning to leave the following week. I wasn't adjusting and couldn't find work. I was planning a road trip. Tamara was one of the few friends I had made up there, and she actually wanted me to stay. I'd been out of the military for almost two months at the time, and I was already miserable. We made it to the party around ten p.m., and the place was packed. It was on the seventh floor of an apartment building in Brooklyn. The residents had moved out but hadn't turned in the keys.

"The music was loud, and you couldn't walk without brushing against people. Couples were making out everywhere. The smell of weed was thick in the air, and everyone looked drunk. I found myself getting sweaty hands. My heart rate increased, and I knew I was having a panic attack. I was feeling claustrophobic, and my senses were in overdrive. I had lost Tamara as soon as we walked in. I tried to head toward the door, but people kept grabbing and pulling at my clothes.

"I eventually made my way to the back and found a fire escape. I just wanted to get some fresh air before I broke down in the middle of the crowd. I swear I never meant to hurt anyone." I had never told that story to anyone. My palms were sweating again, and tears were rolling down my cheeks.

"What happened next?" Death was so still, it was overwhelming. I wasn't sure why she'd asked; by the look on her face, she already knew the answer.

"The window was open, so I climbed out. Unfortunately, when I was trying to get up, I accidentally knocked someone down. It all happened so fast. At the time, I had no idea what I pushed. I tried to catch it. It was followed by a loud scream. By the time I made it to the ledge, there was a body on the ground. Please believe me; it was an accident. I went back inside and rushed back down. I wasn't sure how safe the fire escape was. The apartment was even more crowded. It took me longer than I expected to get down. When I got to the street, the body was gone." I was nervous. I knew I was rambling, but I couldn't stop talking or crying. I was trying to calm down while Death continued analyzing me. "Is he dead?"

"Unfortunately, dear, yes he is. No human can survive a fall like that. And he is the reason I'm here." Death shifted her body. I had the full weight of her stare on me. "The young man you killed was my intern."

"Your what?" I was grateful I was standing, because I was getting ready to bolt for the door.

"Relax, Isis, and please sit down before you faint." The statement was more of an order than a suggestion. Her demeanor was strong, and I felt as if I were in Death's house instead of mine. I pulled up one of the folding chairs and dropped myself down. This was so bad; it was hurting my head.

"So, are you here to take revenge for your intern?" That was all I was able to say very softly.

"I told you already, I'm not here to kill you." Death was getting annoyed. I could tell, but I wasn't sure what to say.

"There are things worse than death." I had heard stories of pure damnation.

"That is very true, dear. Hopefully, my proposal won't sound that bad." Death took a breath, not because she needed it but more for emphasis. "With the loss of my intern, I'm in need of a new one. Since you killed him, the job is now yours."

"Say what? What job? Wait. What are you talking about?"

Death actually smiled at me. She probably was thinking I was mentally challenged. "The rules are simple, dear. You kill my intern, and in turn, you take his place. That is, if I find you an acceptable candidate. You passed."

I was starting to feel like Tim Allen in *The Santa Clause*. Granted, I was sure Tim had a much better deal than mine.

"Rules? Who makes these rules? This is nuts." I was yelling and pacing in front of Death. I wasn't sure when I got up from my chair, but this was madness.

"You can call it cosmic law—an eye for an eye, a tooth for a tooth. Or just karma. Whatever you prefer. Unfortunately, that's the rule." I was getting ready to interrupt her when Death raised her index finger, and I stopped moving—even breathing. "I do believe in free will, dear. I don't want people working for me who don't want the job. But before you decide, I want you to meet a few friends of mine."

I had an incredulous look on my face. Death smiled gently at me. I wasn't sure whether I was supposed to say anything.

Death continued. "You might actually enjoy the fringe benefits of the job. Even more, you might find purpose again."

"With all due respect, Death, please don't act like you know me. You know nothing about what I want or need." I hated when my elders tried to put me in their boxes. I didn't care that it was Death making the assumptions.

She just kept giving me that infuriating smile. "Whatever you say, Isis. Please have a seat." Death's voice was even gentler, but it left no room for argument. I felt myself drawn to the chair again. "You will meet with my friends tonight, and you will have three days to decide whether you will take the job. The boys will fill you in on all the details."

"What makes you so sure I'll take this job?" Why was I arguing with Death? Oh, yeah. It was that horrible streak in me that hated being controlled.

Death got up from the futon and smoothed down her suit. She looked around my apartment, taking inventory. I felt offended.

"Things have been arranged, dear. Trust me, it will be your choice if you come work for me, but I'm sure it's a much better offer than what you have right now." Death walked around the table and stood next to my chair. She smiled down at me and then went over and kissed my forehead. Before I could complain, I felt my body shutting down, and I was slowly falling. In a blink of an eye, I blacked out.

Chapter Three

I heard voices, but I couldn't make them out. Was I dead? My eyelids were heavy, and there was a heavy weight on my chest. Death said she didn't kill people; maybe she had made an exemption.

"Constantine, get off her. You're killing her," I heard a man say. Or was it a boy?

"No way, dude. I don't weight that much," another male said—the one who was sitting on me. I tried to move but couldn't.

"You're at least fifteen pounds of solid fur, with pressure points directly on her chest." What was the boy talking about? Why was a man in a fur coat sitting on me? How does a grown man weigh only fifteen pounds?

I was finally able to open my eyes.

"Ahhhhh." I couldn't help it. I was staring at a pair of feline eyes inches from my face.

"See? I told you. She's not dead." It talked. The cat on my chest was talking. I was dead. There was no other explanation.

"Fine. You're right. Not dead. Can you get off her now? She might like to breathe properly now." The boy was sitting in front of three computer monitors to my left.

I was lying on a black leather couch. The cat jumped up and sat on the back of the couch glaring down at me. Directly in front of the couch was a fifty-inch flat-screen TV mounted on the wall. Above the computer stations, at least a dozen security monitors were mounted to the wall, each with a different image that changed every fifteen seconds. Instead of a wall on the right-hand side, there was wall-to-wall glass. The bottom half of the glass was darker. From my location I noticed we were on the second floor of a building. I guessed the boy and the cat were staring at me.

"Hi, I'm Bartholomew." The boy walked over to me and extended his hand. He looked to be around eleven, maybe five feet and less than a hundred pounds. He had wavy brown hair and hazel eyes.

After several long moments, I shook his hand. "Hi, I'm Isis." What was going on here?

"Isis? Like—"

"Not like the terrorist group."

"I was going to say like the Egyptian goddess," he said with a smile on his face. "You're a little too old to be named after that group."

"Oh, I'm sorry. Yes, you're right. Nobody ever guesses that." First person who had gotten it right, and I sounded like a royal jerk.

"I'm impressed. She's willing to apologize," the cat said.

I stared at him. My head was going to explode if I took any more of this. He was a handsome cat, a tabby with gorgeous stripes, but he was huge.

"Please tell me what's going on." My voice cracked, but I was too stunned to care.

"Like I said, I'm Bartholomew, and this is Constantine. Death brought you over." Bartholomew sounded way too cheery to be talking about Death.

"Am I dead? Or are you part of my three spirits that are here to tell me how to change my life?" Because my life had turned into a horrible Lifetime movie.

"Kid, you've been watching way too much TV. Death told you the deal. You kill her intern, you take his place. We're here to guide you," Constantine said very matter-of-factly. I was never going to get used to a talking cat.

"Constantine is the guardian. He's your walking resource guide to the supernatural world. Trust me, when it comes to that stuff, he's better than Google," Bartholomew said as he went back to his computer area.

"And what is your job here?" I needed to work on my people skills, but I had a talking cat on my left. At this point, I was too stunned to care.

"Your supply guy. Anything you want, I can get," Bartholomew said.

"He's also a hacker and a genius. If Death weren't his legal guardian and kept him off the grid, he would be on every watch list in the world," Constantine said, sounding very proud of the boy's skills.

I ran my hands over my face and hair. This was too much. I got off the couch to get my blood flowing. I could see the rest of the room. It was at least forty-five feet long, with a kitchen area on the far side and a dining place in the middle. A door on the right side led to what I assumed were bedrooms. A door on the left led to the staircase down. The building had a balcony that ran the whole perimeter of the building on the inside. It was about four feet wide. The first floor didn't have any windows; there were a few on the second floor above the balcony. The first floor was open space, and it looked like a house with a mechanic's workshop on one side and an impressive gym on the other. The greenish-yellow mustang was parked inside as well.

"Where are we?" I asked Bartholomew. I wasn't ready to talk to the cat.

"At Nash Business Park," he said, as if it were a normal thing.

"They let you build a house at the business park?" I obviously had not heard him right.

"She's a little slow. Maybe we got a damaged intern." Constantine actually looked concerned.

"From the outside, this looks like all the other warehouses here. Maybe a little bigger. We're forty-five by a hundred and ten feet, reinforced ballistic steel and concrete. Not to mention we're a registered business. We're Reapers Incorporated," Bartholomew said. I was totally lost.

"I'm in shock. I probably hit my head somewhere, and I'm hallucinating." My head was spinning. This was crazy.

"Oh, please don't faint." Bartholomew ran over to me and sat me back down. "Breathe in and out. Slowly." He was waving his hands trying to air me out. Any other time, I would have laughed.

"Bartholomew, get her the handbook," Constantine said from the couch.

Bartholomew hurried back to his desk and pulled a thin folder from his drawer. He gave Constantine an odd look. The cat nodded at him. With that blessing, he came over and handed me the folder. The thing looked like a brochure you get at a travel agency, but it read *Intern's Manual*.

"Are you serious?" I was holding a five-by-eight manual on how to be Death's intern.

Constantine jumped down from the back of the couch and stared at me. It was impossible, but it really felt as if he were staring down at me.

"You have three days to decide, and you have already wasted five hours. So, let's get to the rules. Rule number one: you cannot tell anyone you work for Death. Rule two: you cannot kill anyone unless it's in self-defense. Rule three: you cannot contact Death to get you out of trouble unless you are actually dying. At that point, it wouldn't matter because she would be around the corner. Rule four: This is your primary job. If you decide to have other employment—which I don't know why you would—those hours cannot conflict with ours. Rule five, any romantic relationship cannot interfere with your job. You'll find all the rules on page two of the manual." Constantine was not even taking a breath. Of course, he was a talking cat, so probably normal rules did not apply to him.

"Wait a minute. I haven't agreed to anything. I don't even know what Death's intern does. Why does Death need an intern to begin with?" I needed the insanity to end so I could go home.

"Finally, a reasonable question. We are in the *soul* business." Constantine had said *soul* very dramatically. If he had fingers, he would have made quotation marks with them. "Death delivers souls from this lifetime to their final destination."

"Where exactly would that be?" I had to ask. Honestly, that explanation made no sense.

"It depends on the person and how they lived their life. In your case, you would go to purgatory." Constantine delivered that news with no emotion.

"What? Why?" OK, I was outraged. How did he know that?

"You're Catholic, right?" Constantine asked, and I nodded yes. "OK, you killed a man."

"It was an accident." Did everyone know about that?

"Exactly. If you had actually wanted to murder him, you would be going to hell. Since it was an accident and you're an OK person, purgatory it is." Constantine obviously had practice in delivering horrible news. He wasn't even blinking.

"But don't I have a chance to repent or do something?" I was feeling pretty sick now.

"Listen, child, there are no lawyers in the afterlife. This is your dogma, not mine. We're in the business of helping souls move. What have you done to repent for your sins? When was the last time you went to confession? Those are the questions you should be asking yourself. So, back to business."

I was speechless. Constantine was right. In the last six months, all I had done was run away. I had never gone to confession, and I had been to Mass maybe a handful of times. I didn't have the excuse of not having any churches nearby. For being in the middle of the Baptist Bible Belt, Texarkana had two Catholic churches, one in each state. The churches were less than ten minutes from each other. Catholic churches were very rare in the South. Based on Constantine's speech, I was feeling like a horrible human being.

"Constantine to Isis; come in, Isis." Constantine had actually slapped me out of my pity party. He had the softest paws on the planet. "Are you listening to me?"

"Sorry; just contemplating my afterlife." My afterlife was looking pretty depressing.

"That's great, but you're not dead yet, so do that on your own time. The intern's job is easy. You monitor abnormal activities that might interfere with Death doing her thing." With that, Constantine leaned back and started licking his paw. I looked between Constantine and Bartholomew, totally lost.

"One more time, and in English this time. Abnormal activities?" These two were nuts.

"Bartholomew, break it down for her, please." Constantine didn't stop cleaning his paw when he spoke.

"Isis, it's simple. When people die, their souls separate from their bodies. Death is there to collect them. Souls are powerful, and, at times, other entities try to steal them. Death doesn't have time to track those incidents down, so the interns do." Bartholomew actually believed that made sense. Somebody help me!

"Interns? There's more than one intern?" Of all the things I had heard, why did that bother me?

"Of course, silly child. There's one per continent. Do you honestly think you could monitor the whole world? We're responsible for North America. This is going to take us a while." Constantine gave me that bored looked again, but at least he was done grooming himself.

"If you're responsible for all of North America, why would you pick Texarkana for a home base?" I was trying to sound just as snotty as Constantine.

"We didn't. You did. We're here because you're here," Bartholomew said very softly, trying to avoid my glare.

"We were doing fine in New York. You know how hard it is to find gluten-free food for this boy?" It was Constantine's turn to sound snippy.

There was no way I was responsible for them being there. "OK, this is crazy. I need to get home. I can't take any more of this." I got up to try to find the exit.

"Don't forget your manual. Your minivan is outside with the keys in the ignition. By the way, why does a twentysomething girl drive a minivan?" Constantine asked as he curled up on the couch, ready for a nap.

"It can carry a lot of stuff," I replied weakly as I got my bearings again. I slowly walked toward the door.

"Still odd, unless you were planning on starting a band." Constantine chuckled to himself.

I looked over my shoulder, and Bartholomew was busy scanning his monitors.

"Bye, Isis. See you tomorrow!" Bartholomew yelled, not even looking up from the screens.

"Bye," I whispered. I prayed I would never see either of them again.

Chapter Four

I was late for work. I was never late for work. Thanks to the army, I was brainwashed to believe that being on time meant late. Everywhere I went, I was at least fifteen minutes early. Today, I was barely moving. As my drill sergeant used to say, I was moving like pond water. My shift at Abuelita's started at 4:00 p.m. It was 4:45 p.m. by the time I showed up. Honestly, it wasn't as if anyone could blame me, if I could tell a soul.

I had managed to crawl back to bed by 7:00 a.m. The sun was coming up when I drove home. I hadn't done an all-nighter in years. My party days were over. At least when I was partying, I didn't end up feeling depressed and overwhelmed. I prayed for sleep, but all I got were nightmares. I had been plagued by nightmares since my parents' death. The nightmares were worse after the military. The ones this morning were not any better. I popped an Ambien at eleven o'clock after waking myself up screaming. Thanks to the VA, I had more pills than a pharmacy. Why cure the problem when you can knock it out?

The Ambien did the trick. I had a dreamless slumber. Unfortunately, it was hard to wake up from a drug-induced sleep. It was 4:16 p.m. when I woke up. My head was pounding, and I felt as if I had run a marathon. My body ached everywhere. I took a military three-minute shower and was out the door by 4:35 p.m. The blessing of Texarkana was that there was very little traffic, and you could get anywhere in less than ten minutes. Even speeding, I was still very late. It rankled me. I hated being late.

Saturday at Abuelita's was our busy night. Abuelita's offered a half-off menu from 4:30 to 7:30 p.m. As I pulled up, I could see that the place was packed. The three tables were filled with families, while the bar was packed with people waiting for carryout. I ran out of the Whale and went in the back door. No need to try to fight with the crowd.

"Girl, late night? Where were you partying? You look like hell." Angelito was back in his usual mood, very mischievous.

"Hi to you, too, Angelito." I didn't even try to smile.

Angelito was beaming like firelight. He'd had a great night, by the look of his neck. Some poor soul had left her mark on him. He was shameless, wearing them like a badge of honor. I passed him and headed straight for the kitchen counter. Abuelita was by her double stoves cooking away.

"Isis, are you OK? We called four times, and you didn't answer." There was concern in Abuelita's voice.

Great. Now I felt like hell. Another thing I hated was having people worry about me.

"Yes, I'm sorry, Abuelita. I couldn't sleep, and I took an Ambien this morning. It knocked me out, and I missed my alarm." That was the truth. No need to explain the reason for my lack of sleep.

"Child, I told you, those pills are going to kill you. I got a tea you should try. It's all natural and will help you sleep. Maybe even cure those nightmares for you."

How did Abuelita know about my nightmares? Sometimes, I wondered if she was a mind reader. Before I could wonder for too long, three plates of food were flying at me. On Saturday nights, Angelito and I took turns serving and cleaning tables. With the two of us handling the customers, Abuelita pushed more food out than most McDonald's fully staffed.

Saturday nights were my favorite night at work. We were busy most of the night, the tips were great, and time flew by. This was not one of those nights. My head pounded most of the night, and my vision was blurry. I had floaters in my eyes—those little specks you get with age. At my age, I was blaming too many bad parachute landings that had resulted in too many hits to the head. No doctor would confirm my theory, but I was sticking with it.

The rush hour finally ended. Our regulars, a group of about ten or so, avoided that crowd. Most of the regulars were loners or quiet couples with no kids. Not the crowd you would find at Walmart in the middle of the night. They had a quality to them, that of knowing and distance. They all loved Abuelita. It wasn't just for the food that they came; most wanted private talks with her. During those times, Angelito would prepare the food while I managed the serving and cleaning of the tables.

By eight o'clock, the happy-hour crowd had left. The first of our regular customers walked in. The couple was in their early thirties. The lady had flowing dark hair and always wore a peasant skirt. My godmother and she probably shopped at the same stores. The gentleman, on the other hand, had the best collection of Hawaiian shorts and sandals I had ever seen. Even in the winter he wore them. Today he wore a blue pair with a midnight-blue shirt.

The couple always sat at one of the tables by the large windows. She always looked even paler standing next to her man, with his perfect tan. If he wasn't Hawaiian, the man was probably Filipino. Seven years in the army had a way of expanding your horizons when it came to ethnicity. They always ordered the same: horchata to drink and enchiladas with corn tortillas. It was rude to assume, so I stopped by their table to check on them. I brought them the horchata anyway.

Horchata was a typical Mexican drink made out of rice. Few people ordered it unless they had had it before. Sweet and very refreshing, it was our number-one seller with our regulars. I placed two glasses down and smiled at the couple. The lady looked up at me and smiled. The moment our eyes met, I felt a sharp pain in my forehead, almost between my eyes. I took a deep breath and leaned on their table.

"Isis, are you OK?" She touched my hand as she spoke. Her hands were hot, almost burning.

I pulled away without thinking. I tried to speak, but her eyes were glowing. I looked at her man, and his eyes were catlike.

"Oh God." My mouth went dry, and my hands were sweaty. I bumped against the table behind me as I backed away. "I'm so sorry. I'll be right back."

I ran past the kitchen and out the back door. Deep breaths were not calming me down. I rubbed my face with my hands, trying to erase what I had just seen. What had I seen? Nothing made sense. My headache was worse. The back door opened, but I didn't dare turn around.

"Isis, are you OK? The Joneses just told me you ran out the back. What's going on? You've been acting weird all day." Abuelita had her arms crossed over her chest when I turned to face her. She looked younger and stronger. There was a faint glow to her. She always radiated heat. I couldn't focus on her face. "Isis, are you listening to me?"

"I'm sorry, Abuelita. I really don't know what came over me. My head is just killing me." I looked at the ground as I spoke. Abuelita was too much to look at now. It was probably the light overhead that gave her that weird glow.

"Child, you need to start taking better of yourself. If you're good, let's get inside. The regulars are hungry." She walked back inside and held the door for me.

I took another deep breath. I needed to get it together. In less than twenty-four hours, I had been followed by Death, met a talking cat, and hung out with a boy genius. At this rate, I was going to go nuts before my three-day deadline—if it was actually real and I hadn't been just dreaming or hallucinating. To top off this crazy day, I just needed Samuel L. Jackson to walk in and recruit me for the Avengers or XXX.

Breathe. Just breathe, Isis. You're going to be OK. Why did we talk to ourselves as if we were three years old when all hell broke loose? That was one of those horrible habits I couldn't break. I steadied myself and picked up the plates of enchiladas. The Joneses were creatures of habit.

"Hi, here is your food. I'm so sorry about earlier. I'm having a horrible headache." That wasn't a lie, but I made sure to keep my eyes on the plates when I talked to them. Whatever was going on, I didn't want a repeat of it.

"Oh, that's too bad. Are you going to be OK?" Mr. Jones sounded very sincere. I nodded and slowly walked to the bar before one of them tried to touch me again. I still felt the heat on my hand where Mrs. Jones had touched me.

"Isis, come over here and help me with this pot," Abuelita said from the back of the kitchen. The kitchen area of Abuelita's was larger than the front. She had three large fridges and two deep freezers. The cooking area was to the left of the building, and a sink sat all the way on the far right. The back door was in the middle of the back wall. Abuelita always made extra beans and rice on Saturdays to donate to the shelter downtown. She was struggling to put the bean pot in the fridge.

"Angelito, watch the front for now. Isis can handle the back." I was so grateful to Abuelita. She was truly a caring woman.

"Thank you, Abuelita." I really meant it. Her compassion for people was probably the reason I never looked for another job. I was making a little less than minimum wage, right at $6.50. With the tips, the money balanced itself out. I wasn't getting rich, but I could afford rent and was comfortable for my standards.

For over an hour, I scrubbed pots and pans. Angelito brought in a steady stream of plates and dishes. At one point, I wondered where he kept finding them. I was washing the big items and running the dishwashers for the plates and cups. Thank God we had two. Fortunately, the work was calming my nerves. Instead of complaining, I enjoyed the peace of the simple action and the running of the water. My fingers were prunes by the time I finished with all the dishes. It was still early, and our regulars would be coming in till we closed at midnight.

With the water off, I could hear Angelito's conversation at the bar. One of my favorite customers had walked in. I recognized Gabe's voice. He had that Barry White voice, with smoldering blue eyes that were incredible with his jet-black hair. If Michelangelo needed a model for *David*, I was sure Gabe would have qualified. It had been years since my last date, and I felt clumsy and young around Gabe. Maybe Gabe was the reason I loved Saturday nights. I was told he came in Monday and Wednesday night as well. Too bad; I only worked Thursday to Sunday. Abuelita's nieces handled the rest of the week.

He was great eye candy. I knew Gabe's order by heart. He always sat at the bar—something about the tables being too tight. I didn't care about the reason; at the bar I didn't need a reason to talk to him.

Angelito put in his order, and in less than three minutes, Abuelita was ready. Carnitas asadas with rice and beans, no tortillas—that was his usual. I wasn't a meat eater, but watching Gabe enjoy his food made me want to try the pork at least once.

My earlier incidents were forgotten, and I rushed to take his plate from Abuelita. Angelito smiled and bowed down when I walked by him.

"Do your thing, little mama." The child was unstoppable with that mischievous smile. I turned around to face Gabe, who was looking at me.

"Oh God." I dropped his plate. Gabe was glowing, and he had wings. Not the fake plastic crap people use for Halloween. Oh, no. These babies were real and at least five feet from his shoulder down to his legs. No wonder the boy couldn't fit in a chair. He was a freaking angel or demon—oh God, I had no clue. I looked over his shoulder, and everyone was staring at me. They looked like my regular night crowd except they were not humans. I had a three-eyed monster in one corner and a pointy-eared couple in another. Everyone was glowing. Their eyes were inhuman.

I was having a panic attack. I couldn't breathe. My mind was in overdrive. I was nauseated, and the room was starting to spin. Angelito put his hand on my shoulder, and I bolted for the door. The tears came down before I could stop them. I was trembling all over. Even the woods behind Abuelita's looked alive. There was so much movement out there.

"Isis, sweetie, you need to go home." I barely heard Abuelita's voice. It sounded muffled and very far away. "Honey, you need sleep. You're sleep deprived. Can you drive yourself home? Or I can have Angelito take you."

Abuelita was careful not to face me. She walked up behind me and slowly guided me toward the Whale out front.

"Sleep deprived. That's it. I'm hallucinating." I sounded drugged, even to myself. "You're right. I just need to go home and sleep. Are you sure I can leave?" I felt guilty leaving, but I knew I couldn't stay.

"Sweetie, I'm afraid you might dump a plate on top of a customer. Are you sure you can drive?" Abuelita didn't sound mad, just truly concerned. I climbed into the Whale and waved at her without looking. Home was not going to help me now, but I had a feeling I knew a pair who could.

Chapter Five

Like everything else in town, the business park was less than six minutes from Abuelita's, heading west on 82. I was there in less than four. The outside looked like all the other metal buildings in the parks, just taller. No windows on the front, and the ones on the side were too high for anyone to climb. Unless you had wings, like Gabe. I was still in shock, and I prayed this was all a bad dream. They were going to dehypnotize me, and life would go back to normal.

I slowly climbed out of the Whale. The sign on the building, *Reapers Incorporated*, was written in gothic red—blood red, to be precise. Who said Death didn't have a sense of humor? If not Death, at least her people did. There was something eerie about the building. Almost like a sensation that made me want to turn around. There was a door on the left-hand side and a doorbell. I rang the bell and heard a soft voice say, "Come in."

I stepped into a narrow hallway, four feet wide by six feet long. The door behind me closed on its own, and I heard a lock kick in. There was another door at the end of the hall. When the first door closed, the second one opened. Weird blue lights illuminated the place. I understood what those kids in *Willy Wonka and the Chocolate Factory* felt like. Too bad the end of this tunnel didn't lead to a river of chocolate. I had really been out of it when I left that morning; I didn't remember any of this. To my right was a glass wall. These boys were nuts about their glass walls. This one didn't let you see inside.

The way my night was going, I steadied myself before leaving the hallway. The first floor of the warehouse was empty. A few lights were on, illuminating the shop and the gym area. I looked behind me, and there were two rooms parallel to the entrance hallway. I wondered what was inside. The eerie sensation had left me, but I wasn't sure whether I really wanted to keep walking. I saw Bartholomew wave at me from the second-floor balcony. As I had suspected, the bottom of the glass was a one-way mirror. From the ground it looked like steel.

I was wasting time. I swallowed my fears and headed to the staircase on the other side of the warehouse.

By the time I reached the second floor, Bartholomew was back at his computer station. Constantine was napping on top of the couch. I started talking even before I reached them.

"What have you done to me? I'm broken. For the past four hours, I've been seeing things. The world looks weird. This headache won't go away. This is all your fault. I was fine before I got here last night."

Constantine jumped up. I guessed he wasn't used to waking up to screaming girls.

"Wow. Do you normally talk that fast?" He yawned lazily.

Bartholomew just looked over his shoulder and kept working.

"When I'm mad or nervous." I sounded like a five-year-old. It was unnerving, but I was sure Constantine could see into my soul.

"Good to know. Now, one more time. This time slowly, and from the beginning. What's going on?" He laid his head on his paws and stared at me very closely. Note to self: never get into a staring contest with Constantine—I would lose badly.

"I'm going mad. I saw a guy with wings. Not the fake kind but honest-to-goodness wings."

At that Constantine's head snapped to attention, and this time, he was fully awake. Bartholomew also stopped what he was doing and was staring at me.

"Constantine, is that possible? It's way too early." Bartholomew sounded worried, and Constantine looked at him in silence. It's really hard to read emotions in a cat.

"Where were you, Isis?" Constantine was back to staring at me with those penetrating eyes. I hadn't noticed, but Constantine had a blue eye and a green eye. At least he wasn't a black cat. I would bet money that he thought his stripes made him a tiger.

"I was working at Abuelita's." Didn't they know I had job?

"That explains it. Abuelita's is the Starbucks of the supernatural community in this area, without the coffee." Constantine was nuts. That did not explain a thing to me.

"OK, little Yoda, what are you talking about?" I was not a patient person at times.

"Your third eye has opened. It didn't help being around so many magical beings all at once. But Bartholomew is right—it is very early." I probably looked totally lost, because Constantine kept talking. "When Death kissed you, she transferred some of her powers to you. Typical part of the process. A very small amount, nothing major. But now you are able to see the other side. It should have taken weeks, if not months."

"Constantine, Death marked her the night she killed Teck. It's been six months." Bartholomew delivered that line very seriously. It sounded like a death sentence; no pun intended.

"Third eye, like in the chakras' third eye? Never mind; it doesn't matter. I haven't agreed to any of this. Can you just make it go away?" I was ready to beg.

"You are correct. It is your frontochakra. One of the seven main ones. Unfortunately, no. Once it's open, you can't make it go away. I can help you control it." Constantine was looking up at me from the couch.

"It sucks. When you see them, they acknowledge you as well. I avoid the outside world as much as possible for that reason. Besides..." Bartholomew's computer beeped, and he turned back around without finishing his sentence.

"OK, let's get this lesson going. Sit over here and face me." Constantine took on a very authoritarian air.

I had nothing to lose, so I followed orders. At times, I could still do that very well, just not as often as I should have.

"So, why are you two not glowing?" I asked Constantine after I settled down.

"I'm a talking cat. What else do you want to see?" He did have a valid point.

"A very old, talking, magical cat, for that matter," muttered Bartholomew from his seat.

"OK, you're right about how impressive a talking cat is. But what about Bartholomew?"

"You haven't actually looked at him. Go ahead and do it." I was starting to dislike that he was right so often. "Isis, it's going to be OK. Just look at him."

I took another deep breath and looked up. He looked the same. He had a slight blue glow around him, but other than that, he looked normal.

"What do you see?" Constantine asked, fairly patiently for a cat.

"Just a blue haze over him." I looked at Constantine for confirmation.

"Good. All you're seeing is his aura. Most of Death's interns and the guardians he chooses have a bluish aura. Around other interns, guardians, and Bartholomew, you will see only auras. Same as most humans." Constantine scratched his ear. It was creepy how normal he looked at times.

"Wait—Death is a woman." I was pretty sure it had been a woman who had completely messed up my life last night. Why was that such an important fact for me, above all things?

"Death is whatever your mind and soul decide it is. You've spent a long time courting death. Death to you looks like an old friend."

My mouth was hanging open.

"Death is a woman for me, too, Isis. I think it's because we're both orphans. We see her as a parental figure." Bartholomew's explanation was even more disturbing than Constantine's.

"You're procrastinating. Can we start?" Constantine was annoyed.

"Is it going to hurt?" I was stalling. But hey, this was scary stuff.

"Did it hurt when it opened?"

I gave him a confused look.

"If you can't remember, then probably no. Pay attention now." Not the most convincing argument, but I stopped fighting. "OK, close your eyes and visualize a window between your eyes. This window has large curtains on either side. You want to mentally close the curtains on the window. Imagine yourself pulling them shut."

I took deep breaths and calmed my heart rate down. I wasn't sure what I was doing, but I followed Constantine's instructions. I kept repeating the exercise over and over.

"How do I know if it worked?" For a mind exercise, this was exhausting.

"Open your eyes and look at Bartholomew. Can you still see his aura?"

I followed Constantine's instructions. "He still has a haze, but it's not as defined as before." I was out of breath by now.

"Good. You're getting there. You need to put more of your willpower into it. Almost like you're slamming the window shut."

It was easier said than done. I took another breath and tried again. Around the tenth time, I felt a sensation that ran down my body. The pressure in my head stopped, and my muscles relaxed. I opened my eyes, and Bartholomew was normal.

"Thank the Lord; it worked." I couldn't stop smiling.

"Great. It took you only an hour. Now open it back up and close it again."

My jaw dropped. "In the name of all that is good and great, why would I want to do that again?" This cat had lost his ever-loving mind. I was not going to do that.

"Because you need to control it. Do you want it to fly open in the middle of the mall? Do you know who hangs out at the mall?"

I almost choked on my saliva at that thought.

"I'm glad you see my point, Isis. You need to practice till this becomes second nature. Today, we just need to make sure you can close it and open it at will. So, go back to the window, and this time, open the curtains. Got it?"

I nodded and went back to work. I had always been good at playing make-believe, but this took concentration. I tried opening the curtain and then opened my eyes to see Bartholomew. No blue haze. Then back to the curtain I went. This time it took me an hour and a half to open it.

"The first time is the hardest. Do it again." Constantine had very little sympathy for me.

"You're a little dictator. How old are you?" I was exhausted, and my clothes were covered in sweat from the mental hell.

"He's been around since the pharaohs," Bartholomew said from his chair.

My curiosity got the best of me. "Which one?"

"All of them." Constantine did not seem happy when he said that. "I was glad to leave with Death. All those people always wanting to kill everyone and take them with them to the afterlife. Like I wanted to follow them that far."

I had to smile at that. He was right. The nerve of humanity, to assume everyone agreed with their way of thinking. I could imagine an indignant Constantine walking out.

"Constantine, another one went missing."

I had no idea what Bartholomew was doing at the computer station, but he was upset. Constantine jumped off the couch and made his way toward him. With another leap, he was at the monitors.

"Where this time?"

Bartholomew pointed at a monitor on the top right, and Constantine followed his gaze.

"Downtown again." Bartholomew looked at Constantine.

"What went missing?" I couldn't help myself. I was curious by nature.

"Nothing. Back to practicing. You have other issues to worry about now."

I wanted to argue, but my eye was still open, and the headache was kicking in.

Constantine was right. The first time was the hardest. After three hours, I was able to open it and close it in less than ten minutes. At some point during my session, Constantine left for a recon mission. Bartholomew relayed the message from the little dictator that my homework was to practice. I needed to be able to open and close it within seconds. I could barely move. I wasn't sure how I was going to get home. I tried to get up but fell back on the couch.

"You should really rest before leaving. Your room is the first one on the left on the other side," Bartholomew said without looking up.

"I don't live here, and I haven't agreed to anything." My words came out slurred.

"OK, Isis. Whatever you say." That was the only reply I got. Bartholomew came around the computer area and laid me back down on the couch. He grabbed a blanket from somewhere and draped it over me. I was too tired to even argue.

"What are you monitoring?"

"People are disappearing from the area. Mostly homeless, so the reports don't have a lot of information." He sounded a lot older than eleven.

"Are you sure your boss isn't taking them?" Morpheus was pulling me to slumber, but I still tried talking.

"That's the problem. They're not dead—just gone. Just like New York..."

I faded to sleep while Bartholomew was talking.

Chapter Six

These late nights were going to kill me. I was used to at least eight to nine hours of sleep a night. Granted, most were Ambien induced, but I was sleeping. Lately, I was averaging less than five hours a night—not good. My Sunday alarm was set on my watch for 10:00 a.m. I woke up completely disoriented. It took me a minute to remember where I was. Blessings for the alarm, since I had to head home to shower and get ready for work. My shift at Abuelita's started at 11:00 a.m. Abuelita's offered a brunch special on Sundays for the church crowd from 11:30 a.m. to 3:30 p.m. We were closed for dinner on Sundays.

We didn't have uniforms at Abuelita's, but I always wore black pants with a black shirt. Made dressing quick and easy. I made it to Abuelita's with fifteen minutes to spare. I parked in my favorite spot. Nobody ever took that one—it was the farthest spot from the restaurant. On most days, I combat parked, which meant I backed into the spot so the front was facing the entrance and the back bumper was parallel to the line of trees on the left-hand side. I liked to practice my driving skills, and one day I actually parallel parked the Whale. It was Texas. We had so much space everywhere that nobody parallel parked around there. I was still proud of my accomplishment.

Today, I was so tired that I didn't bother to combat park. I pulled into the space and was grateful the Whale looked fairly straight. I locked the Whale—nobody was ever going to steal it, but why tempt fate?—and walked to the back of the restaurant. Abuelita was busy stirring a pot of crispy southwest potatoes for her huevos rancheros when I walked in. Her huevos rancheros were a house favorite. Most of our clients had their huevos with chorizo, but they were still amazing without the meat. Maybe I just worked at Abuelita's for the food.

"Isis, I wasn't expecting you this morning, but I'm so happy you came. Angelito was out with his new girl and didn't come home last night. He probably will be late if he makes it in. This is not like him." Abuelita was right. Angelito was a player, but he always put Abuelita first. For him to not come in when he was scheduled was not like him.

"He might come in before we open." I had barely made it in time myself, so who was I to judge the boy?

"How are you feeling, dear? You looked awful last night. You're not looking much better now." Abuelita was trying to sound normal, but her voice was lined with worry. I noticed she was trying not to stare at me. I appreciated the space, but I knew it was taking a lot of effort for her to hold back.

"My headache is gone. I'm tired but OK. You were right—I was just tired." No need for all the details from last night. The less Abuelita knew, the easier it would be. At least I hoped. "I'll get the dining area ready to open. Do you need any help back here?"

"I think I got it. But would you like to work the rest of the week? My nieces are heading to Mexico on vacation, and I need extra help. What do you think?"

"Sure thing, Abuelita, I could use the money. Thank you for asking." That wasn't a lie; I really could use the money. Especially after I'd left early yesterday and missed all my tips. Besides, I would do anything to help Abuelita.

"Oh, good. Now I don't have to ask that crazy cousin of mine. She's a hot mess on a good day." That was the understatement of the century. Cousin Maria was a mixture of *Days of Our Lives*; *Beverly Hills, 90210*; and *Jersey Shore* all rolled into one. If she didn't have drama going, she was making some up. With three baby daddies, that woman made the rest of the world look boring.

I left Abuelita to her brunch extravaganza, as she called it. "All-You-Can-Eat Mexican Brunch" involved a lot of food. Our bar doubled as a buffet table on Sundays. So, my job was to set up all the warmers, plates, utensils, and all those little things you needed to eat. I always wondered how many steps I took in this small space, but I never wanted to spend the cash for one of those fancy watch/pedometers. I was convinced I was at least at 2,500 before we opened. I kept forgetting something for each area and table.

Right before we opened, I heard Abuelita talking. By the sound of it, she was on the phone with Angelito. It was not a good talk.

Abuelita walked to the bar from the kitchen. "OK, Isis, it's just us two. Are you sure you can handle things today?"

"I'll be OK, Abuelita. It's only a few hours. Where's Angelito?" I was hoping he had a really good excuse for bailing on us.

"According to him, just getting home from driving all night. Something about going to Dallas with his girl. He sounded exhausted. After your spell yesterday, I was afraid of having another tired server around the customers." Her expression turned sour. She was a very loving woman.

"Abuelita, I got this. You're right. We don't need him falling on people. The Sunday crowd serves themselves, so it's easy." I gave Abuelita my best Shirley Temple smile. She didn't buy it.

My words came back to haunt me. There was nothing easy about the crowd. They were coming in all day, nonstop. If I wasn't refilling food, I was busing dishes back and forth. In between the stampede, I ran the dishwashers. I was so grateful for the little things in life. I wasn't sure how Abuelita did it. The food never stopped coming, and it was always delicious and hot. Even the people with special plates were impressed. The drive-through was killing me. By the time I got one order delivered, another car had pulled up.

Four hours on my feet moving like Speedy Gonzalez took its toll on my poor feet. I didn't fall asleep on anyone or drop any more plates. I was too busy to even daydream. My only goal was to head to bed the moment I left Abuelita's. It was 3:45 p.m. when the last customer left. Cleanup on Sunday normally took about an hour, but that was with Angelito here. I braced myself for at least two hours of hard-core manual labor. Abuelita was in a fabulous mood. She was singing an old salsa song to herself.

I was hurting everywhere, but slowing down was not an option. All warmers, plates, and utensils had been cleared from the dining area and moved to the back. That was my normal pattern—clear the dining area and then worry about all the kitchen stuff. With just one person working, dishes had accumulated everywhere. It took forever just to get all the horizontal surfaces cleared and ready to disinfect. I went by the window to wipe the tables. I looked over at the picnic table, and Bob was settling down. Bob normally showed up around five-ish to look after the place. He was early today. I wondered why. I planned to check on him when I went out to take the trash. Abuelita normally had a plate ready for him around five-thirty.

My adrenaline rush from earlier was now gone. It took me over twenty minutes to wipe everything up in the dining hall. The last family with kids had spilled beans on the table and all over the chairs. I wasn't even sure how that was possible. The kitchen was my next target. I decided to take a break and delivered food to Bob instead. I walked over to the window and saw two men carrying Bob to the door of a van. He wasn't dead, I hoped. They looked as if they were helping him walk. What in the hell was going on? I ran to the door just in time to see a brunette girl in her late teens close the van door.

"Hey, bring back Bob!" I yelled at the top of my lungs. OK, so my comeback lines under stressful situations were not that great. I searched my pockets for my phone, but I had left it on the kitchen counter.

I ran back inside. Abuelita had probably heard the door open, since she was standing by the window when I came in. I got my phone and ran back to the dining area. My fingers were already dialing by the time I reached Abuelita.

"Hi, yes, I need an officer. My friend Bob has just been kidnapped." I was nervous and talking way too fast for down South.

"Ma'am, please slow down, and repeat that again." The female dispatcher sounded patient but confused.

I took a breath before starting. "Sorry. My friend was just abducted by three people in a van."

"OK, ma'am, what is your friend's full name?" I could tell she was taking notes.

"I'm sorry, but I don't know it." I had never thought to get Bob's full name.

"You don't know it? Was he resisting?" The dispatcher was starting to sound confused.

"I'm sorry. I never asked him. He didn't look like he was resisting. They were almost carrying him; maybe they drugged him." I was frantic and wanted to scream.

"Are you sure it wasn't his family?" She was still taking notes.

"I don't think so. Bob is homeless, and I'm pretty sure he doesn't have any family in this area. He doesn't even have many friends, especially ones that drive a van."

"But you can't confirm that he was going against his will or that it was family taking him. Is that correct?"

I really wanted to choke this lady. "Yes, ma'am. That is correct. But can you help me?"

"OK, how long has he been missing and from where?"

"Less than five minutes ago, from Abuelita's on 82." I prayed she was taking me seriously.

"OK, ma'am, he is not technically considered a missing person just yet. Since you have no idea whether those people were not his family, it's hard to tell if something actually bad is taking place. I'm going to send an officer down to take your statement. What's your name?" She thought I was crazy.

"Isis Black."

There was silence on the other end of my phone.

"Are you serious?" The dispatcher thought I was prank calling her. Damn terrorists! Now nobody takes me seriously because they stole my name.

"Yes, ma'am. Please hurry." I hung up the phone. I knew she wasn't listening anymore. I slammed my fist down in frustration.

"Don't get mad, dear. Nobody is paying attention to people like us and Bob. Society has forgotten about us. Bob is smart. He's going to be OK."

I looked at Abuelita. Fear was written all over her face. I couldn't just sit around waiting for police who might never come. I needed to do something.

"I'm going after them." My keys were in the kitchen area. In less than a minute, I had all my stuff in my pockets. I never carried a purse. If everything I owned couldn't fit in my pants, I probably didn't need it. My wallet was a man's billfold, compact and practical. "Abuelita, are you going to be OK finishing up by yourself?"

"Isis, this is crazy. You don't know where to find them." Abuelita kept glancing out the windows, almost willing Bob to come back.

"I know, but I need to try. Please call Angelito to meet you. Don't leave alone, please." The last thing I needed was to lose her, too.

"If you are going to do this, go. I'll call Angelito, and I'll be OK. Please be careful." Before I could walk around her, Abuelita pulled me close to her and said a silent prayer with her hands on my forehead. I hoped it was a prayer.

When she was done, I hugged her. I wasn't sure what else to do, and I ran out the door.

Chapter Seven

Texarkana was not a big city, but when you were wandering around with no clear direction, it was a huge place. The adrenaline rush had passed, and I was worried to death. I drove for over an hour, going to Liberty-Eylau, Wake Village, Nash, and Beverly Heights with no luck. My last resort was to head toward downtown. My plan was to check out the shelters. Maybe the dispatcher was right and they were family or friends. I highly doubted it, but I was out of options.

I was too tired to notice how fast I was going. Granted, most minivans were not known for their speed, but they can hit fifty pretty easily. The speed limit for most of Texarkana was forty, and I had no reason to speed. It wasn't till the red and blue lights were behind me that I noticed my speed. I pulled over across Wadley's Hospital on Texas Boulevard. On Sundays, this part of Texarkana was empty. Downtown was home to several court systems, the police department, the city hall, the local jail, and plenty of bail bondsmen. On weekends, the only people working downtown were the cops. I took a deep breath and waited for the officer.

By the time he came over, I had my window down. Just my luck—the cop who walked to my window was gorgeous. How was that fair? He was at least six feet tall, with a muscular body and brownish hair and matching eyes. He even had a chiseled face with full lips. I saw my reflection in the mirror, and I looked as if I had stuck my finger in a light socket. My hair was messy from all the times I had run my hands through it. I saw grease on my face. I even smelled like Mexican food.

"Ma'am, do you know why I stopped you?" He even had a sexy, smooth voice. I wanted to smack my head on the steering wheel.

"I was probably speeding, Officer." Why lie?

"Yes. Can I see your driver's license and registration?"

I was pretty sure that was just a formality. He had probably pulled all my information while he was sitting in his car. I handed him the license and registration and waited.

"Isis Black? Didn't you just call 9-1-1 for an abduction?"

My mouth just dropped, and I nodded.

"I went to Abuelita's, but you were already gone. Abuelita gave me her statement. What do you think you're doing?" The officer was giving me a lecture. I wasn't sure whether he was also giving me a patronizing look or one of condolence.

"I didn't think anyone would come. I just couldn't stay there doing nothing." I didn't look at his eyes when I spoke. I felt ridiculous admitting that.

"Did you find anything?" He was still holding my information.

"Besides that Texarkana is deceptively large, not really." Unfortunately, on top of talking really fast when I got nervous, I also became a smart-ass. Not the best idea when you were faced with police officers or doctors. He didn't look amused.

"No kidding. Would you care to give a statement now, or are you just planning to drive all over Texarkana?" I wasn't sure whether he was being helpful or was just annoyed by me.

I took a deep breath and related my story to Officer Hottie. My godmother always said that my downfall would be men in uniform. I was not going to tell her she was right, but he was hot. He asked a few pertinent questions at all the right places.

"Do you remember what type of vehicle they were driving?" He had been taking notes the whole time.

"One of those Dodge sixteen-passenger vans. The old model with the bench seats in the back. The windows were tinted to match the black paint job. It was hard to miss. Nobody drives those things anymore besides construction crews." In Texas, where everyone had a truck, vans were rare. Most families had SUVs nowadays.

"OK, I'll pass this information to the other officers." He sounded genuine, but I wasn't sure.

"Why? Do people really care if one more homeless person disappears in Texarkana?"

"I don't know about people, but I do." I met his eyes, and they were unnerving. He had an intensity that I couldn't explain.

"I'm sorry." I actually meant the apology. I wasn't a total ass, and I didn't want to be rude just because I was pissed.

"Don't be. You're upset about your friend. But you're not going to find him speeding through town, being a menace to the other drivers. Go home and let us do our job."

OK, Officer Hottie was not that much older than me—maybe four or six years. Why was he talking to me as if I were five? I wanted to argue just to have the last word, but I didn't know what to say.

"Are you going to let me know?" I was working hard to sound as innocent as possible.

He shook his head and smiled. God was definitely not fair—the boy had dimples. How was that possible?

"Yes, I will. Give me a number where I can call you, and I'll keep you informed."

I was speechless. I didn't want to lose my chance, so I found a scrap piece of paper in my glove compartment and wrote my cell phone number. I handed the paper to Officer Hottie, and he handed me back my license and registration.

"As soon as I find something, I'll personally let you know. Now please head home at a reasonable speed. Leave the police work to the professionals." He was trying his best to look trustworthy and not intimidating.

"You're not going to give me a ticket?" I was pretty sure I was missing something, as if he knew something I didn't.

"Do you want one?"

"Not particularly. Thank you, Officer..." I left my sentence hanging because I couldn't read his name tag.

"Smith. That's my last name."

I had a few *Matrix* comments to go along with his name. I decided against it—if I was planning to leave without a ticket. I couldn't afford a ticket with my paycheck.

"Thank you, Officer Smith. Please call me if you find out anything."

He nodded and went back toward his car. I'd had very few encounters with cops, but I was sure this one was not normal.

"Head home, Ms. Black, and please stop drag racing on my streets." He was saying that over his shoulder. I was sort of listening, more focused on his nice ass. He was even fine from behind. I wished I had been drag racing. That would translate to being close to finding someone. Right now, all I had done was get a warning.

I was completely lost and defeated. I turned around and headed back toward home on Texas Boulevard and then turned left on New Boston Road. I was heading east on New Boston Road, or 82. Not sure why some streets in Texarkana had multiple names. At the intersection of Summerhill and New Boston Road, instead of turning right to head home, I kept going straight. I had no idea why, but I couldn't give up so soon. I drove less than a mile and turned right at Beverly Park.

Beverly Park wasn't much to look at. Right next to Big Jake's BBQ, the so-called park was just a couple of picnic tables with benches and a small kids' playground. I remembered Bob mentioning this place. He used to hang out here with an old buddy under the shady area. I drove slowly, so as not to scare anyone away. When I reached the picnic tables, I got out. The place looked empty at first glance, until I looked closely. In the back of the park, beneath a tree, was a man sitting on the ground, not moving. I prayed he wouldn't run away and that he was still alive. Truly, I wasn't sure if that was Bob's friend, but I needed to try.

By the time I reached him, I noticed he wasn't going anywhere. He was sleeping against the tree, holding a paper bag. I couldn't tell what was inside the bag, but I had a few guesses. The man looked frail. The sun still had a few hours before it set, but the shadows gave the man a sickish look. He didn't look very tall, five-four tops, and maybe 120 pounds soaking wet. I leaned down to tap his foot.

"Who are you? What do you want?" the little guy screamed before I could even touch him. He startled me so bad, I fell on my butt. The little man looked crazy, with wild eyes. I was waiting for him to start yelling "My precious!" I was beginning to question my decision to come here. This man looked insane.

"I'm sorry, sir. I'm friends with Bob." I was trying to sit down without attracting too much attention. I didn't want him to do anything crazy, like stab me or bite me.

He was up on his feet faster than I believed possible. "Liar. Bob has no friends. Are you here to take me?" I guessed he had whiskey in the bag, because I smelled it on his breath.

"No, sir, I'm not here to take you. But some people took Bob this afternoon."

That hit him hard, and he stopped moving. I took advantage of his confusion and stood up. At least I could look him in the eyes now.

"I told him to stop asking questions, but he wouldn't listen. He's just like all the rest." Was it the alcohol talking, or what? I wasn't following his conversation.

"Sir, do you know who took Bob?" Please, God, let this crazy drunk guy be semicoherent.

"The witches took him. Like they took all the young and healthy ones. I told him to stop asking questions and stay in his lane. But he just couldn't do it." The little man was pacing back and forth with his arms outstretched. My prayer had failed, because that made no sense. He continued his rambling campaign. "They don't want me 'cause I'm old, but nobody is safe now."

"I'm sorry, but do you know who else is missing?" I was talking to him as if he were a five-year-old. "Please help me. I need to find Bob."

"Girl, he is gone. Let him go. Nobody comes back after they take them." His words chilled me to the core. Those were the first sober words he had said. He delivered them without judgment or fear—just stated a fact.

"Do you know where they took them? Please help me." My voice was shaky and broken.

"Shhhh. Stay away, girl." Before I could say or do anything, he took off. How could a drunk man move so fast? That didn't even make any sense. I had no idea where he was heading, but I knew I was not getting anything else out of him.

I hated feeling helpless. I was overwhelmed, and there was nothing I could do. Bob was missing, and I had no way to find him. The old, crazy guy was even less helpful. On top of that, my own clock was ticking. Death needed an answer by tomorrow. My boring and uncomplicated life was destroyed. I needed to pack up and leave this place. By the sound of the crazy old guy, I was never going to find Bob anyway.

I wiped my eyes and brushed off dirt from my clothes. If I stayed here any longer, I could pass for one of the homeless. I was a hot mess. I had smeared dirt all over my face by accident. It was a blessing I didn't wear makeup, or that sure would have made a worse picture.

I slowly pulled myself into the Whale and headed home. This weekend was ranking in the top three on my list of horrible disasters. I just wanted to crawl into bed and forget this whole mess.

Chapter Eight

On Sunday evenings, I normally brought my dinner home. It was a good thing I wasn't hungry, because I'd forgotten to pick up food today. Fixing meals for one person was more trouble than it was worth. The creation process relaxed me, but the cleanup was too much of a pain afterward. My fridge always had the basics: milk, bread, cheese, deli meat, eggs, butter, and some condiments. I could always make a sandwich and not starve.

After the insane day I'd had, I just wanted to disappear. My shoulders were tight, and I could feel the muscles in my lower back knotting up. On warm days, I preferred cool showers. Today, I wanted a blistering-hot bath. My bathtub was small, but it would do the trick. I filled it up with as much hot water as it could handle. I poured in two cups of Epsom salts and some lavender oil. I climbed into the tub, and the heat from the water boiled my legs. With baths, the worst part was always getting in. After a few moments, the body adjusted. I was relieved to have something else to think about, at least for a few minutes. Tears were rolling down my face, but this time I let them. Maybe that was the only way to empty myself and let go.

An hour later, I crawled into bed, wearing a large nightgown, a purple-and-yellow one my godmother had sent me last year. She had an obsession with nightgowns. Somehow, she thought the rest of the world had one, too. On days like this, I really missed her. Unfortunately, if I called, she would immediately know something was wrong. I didn't need any more people worried. I drifted off to sleep.

It was late afternoon, and I was standing in the middle of the road. The car was wrapped around a tree. Fumes were coming out from under the hood. It took me a minute, but I knew I was dreaming. It was a weird sensation, knowing the place was not real but not being able to wake up. I had been having this dream most of my life—or, more accurately, this nightmare. I was six then, watching my parents die inside the vehicle, too young to help. I was told that the impact had thrown me from the car.

"Isis, don't cry. You are not alone."

I looked up and saw my mother standing over me. I couldn't remember much of her, but I could see her so clearly. Today, her dark hair was wrapped in a bun on top of her head. She wore no makeup, but her eyes had a natural outline that made the almond shape stand out even more. She was wearing a white shirt and jeans, and she smelled like jasmine. My mother had a light tan, and she was beautiful.

"Mom, please don't leave me again." I reached for her but couldn't touch her. I was crying.

"Baby, you are stronger than you think. Don't be afraid. I'm always with you." She kissed my forehead. I closed my eyes to take it all in. That part was new. I had never seen my mother in this dream. I had always ended alone and small.

I opened my eyes, and I was no longer standing in the middle of the road. I was in Fallujah, Iraq. I was wearing my military uniform, including the Kevlar. I closed my eyes, forcing the dream to change again. Nothing happened. I was still in Iraq watching the inevitable. My heart was pounding, and my hands were sweating. I waved my hands as the convoy passed by me.

Like clockwork, the gunfire started. The drivers performed defensive maneuvers. Instead of avoiding the incoming danger, they drove, without knowing, directly over the IED.

"Nooooo! Please stop!" I was screaming at the top of my lungs. Our HEMTT had flipped over. I saw myself pulling the dead body of my friend out. I was holding Sergeant Richardson's body.

"Isis, let me go. It wasn't your fault." Sergeant Richardson was standing next to me on the side of the road, smiling. That boyish smile played on his face as he spoke. We were band people. We had no right to be in a convoy. But we were soldiers first; everything else was second.

The pain was too intense. I fell to my knees, and more tears kept coming. He'd never said those words to me. What was going on?

For over a year now, I had been having this nightmare. Why was it different now? I kept trying to wake up, but I couldn't. I could smell the blood on me. I closed my eyes and sobbed.

"Aghhhh." I knew where I was before I opened my eyes. That cry was imprinted in my memory. This time I was back in Brooklyn, staring down the fire escape. The mangled body of the intern lay on the ground. He wasn't moving.

"Oh God, please let him be OK." Please make this stop, God. I begged God and all the saints. I was flying down the stairs with my dream self. This time, the intern was sitting up looking at me when I reached him.

"You need to get ahold of yourself. Learn to control your emotions and forgive yourself, or you will go crazy."

The intern vanished.

"Wait. Come back." What was going on? I started having a panic attack. Maybe it was too late and I was already going crazy.

"Let me out! Let me out!" My screams woke me up. I was covered in sweat, sitting straight up on my bed.

"Oh God, help me."

"He is trying to help you. Maybe you should let him." The voice came from the corner of my room.

"Holy cow!" I screamed at the top of my lungs. I pulled my sheets over me, as if they were going to save me. I wasn't judging my courage. Trust me, at two in the morning, nobody is brave.

From the shadows, Death appeared. She sat on the director's chair I had in my room. She made it look like an executive chair. With an incredible grace, she crossed her legs.

"How did you get in?"

Death just arched an eyebrow and smiled. OK, so I was a little slow in the middle of the night. Not my fault.

"Do you honestly think doors and locks can stop me?"

"Good point. Disregard that question. Why are you here?" I wasn't sure whether I was ready to hear the answer to that.

"Dreams can be powerful tools. At times, those who have passed have used them to communicate with the living. Your subconscious is more open to the supernatural during sleep. Especially now that you have been blessed by me," Death said, as if it actually made sense.

"I'm not sure if my definition of 'blessing' is the same as yours. What do you mean 'at times'? What about the rest of the time?" I'd had dreams with people who weren't dead. Were they foretelling my future? I hoped not.

"The rest are just random thoughts running through your mind. Some people have gone mad trying to interpret them all. Looking for meaning in the nonsense." She was not offended by my comment.

"Great. So, am I dreaming or awake?"

Death gave me that knowing smile. "You tell me."

"Definitely awake. In my dream, I wouldn't be getting a lecture or intimidated into working for you." I was feeling brave—or just too tired to care.

"Sorry to disappoint you, dear. I don't need to terrorize anyone to work for me. I'm just following one of your laws: for every action, there is an equal and opposite reaction."

Oh, great. Death was quoting Newton on me. It was either way too early or late for this.

"So, if you're not here about the offer, why are you here?" This was the longest day ever.

"You called me." Death was serious, and I was speechless.

"I did what? No way." I was officially crazy.

"You wished you would die and quiet the voices." Death inclined her head and waited for my answer.

"OK, hold up. A lot of people say things like that. Do you appear to everyone who mutters that statement?"

"Only to those who put actions behind the words. But you are different. I have a link to you. So, your voice is a lot clearer. Didn't Constantine tell you not to call on me? Rule number three—remember?"

Was she serious? Constantine had not explained rule number three very well.

"I have a feeling he forgot to tell me why. I'm sure I would remember if he mentioned that Death would appear." I needed to have a few words with that fur ball.

"Strange things happen when I'm around. It would be unfortunate if you called me in a crowded room and people randomly started to have strokes and heart attacks. The body is a complicated machine and reacts differently in my presence."

Death technically did not kill people, but some just managed to die when she was around. Good to know. Don't call Death at a hospital—check.

"OK, I'm not planning to kill myself. I just had a really long day." Not to mention I hadn't slept since I'd met her, but who was keeping track of that?

"I'm glad. But you still need to control your dreams and put some barriers around yourself. If you're not planning to stay at the safe house, at least get this place blessed." Death looked around the room with a measuring air. "Tell me, Isis, what is your purpose in life?"

"That's ironic coming from Death. Do I need a purpose in life?" I didn't want to answer this line of questioning.

"At some point in your life, you will need to stop running. According to your faith, God won't make things easy, but they will be possible. Your martyrs claimed those who don't stand for something will fall for anything." Death sounded like a college professor delivering a well-rehearsed lesson.

"Well, I might be dreaming after all. You're lecturing me."

Death smiled. "Not lecturing, Isis. Just pointing out that you are not living—just waiting to die. When things get tough, you run." How long had Death been watching me?

"Just because you are Death, that doesn't mean you know me. You don't know how it feels when everyone you loved dies around you."

"Now, child, don't give yourself that much credit. That's my job, remember?"

Oh God, I had no arguments about losing people when Death was the one taking them. She knew exactly how I felt, because she had to make the delivery herself. Death's eyes shone with understanding.

"I'm a jackass." I dropped my head down and slumped on the bed.

"At times your mouth moves faster than your brain." She was laughing at me. "Wisdom come with age; remember that."

"Yes, master."

Death gave me an interesting smile. "I haven't been called that in years. Of course, back then it had less sarcasm." Damn, she didn't miss a thing. "Isis, I'm offering you an opportunity to make amends for your mistakes and to find purpose in your life. Isn't that why you joined the military? To do something great?"

I was fidgeting with my fingers. I wasn't sure how to reply, so I listened.

"Ask yourself what brought you to Texarkana. The spirits have been calling you. Why have you followed?"

"Hey, wait a minute. Nobody has influenced me. I just like it here." That sounded weak even to me. I honestly had no idea what had drawn me there. I had just known I needed to come.

"You are intuitive and gifted. Your skills, if you develop them, could serve a greater purpose. You could save your friend and many other souls. Right now, you are wasting away in this dump. Is that how you want to spend your life?" Death did not fight fair. I wasn't sure whether I was ashamed or angry.

"Are you trying to guilt me into accepting?"

"No, Isis, just telling you the truth. Sometimes, the truth hurts. You must face it."

I didn't want to face any truth. Denial was not just a river in Egypt for me; I spent a lot of time there.

Death rose from the chair and walked over to my bed.

"What are you doing?" I pushed myself as far away from her as possible.

"I'm going to help you." She was standing over me.

"Listen, lady, last time you kissed me, I was seeing all sorts of crazy things. I don't need a replay of that." I was barely able to open and close my third eye. Another kiss might go supernova and never close it.

"Shhh. Isis, you need sleep." With that she patted my head. I wasn't sure what Death did to me, but it felt as if a hundred-pound sack was lifted from me. I took a deep breath and felt asleep.

Chapter Nine

I had no idea why I was there. It was eight in the morning, and I was parked in front of Reapers Incorporated. Maybe I wanted to say thank you to Death for the best night of sleep I'd had in years. Or maybe I had lost my mind. What was I doing there? Not sure why, I got out of the Whale. I slowly walked toward the door but turned right around as soon as I reached the call button. This was insane. The best course of action was to go back home and back to bed. It was almost as if I had been sleepwalking when I dressed and drove there. For whatever reason, I paced back to the door and then back to the Whale. It was a blessing the building was at the back of the business park, because I looked fairly crazy. On my third lap around, I heard the buzzer go off.

"Isis, pull your van around the back and come in." It was Constantine, and he sounded bored. "I don't need a trench in front of the door."

I pressed the speaker button. "I'm so sorry. This is a mistake. I really should be heading home."

"Woman, stop wasting my time and get your skinny butt in here. What else do you have going on now?"

Did I just get cursed out by a five-thousand-year-old cat? What was the world coming to? I wanted to be mad, but he had a point. Like a whipped puppy, I got in the Whale and drove around the building. On the back side, there was a large commercial garage door. I had wondered how they got the Deathmobile inside.

The door rolled up, and I slowly drove the Whale in. Just like the front door, this had another set of rolling doors on the other side. As soon as the Whale was completely in, the first set rolled down. The weird lights were on, and then the second set of doors rolled up. I slowly pulled the Whale into the building. I drove up next to the two other cars. They were both covered with tarps. When I climbed out of the Whale, Constantine was standing behind me, looking completely bored.

"It's about time you got here. What took you so long?" This cat was crazy. I had just decided to come there that morning.

"You don't know why I'm actually here." I put my hands on my hips and took a pose. I probably looked like a spoil brat, but I didn't care. I was not backing down.

"Isis, you have no life. You live in a shit hole. You have a minimum-wage job that barely pays your rent, and the only nice person who doesn't judge you just got kidnapped. Should I go on?" Constantine was ruthless and brutally honest.

"Ouch! Has anyone ever told you that your bedside manner sucks?" My ego was crushed.

"We have no time for sugarcoating. People are disappearing, and you took your sweet time deciding. Let's be honest, girl. What are your other options?" If Constantine could have crossed his arms, he would have. Instead, he jumped on the hood of the covered car to glare at me. I knew I was not going to win a staring contest with him. I dropped my head and just addressed the floor.

"How sad is it that my best offer in life comes from Death? Do you see the irony in that?" He was so right—my life sucked.

"No. No, I don't. Humans are odd. You pray for miracles, but when they arrive, you don't want them. Just because they're not wrapped the way you expected them." Constantine was profound. "You search your life for purpose, but when the army got bloody, you ran."

"I can't guarantee I won't stop running." I was at least honest with myself.

"Fair enough, but at least you're trying. So, enough talk. Let's get started." An evil grin crossed his face. Cats were not made for smiling.

"Right now? What are we doing?" OK, so I was a little nervous. The crazy cat had dangerous plans for me. Self-preservation was kicking in.

"*We* are not doing a thing. *You*, on the other hand, will start training. I'll supervise. Follow me to the training area." In one smooth jump, Constantine was off the car and strolling across the room to an exercise area.

I knew there was exercise equipment there. What I hadn't realized was the extent of it. For all the gym rats and cross-trainers, this was a wet dream. For me, on the other hand, it was a bunch of high-end torture devices. Constantine had everything, from spinning bikes, treadmills, free weights, some weird inverted benches, and even large tires. I was sure he had stolen those from a five-ton truck. They looked awfully similar to military-issue tires.

Constantine's training area had racks on the wall that reached to the second-floor balcony. There were jump ropes, elastic bands, and some weird cable with a sign that read Pilates. I looked around to see if other people were coming, because this place had two of everything. From across the room, it didn't look large, but appearances were deceiving. My heart rate had increased, and I wondered how quickly I could clear the double doors.

"Why do you have double doors at each entrance, and what's the deal with the lights?" I tried to sound normal. I needed a distraction before I passed out.

"Stop stalling and get over here. You want answers, you will earn them. At least you're dressed appropriately." Constantine was an evil dictator. Granted, all dictators are evil, just by the nature of it. So, more accurately, he was an evil overlord. "Put on that vest, and let's get you warmed up on the treadmill. Do ten minutes at a brisk pace."

Like magic, a vest was lying by the rack of free weights by the wall. I walked carefully across, praying I wouldn't kill myself in the process. The thing looked similar to the ones issued by the military. I wondered if it had steel plates. My answer came quickly when I picked up the demonic thing and put it on. It weighed at least twenty pounds, and yeah, it had steel plates. I was glad I had decided to wear yoga pants and a thin T-shirt.

"You should be familiar with the design." Constantine made himself comfortable across from me on one of the benches.

"Oh, thank you. I'm very moved." My words dripped with sarcasm as I started walking on the treadmill.

"Pick up the pace. If you're able to talk, you're going too slow. I said brisk walk."

I glared at Constantine, but he ignored me by licking his paw. I guess he was practicing his yoga moves. He had his back leg straight in the air, with not a care in the world. Show-off!

In less than five minutes, I was drenched in sweat. I was breathing heavily enough that Constantine looked at me.

"Oh, good. We're getting somewhere now. So, about the doors—where to begin? Remember we mentioned the building is reinforced, right?"

My brisk walk was kicking my butt, and I couldn't answer. I made a grunt sound and nodded.

"Good." I wasn't sure whether he meant "good" that I remembered or that I wasn't talking.

"We're in a dangerous business, so multiple layers are in place. The outside has been blessed against demons and evil spirits, it's enchanted against wandering humans, and it's reinforced against fifty-caliber rounds." I arched an eyebrow in astonishment. I was truly impressed. "We can't take any chances, and we don't believe in overkill. The lights are full-body scan or vehicle scan against everything. Just small precautions. We do work for Death." Constantine jumped off the bench and onto the treadmill. He looked at my time and hit the stop button.

"Lunges are next. You're going to lunge from one side of the room to the other, five times each way." He jumped down and walked over to the edge of the gym area. "Start here and go all the way to the far wall. Start."

My jaw dropped. "Are you serious?" I prayed he was messing with me.

"Like a heart attack. So, stop wasting time. We got tons more." The wall Constantine was pointing to was at least thirty feet away. It was not too late to quit. I could walk out door.

"So, the doors are like the TSA screening detectors, except better?" I needed a distraction to handle the painful exercises, and random questions would help.

"The passage includes X-ray scans, spell detectors, and, of course, confirmation of being alive. It would be really painful for you if you were a demon crossing that entryway." I was lunging back toward him when he finished. He looked really pleased with himself.

"So, are you going to buzz me in every time?" I was breathing heavily as I spoke.

"Do I look like your servant? Of course not, silly. Besides, that takes too long. Bartholomew will get you in the system, so all you'll have to do is scan your hand and get in." He was sitting perfectly still, with his tail wrapped around him. I wondered if the ancient Egyptians had based the sphinx on him.

"Really? Hand scan, not retina?" I was trying to be funny.

"We could, but I figured getting your hand chopped off had a greater survival rate than getting your eyeball ripped out of the socket." He said that without blinking an eye, totally serious. I stopped in mid-lunge and swallowed. He didn't take jokes well.

"OK, I can't argue with that logic. So, why not just keys?" I liked my hands and eyes attached to my body. We could find option three.

"Those are easily stolen or copied. Can't take any chances. We have some *smooth criminals* out there." On that note, Constantine did a head shake that would have impressed Michael Jackson. If he had moonwalked, I would not have been surprised.

Constantine wasn't kidding when he said we had a lot to do. Three hours later, we were finishing up his torture session. I'd had drill sergeants and jumpmasters who were nicer than he was. Constantine took his training sessions seriously. We were going to finish with push-ups. I hadn't done a push-up in almost a year. I got down army-style. Before I could lower myself, he jumped on my back. I nearly lost my balance.

"What are you doing?" For a bunch of fur, the cat was heavy.

"Developing your resistance and focus. Your adversaries are not going to play fair. A push-up should teach you not just to carry your own strength but how to get out of sticky situations." I swear he was making that up. I struggled to get down.

"Girl, when was the last time you went to a gym?" He at least was lying down instead of having his four paws on me like pressure points.

"Gym memberships are expensive," I barely said. I struggled to finish my ten push-ups. Constantine was keeping count and jumped off as I finished. I was glad we had lost the vest after the lunges. My whole body ached.

"Please tell me you did the same thing to the other intern." I was sure I looked like a sack of potatoes. As soon as we were done, I dropped to the floor unceremoniously.

"Teck was a ninja. He had his own strict regimen. OK, you need to start stretching before you cool off."

"A ninja? You've got to be kidding me. Anything else Boy Wonder did?" I started doing calf stretches, and my muscles were on fire. I was going to be sore for the next week.

"He was also an alchemist." Constantine actually said that a little apologetically. He almost looked sorry for me.

"Are you serious? How do you follow in the footsteps of that?" I rolled over and stretched my hamstrings and back by bending my waist and reaching down to my toes.

"Easy. Don't get killed."

I laughed at that. At the end of the day, life was that simple. I had no idea how Ninja Boy had fallen down the ladder. All it had taken was one minute of distraction.

I reached my arms over my head, bent at the elbows, and stretched my biceps. One thing was certain—the military had shown me how to stretch.

"When you're done, make sure to drink your shake and take a hot shower. It should loosen those muscles." Constantine got up and stretched his lower and upper back. He even looked better than I did. Damn feline flexibility.

"Can I take it to go? I need to go home and clean up." I didn't get up as gracefully as Constantine.

"No need. We have clothes for you in your room already. Bartholomew sent the cleaning crew to pick up your stuff at your apartment and close your lease. Your possessions should be here this afternoon." He was heading to the loft as he spoke.

"The 'cleaning crew?' Constantine, I can move myself. Besides, I just got here. How is it already done?"

"We got people. Your stuff has to be inspected for spells and tracking devices. The crew handles all that. We can't take any chances." He stopped long enough to look back at me and said, "Besides, it wasn't like your apartment was Fort Knox. Don't look so shocked, Isis. I've been around for a very long time. I can read people very well. Welcome home, Isis."

Home? I had never been in one place long enough to call it home. Constantine was very sure of himself. What did that crazy cat know?

Chapter Ten

It was afternoon by the time I dragged Bartholomew out of the building. Constantine was right—they had jeans and T-shirts in the room for me. I hadn't been that sweaty since Iraq. My clothes were sticking to my body, and I stank. I ran to the room and took the longest shower I had in ages. It was hard to admit it, but I really liked the room. It was fully furnished, so all my old stuff was going to storage, according to Constantine. After checking out the room, with its own bathroom and walk-in closet, I wasn't going to need anything besides my clothes. The bedroom was bigger than my old one.

By the time I dressed and combed my hair, I was starving. Unfortunately, the fridge at Reapers was in worse shape than my own. I made the fatal mistake of having some of Bartholomew's cereal. No wonder the boy was so thin—that stuff was nasty. I didn't know much about gluten issues, but my heart went out to all those who suffered. Food options were extremely limited; forget most processed foods—which translated to all the stuff that tasted good was out of the question.

Bartholomew hated going out. He had really good control of this third eye, but the idea that the creatures could see him terrified him. Not to mention his huge dislike for people in general. He believed stupid people in large masses were a force of disaster. Couldn't argue with his logic. I guessed it was a good thing Texarkana was not a huge metropolis. At the same time, options for healthy foods were limited. We didn't have a Whole Foods or Trader Joe's, but we did have the Granary, a local health store that carried an eclectic collection of foods, vitamins, and oils for every hippie in town. If you shopped at the Granary, you were definitely a "tree-hugging hippie" or on your way to becoming one. I really loved that store.

Besides the selection, the Granary was a safer option than going to Walmart. I was sure Bartholomew would not handle Walmart well. I didn't want him having a panic attack. It didn't matter the state; somehow Walmart had a way of attracting some of the shadiest people in town. To some extent, Walmart was a great commentary on the makeup of America. I wasn't sure I could handle the clientele of Walmart.

"OK, I think I have enough money to get us enough groceries for the week." The awkward silence was driving me nuts. I had to say something, since Bartholomew looked a little pale staring out the windows.

He gave me a strange look. "Why are we not using the corporate card?"

OK, it was my turn to look dumbfounded. "What corporate card?" I had missed something.

"You haven't read your manual." It was a statement. He didn't even bother asking me.

I was embarrassed to admit he was right. "I've been busy the last couple of days."

Bartholomew shook his head in disapproval. "You are so behind the curve here." He was looking a little smug as he spoke.

"Fine, boy genius. Give me the CliffsNotes. What am I missing it?" I tried not to glare as I drove down the street.

"You really need to read your manual. I won't be able to do it justice. But we get a corporate card to cover all house expenses, which includes unlimited food."

My jaw hit the ground. I was sure I looked like a cartoon character. "So rent, utilities, cable, Internet, and even food are all covered. Please tell me you're not messing with me." I waited patiently for the horrible truth.

"Those are the essentials. You also get your monthly stipend as well as a monthly clothing allowance. I guess it's almost like the military." Bartholomew looked as if he was comparing numbers in his head.

"How much is this clothing allowance?" I knew I was not hearing him right.

"Five hundred dollars, and you get it on the fifteenth." He looked worried.

"Definitely not like the military. I got a clothing allowance only once a year."

"Try not to spend it all. Requesting an increase is very time-consuming and requires lots of paperwork." He made a face that looked highly annoyed.

"Why would anyone need that much money for clothes each month? That's crazy." I couldn't remember spending that much in a year. Most of my clothes came from thrift shops. I thanked my godmother for passing down some of her shopping habits.

"Teck went through his in less than a week each month." Now that was one piece of news that made my day.

"Ninja Alchemist was a fashionista? That is precious." I started laughing. I couldn't help it. I had a mental image of a metro-ninja in leather pants fighting the forces of evil with Gucci shoes.

"He liked his clothes. So, he spent his stipend and allowance on clothes and accessories. New York was dangerous for him." Bartholomew looked sad.

"That's an understatement." I felt guilty and needed to change the topic. "So, how much is this stipend?" I had known some interns in college, and they never made any money.

"Your first year is $5,500 a month after taxes, and you get it on the first. If you're really good, you can request an increase in six months. But you'll get a raise of at least five percent each year."

I was dumbfounded. I knew I wasn't hearing right. "Are you serious?" I was using that phrase a lot lately, but I couldn't help it. I was in shock. I had never made that much money in a month.

"Hey, this is a dangerous job. You have to be compensated."

"OK, Bartholomew. Wait, can I call you Bart? Bartholomew just seems so grown."

His eyes lit up as if it were Christmas morning. "Sure thing. I've never had a nickname. Pretty soon I'll have a secret identity and—"

I had to stop him before he decided to leap buildings in a single bound. Bartholomew really needed friends his age. "Slow down, now. One thing at a time. Let's stick with the nickname. So, tell me, where does the money come from? I mean, we pay taxes; there's insurance. This looks pretty legit."

"Have you heard of the Boatman?"

I had no clue what he was talking about. I shook my head, and my miniature professor continued.

"Back in ancient times, people used to bury their dead with a coin in their mouth, so the ferryman would carry them to the afterlife. Over centuries, many forms of that ritual have evolved. Who do you think the ferrymen work for?"

I was in awe. "Really?" I was trying hard not to ask him if he was serious again.

Bart smiled. "Add a bunch of people dying to the power of compound interest, and you have one super-rich entity." Lectures made Bart glow with information.

"So, we are actually a real company?" That was insane.

"Money has always meant power. As long as you're paying the appropriate Caesar of the times, have all your documents in order, and have a simple backstory, you'll be surprised how the world looks the other way."

I had pulled up to the Granary while Bart was talking. I was in shock. "I can see why most people don't turn down the job." I was actually surprised more people weren't taking out interns for the position.

"Yeah. They normally read the manual the first day. The fringe benefits are pretty amazing. There's a short history of the enterprise in the manual as well."

Ouch. I was never going to live that one down.

We parked in front of the store, with an empty space on either side. It would be easier to load the minivan that way. Only two other vehicles were parked in front. I always wondered where the staff parked. For a Monday afternoon, the place was pretty empty. Fridays were usually a nightmare, since most of the workers from the army depot were off on Fridays and were running around town. I was so lost in my thoughts and celebrating having enough money to pay that I ran into a person.

"Oh, I'm so sorry." I had to look down, since I had run into a little girl. Bart had to peer around me.

"It's all good, Ms. Isis." The little girl was probably around ten or eleven, but next to Bart, she looked even younger. Or maybe Bart just looked mature for his age. Being raised by Death and a talking cat probably had that effect on kids. It took me a minute to remember her name.

"Hi, Dulce. What are you doing here alone?" We really didn't need kids disappearing around here.

"Mom is inside. She said I could stay in the car, since it was so nice today. I got bored and was going to find her." Dulce and her family were regulars at Abuelita's. I was pretty sure they were among the human regulars. Dulce had a habit of being easily bored. I was amazed she had agreed to stay outside.

"That's a good idea." I stopped midsentence. Dulce was staring over my shoulder across the street. I turned to follow her gaze.

"Ms. Isis, I think someone is trying to rob that lady."

I prayed Dulce was right. Unfortunately, that evil black van was parked on the other side. The same two guys who had taken Bob were pulling the girl in. This time, I could see two girls in the front of the van.

"Dulce, head inside and stay with your mom. Bart, we have to go."

Bart was already running back to the Whale. Dulce looked way too curious for her own good. I could relate to her. I gave her a look, and she headed inside. At least my sergeant's glare was still working.

Bart and I jumped into the Whale. I was not planning to lose those fools again. By the time we got the Whale turned around and facing 82, the black van had taken off heading west. Fortunately, they were trying to blend in and were not speeding off. That didn't last long. As soon as we started following them, they took off like bats out of hell. The speed limit in this part of town was forty-five, and they were going at least seventy. I gunned the Whale after them.

The black van made it to the intersection with a green light and took a sharp left, heading out of Wake Village and the 59 loop. I was driving like a madwoman, and I took the same turn just as fast, except my light was red. Horns were honked, and Bartholomew was holding on to his door handle for dear life. I finally understood the term "oh shit handle." The black van kept left and headed to the loop. If we didn't catch them soon, we would lose them again. We took the ramp faster than recommended by most manufacturers. The Whale skidded all the way to the left. At least we didn't flip. I had no idea how their van was handling this so smoothly.

The Lord was on our side, since the loop was empty. We caught up with them, and I tried to cut them off to make them stop. OK, so I had no idea what we were going to do after we caught them. I just wanted them to stop. We were moving fast and had passed the Seventh Street exit when the crazy driver chick threw a ball out her window.

"Oh, shoot!" Bartholomew screamed and ducked in his seat.

The weird balloon hit the back door and made a hole the size of a head through it. Bartholomew and I looked at each other.

"That wench just threw acid at us." A smart, normal person would have been terrified. Me, on the other hand—I was pissed.

"She's a witch!" Bartholomew was screaming at me and looking paler than before.

"Witch, wench. Who cares? Look what she did to the Whale." Why was Bartholomew getting technical here?

"No, Isis. I mean she is a witch, a real witch. The 'spell-throwing' kind of witch." Bartholomew pointed at the back door for emphasis.

"What? No way. Please tell me you're lying." This was insane.

He had no time to make me feel better. The black van took a sharp left into our lane.

"Watch out!" Bartholomew screamed as we were heading toward the median, thanks to the witches of Eastwick.

I was thanking the military for my training in defensive driving. That was the only thing that saved us from a collision. I made a few quick maneuvers and pulled the Whale to a stop. The witches had taken the exit behind us at Lake Drive. I glanced behind us, trying to determine how clear our path was.

"Don't even think about it." Bartholomew's voice was ice cold, and I froze.

"We're going to lose them." If we did a quick U-turn, we could catch them.

"We've lost them already. Besides, do you have anything here to fight with or shield us from spells? I don't think so. You're not going to get us killed on your first day on the job." He crossed his arms and stared me down.

"Fine." I beat my head on the steering wheel. This was a horrible day.

"We still need food. Can we finish that part and then head home? Constantine is going to want to hear about this. It's probably a blessing that you don't like to shop much. You're dangerous." Bartholomew's color was returning, and I decided to drive at a moderate speed. He was never going to leave the house after this.

Chapter Eleven

I barely had enough time to drop off Bartholomew and the groceries at Reapers. With the witches and all the excitement, I was almost late for work again. Abuelita's only had a dinner hour on Mondays and closed early. I promised Bartholomew and Constantine I would feed them that night, since we finally had food. As Constantine had promised, my clothes and small items were in my room when I got back. I dressed in my regular black shirt and pants and was out the door.

I walked into Abuelita's exactly at 4:00 p.m. The dinner hour started at 4:30 p.m., and I knew I had lots to do after rushing out the day before. Abuelita was busy making rice and beans. She made her own tortillas, and those were already done. I had no idea what time Abuelita came in, but she always had so much stuff done, it was insane.

"Hi, Abuelita. Hope I'm not too late." I dropped my keys on the back table and grabbed an apron.

"Isis, you're looking much better." Abuelita had a huge smile on her face.

"I finally got some rest last night." I really needed to give Death thanks. Despite Constantine's horrible training session, I was feeling so much better. Even the exercise had my muscles vibrating with new energy.

"You should try doing that more often. You're almost glowing."

I stopped short and took a breath. Was I glowing because of my crazy Death kiss or just because I looked refreshed?

"By the way, Constantine said hi."

What happened next was totally unexpected. Abuelita dropped her wooden spoon into the pot and rushed over to me. In less than three seconds, I was being embraced in a huge hug.

"Thanks to all the saints in heaven you said yes. I was so worried you were going to turn it down. I felt horrible seeing you in so much pain on Saturday and not being able to help." Abuelita was holding my face in her hands. I couldn't move, so all I did was stare at her.

"You knew. I'm not even supposed to talk about this. How did you know?" I had a million questions I wanted answers to.

"Constantine asked to me watch over you when you started working here. They had to get everything ready before approaching you. Buildings are not done in a day." Abuelita made that statement as if it answered all my questions.

"You've been watching over me for the last three months?" No wonder she was always so nice to me.

"Isis, please. We're nice to you because you're a doll, not because we had to."

"Can you read my mind?" I was not prepared for all this.

"Of course not, silly girl. But your expressions are an open book. You need a better poker face. So, don't stand there. Start getting the utensils ready." Abuelita moved back to her stove, and I ran over to the bar to get things ready. We had less than thirty minutes before people started coming. I angled myself so I could work and still see Abuelita.

"Why did you agree to do it?" Was I such a sad case?

"I wasn't planning on it till you came in asking about the opening."

Abuelita had started working the chicken for the tacos and didn't see me staring.

"You weren't?"

She glanced at me, and I started working faster, pretending the answer was not very important to me.

"Most interns are self-righteous, pretentious pricks." Abuelita never cursed, so I knew she was serious.

"Don't hold anything back, now. Tell me how you really feel."

She smiled at me, and I couldn't help but smile back.

"Trust me, Death hires talented, smart, and gifted people. But they're insufferable and downright annoying. You were different. You weren't too good to clean tables and work for a living."

I had never thought she noticed my attitude that much. "Thanks. That means a lot to me." I moved around the bar to get the chairs down and set the tables up.

"So, I guess you won't be working here anymore." Abuelita had moved over to the bar and was watching me. I stopped short. She looked nervous.

"What? Are you firing me?"

"Of course not. But I figured that's why you came in today." Had Abuelita hit her head on the stove?

"Abuelita, you told me to come in this week, remember?" I had my hands on my hips before I could stop myself.

"Yes, I remember, but you accepted the job. That was the message from Constantine. Interns don't moonlight as waitresses in run-down Mexican places." She looked sad.

"Abuelita, I have no idea what interns do. I haven't even read the manual." At that, she gave me a confused look. "Long story. The bottom line is, as long as you still want me, I would like my job. It gives me a reason to run away from my evil overlord of a trainer. As long as you don't mind me missing at times due to soul business."

Abuelita laughed—a rich, powerful laugh that was contagious. The tension in my shoulders melted away. I hadn't noticed I was carrying any. I felt good not being alone with this huge secret. It meant I wasn't crazy.

"That is the best description of Constantine. He's all about soul business. But don't think I'm going to treat you any different now." She gave me a serious glare, but I could see she was trying to hide her smile as she walked back to the stove. "Also, don't tell Angelito a thing. He is clueless. Constantine has already made the announcement, so don't be surprised if people congratulate you. Those who do—you know what side of the fence they fall on."

That cat was fast. In less than ten hours, I had already been inducted into the world of the supernatural. I wondered if that was how those boys in that series felt. My life was becoming a comic book.

"So, basically, I have to wait for people to approach me, and then it's OK to talk shop stuff?" I needed a better guide than the ones I'd had so far. They were too vague.

"No. Not everyone who knows is for you. You don't talk to anyone. You just acknowledge they know and watch your back. Some want your job. Others want you out of the way." Abuelita was great at delivering horrible news with flair. She had steam all over her face as she spoke and didn't even blink.

"I believe that. The benefits package is out of this world."

"That's because you might not last long, so it needs to be enticing. Please try not to get killed. I would hate to murder some people." Now, that was true love, and I was afraid she meant every word.

I had to move a little faster to get the drinks ready. I had left all the plates in the dishwasher the night before, and I needed to get them set up. I prayed the Monday crowd would be calm when I opened the door. I peered outside, and the parking lot was empty. Normally on my nights, we had at least two people waiting in their cars to come in. Maybe this crowd was timid.

"Abuelita, what time do your Monday regulars come in?"

Abuelita had moved to the back to get the roast out of the oven. She had to come to the front to answer me. "Usually between four fifty and five fifteen. They know the nieces are never ready on time." She went back to the stove to prep more food. The blessing of Abuelita was that she had a set menu for each night. So, she always knew nothing was going to be wasted, three entrees per day.

"Why didn't you tell me? I've been killing myself trying to get ready." I now had twenty minutes to kill and not much to do.

"I thought you were making up for yesterday. By the way, did you find Bob?"

My good mood vanished. "Nope. They took another lady today. Bartholomew thinks they're witches." I was heading toward the bathrooms to check the toilet paper levels when Abuelita popped her head around the bar area.

"Isis, witches in Texarkana. Are you sure?"

I had to turn around to answer. Abuelita looked worried.

"I'm not sure of anything. We got hit with some nasty spells on the loop. Bart's the one who thinks they're witches." I was obviously missing something, because Abuelita looked troubled.

"What did Constantine say?"

"No time to talk. I was running late for work. You do realize I barely made it in at four." I knew she had noticed; I was not that smooth.

"Isis, watch yourself. Witches and wizards can be extremely dangerous. The closest registered coven is in Sulphur Springs." Was I supposed to remember that?

"Yes, we've noticed that. I still don't know who they are or what they want, but they're real good at covering their tracks. Bart has been trying to find them for over a year."

Abuelita didn't looked satisfied. I gave her one last glance and headed to the bathrooms.

By the time the first customer made it in, the bathrooms were stocked and cleaned. I had wiped down every table at least twice and even had time to eat rice and beans. My stomach was growling—not the best impression to give paying customers. Angel boy was the first one to walk in, followed by the Joneses. They looked nervous. I guessed interns didn't have a good reputation. All three looked as if they wanted to turn around.

"Hi, everyone. Your usual drinks?" I said from behind the bar.

Everyone gave me a polite nod. Like creatures of habit, they all took their assigned seats. At least that was a constant in my life. Gabe smiled at the Joneses and headed toward the bar. I passed him taking the horchata to the table.

"Mr. Gabe, I'll be right there with you." I gave him my most brilliant smile. Somehow, knowing the man was not just out of my reach but out of my planet made it easier. I had stopped drooling over him.

"Here you go, guys. What can I get you today?" The couple was looking at me as if I were growing horns.

"How are you feeling?" Ms. Jones asked, not really looking at me.

"I'm better, thank you. I had a rough couple of days, but I think things are slowly falling into place." I wasn't sure what it was, but she noticeably relaxed. Even her husband released the breath he was holding. I wondered when I had started noticing those little details.

"We're so happy, and congratulations."

I just smiled back at her. They ordered the Monday carne asada special.

By the time I got back to the bar, Gabe had a drink, courtesy of Abuelita. They were chitchatting merrily. I cautiously walked around her and left the orders on her stand in the kitchen. When I turned around, they were both smiling at me. Abuelita went back to the kitchen, very chipper.

"Isis, I'm so sorry I scared you on Saturday." His smile had changed to a look of concern.

"Don't be. It was probably my fault for not reading the manual." Eventually I would give in and read the damn thing. Maybe.

"You have a manual?" For an angel, Gabe had a fabulous mischievous smile.

"So I've been told. Really, it's all good. Lesson learned. My sergeants would have told me it was good training."

"I'm pretty sure Constantine would say the same." Gabe relaxed, and he radiated confidence and peace. That, I definitely hadn't noticed before.

"Everyone knows Constantine." I said that more as a statement than a question. I obviously knew the answer already.

"The boy has been around. No matter what people say about him, he's good at his job." Gabe's voice had a touch of pride. I was pretty sure they were old friends.

"How long has Constantine worked for Death?" I leaned over the bar and watched him drink his horchata.

"Rumor has it he always has worked for her. Officially, since Cleopatra. Now be nice, and don't try to get an honest boy in trouble. It's bad to gossip." Gabe winked at me and pulled out his phone. "Work calls; be right back." He strode out the front door to take his call. What kind of long-distance plan did God have?

The rest of my night flew by. I was seeing my customers in a new light. As if the veil of reality had been pulled off. At first, everyone was cautious and short around me. I guessed that like Abuelita, they were expecting me to change. I might need to tell people I was too lazy to learn a new personality.

Chapter Twelve

Six hours on my feet were murder. I had purchased really good shoes a while back, but I, obviously, needed new ones. It was still odd—the concept of a steady income. From what everyone said at Abuelita's, interns had mixed reputations and short life spans, so the salary was a great compensation plan. Maybe this week, I could swing by the mall or the Shoe Carnival. I wasn't sure when I would find time, but it was a fun thought.

I pulled up to the car entrance of Reapers. Bartholomew had a hand scanner installed ten feet from the building. That way I wouldn't have to get out to unlock the gate. The boy was impressive—probably dangerous, but impressive. I rolled in slowly and waited for the security system to do its magic. As soon as the second set of doors was up, I rolled down the shop to the car area. The emergency lights were the only lights on downstairs. The upstairs loft gave enough light to compensate.

It was past ten in the evening, and I didn't want to cook. I had cheated and brought food with me instead. I had not been expecting all the advice I had received from everyone. Even Abuelita was amazed at how concerned everyone was for me. I needed to say some extra payers of thanks for all the customers. By the time I reached the upstairs door, Bartholomew and Constantine were waiting for me. Neither was very patient.

"OK, what did I miss?" I dropped the food bag by the counter and waited for the lecture that was coming. When people looked at you so agitated, lectures were coming.

"We need your help. We have no idea how to make any of the stuff we bought today. We've already burned several weird packets of pasta." Bartholomew's face was priceless. He looked like the eleven-year-old boy he was, not like the genius hacker he played most of the time.

My heart dropped. Why did I always jump to the worst conclusions about people? It was a blessing I wasn't a gambler, because I was sucking at discerning people lately.

"Oh, I'm so sorry. Somehow, everyone wanted to talk after Constantine's announcement. Did you tell the whole world?" I was pulling containers out of the bag. "I figured it was a little too late to make food, so I brought dinner instead. Hope that's OK."

Bartholomew and Constantine's jaws both dropped. They looked as if they were almost drooling. I really didn't want to know what they had been eating.

"You brought Abuelita's home?" Bartholomew was now five and looking younger. It was incredible how young he sounded.

"Yes, I did, and I even checked that it was gluten-free." I found plates in the cabinet and made a plate of carne asada, beans, and rice for Bartholomew. I added a side of salsa and guacamole just in case. For Constantine, I skipped the beans and rice but added an extra helping of chicken.

I handed the plates to Bartholomew, who took them to the dining table. Like most of Abuelita's clients, I was nuts for the horchata. I had brought a large container. I poured a cup for Bartholomew and a small saucer for Constantine. They were both waiting for me very patiently. It was weird to have people waiting for me to actually eat, not just to get their food. I gave them both their drinks.

"Aren't you having dinner with us?" It was the first time Constantine had spoken. If I hadn't known better, I would have thought he sounded sad.

"I smell like Mexican food. I'm going to take a shower first. Don't wait for me." Even my hair smelled like it.

"We can wait." Bartholomew put his fork down and took a sip from his drink. I heard his stomach growling.

"If you guys don't mind me stinking, I'll join you." I walked over to the kitchen area and made myself a plate. I had three large containers—one with pork, one with chicken, and the last with rice and beans. I really hoped they were hungry, or we were going to have food for days.

"You smell pretty tasty. But I understand not wanting to walk around covered in it." I was sure that coming from a cat, being tasty was a great compliment.

I took my plate of rice and beans to the table. Bartholomew had poured me a drink while I was making my plate. I had piled guacamole on my plate. Abuelita's guacamole was addicting. I sat down and bowed my head to pray. Bartholomew and Constantine were staring at me with their heads tilted. They had such a similar look that I almost smiled.

"What are you doing?" Bartholomew looked so innocent.

"I was going to pray. Do you guys want to join me?" I was afraid to push my beliefs on them.

"I don't follow a god or denomination." Constantine looked at me as he spoke.

"Neither does my godmother. She claims to be agnostic. So, our prayers, growing up, were directed to a higher power in thanksgiving and grace. No affiliation necessary." That was the best way I could describe it.

"I like that. Could we try it?" Bartholomew looked eager. Or maybe he was just hungry.

"Your godmother sounds like my kind of people. And you grew up to be Catholic?" Constantine was right. My godmother and he would totally become best friends in a New York minute.

"I found the rituals and traditions comforting. Christianity called to me while I was in the military." At first, church was a way to get out of duties on Sunday in basic training. Then I was touched. I was definitely not sharing all that.

"And now you are a poinsettia, lily, and orchid."

Even Bartholomew was confused by Constantine's statement.

"I'm a what?"

"You're a Christmas, Easter, and Mother's Day Christian. The only times you go to church." He was rolling when he said that.

"OK, I like the other way better. Sounds so much nicer." A smart-ass cat was not funny.

"I heard that from a wise man in town. He's devious but oh so clever." Any man Constantine admired as devious and clever was someone to watch out for.

"Can we pray now, before Bart's stomach starts eating itself?"

At that, they both smiled and nodded.

I bowed my head, and the boys followed suit. "Father, we want to thank you for the food we are about to eat. We pray for the people who prepared it. We give you thanks for the new friends you've brought into our lives. Give us health and happiness. For all this we pray."

I finished my prayer with the sign of the cross. Crossing my right index finger over my right thumb, making a cross, I touched my forehead, my heart, my left shoulder, and finished with my right shoulder. The physical prayer made another cross over my body. Silently I repeated the words "In the name of the Father, the Son, and the Holy Spirit." I had done it so often that it took less than five seconds to complete.

"Let's dig in. I hope you guys like it."

Neither one replied. They just jumped on their food. I noticed Constantine had a booster chair to reach the table. At least he ate like a cat. I wasn't sure if I could handle him using a fork, since he didn't have fingers.

Abuelita's food had a way of calming the masses. We were all focused on it for at least the first five minutes.

"So, are you quitting Abuelita's?" Constantine asked between mouthfuls.

"I wasn't planning on it." I was enjoying my beans and rice too much to even look up. When I did, both Bartholomew and Constantine were staring at me. "What? What's wrong with that?"

"Nothing, but most interns said it was too much work to have two jobs." Bartholomew didn't sound convinced when he said that.

"It's a part-time job; come on, now. It's not like we're working in a factory with set hours. Besides, I get all the free food I want. You can't beat that." OK, so maybe I really did work for food, but a girl has to eat.

"Can I work there, too?"

Oh, thank God I wasn't the only one who would work for food. "Or I can just bring food home, and we share."

His mouth was full, but he managed to nod. Was this actually home? The thought scared me. We finished eating with a few comments regarding the food.

"OK, I'm heading to the shower. Afterward we need to talk about those witches and what's going on. You two are in charge of the dishes." With that I dropped my plate in the sink and headed toward my bedroom.

"She's been here less than a day, and she's already bossing us around. That's technically my job. I'm the guardian," Constantine said to Bartholomew.

Bartholomew laughed. "I heard that."

The hot shower did wonders for my muscles. I struggled to get out and get ready. The bed looked so good, but we needed to get to work. Hopefully, one of them would explain the mechanics of it. Twenty minutes later, I was clean and dressed and heading toward the common area.

Bartholomew was at his workstation typing away. Constantine was on the back of the couch talking to him.

"Are you sure you can't find them?" Constantine sounded irritated. "You can track anyone in the world, but you can't find witches in Texarkana."

"I told you, we don't have nearly as many police cameras around town. Makes the work a little harder now." Bartholomew didn't even look at him when he spoke.

"What are you doing, Bart?" I took a seat on the couch. Constantine was hanging on the top of the couch.

"Breaking the law and spying on people." At that, Bartholomew glared at Constantine.

Constantine just smiled.

"I'll take that. Did you find anyone?" I didn't want to know the details.

"Nothing. It's like they dropped off the face of the earth. At least we know what we're looking for now." Bartholomew turned back to face the screen.

"Hold it; I'm confused. You didn't know you were looking for witches. What were you doing in Brooklyn?" I was totally lost.

"We were technically in Chicago. Teck went to New York alone." Bartholomew was still not looking my way.

"So, what did he find?" This was like pulling teeth.

"We have no idea. Teck didn't share much." Constantine sounded bitter.

"Ninja Boy was a lone wolf. Great. In that case, what do you know?" It sounded as if Ninja Boy had been your typical intern—special and not well liked.

Constantine stretched out and started talking. "There was a report of a mass grave with over sixty bodies in Los Angeles. Death had no record of any of their passings. It looked like the bodies had been dead for over twenty years. But when Death arrived at the scene, she established that they had been dead only a couple of days. Bartholomew compared their fingerprints to those in the system, and they were a match for missing people. Except the people had been missing only a couple of months."

"Death had no record of their passing? Where were the souls? Doesn't Death know when a person is about to die and is there to escort the soul?" Was that lesson in the manual, too?

"That's the mystery. Death didn't sense their passing. By the time she arrived, the bodies were empty of souls." Bartholomew's voice came out as a whisper.

"How is that possible?" My voiced sounded hoarse.

"It's not. None of it is natural. Something or someone stole years of life and the souls out of them. We had no leads, and Death was mad." Constantine was angry. "So, Bartholomew started monitoring the missing person reports across the country. But as you probably know, very few reports are filed on homeless or runaways."

"How did he end up in New York?" I was still not following that part.

"A couple of shelters in the city started reporting suspicious people and their clients missing. It was the only lead we had." Bartholomew looked at us this time. "Teck went to New York to track leads before more souls were lost."

"Then I threw him off a balcony, and that never happened." My cheeks were burning in shame.

"In a nutshell. The next day, the police had a report of twenty dead bodies in the ground at a Catholic church. We assumed cult killing." Constantine was focused again.

"Why not witches?" I needed the CliffsNotes on the supernatural world.

"Witches were an option, since it took place on Ostara," Constantine said. "The spring equinox and a major Wiccan celebration. But the Catholic angle made that hard to connect."

"So, what do we do now that we know witches are involved?" I needed marching orders before I went crazy.

"Constantine contacted the Order of Witches, but they're a little short staffed, with Mabon being this weekend." Bartholomew was pulling up a calendar on his monitor.

"Let me guess—the fall equinox." Both Bartholomew and Constantine looked astonished. "Don't be too impressed. My godmother knew a little bit about every major religion and its practices. That included major holidays. So, what does that mean for us?"

"It means we need to find them before Saturday and stop them. With Texarkana being a much smaller city, a large group of people missing, even homeless, would be noticed. So far, we're tracking seven, including the girl from today and your friend Bob, but there could be more." Constantine hopped over to Bartholomew as he spoke.

Bartholomew pulled up a series of photos of the missing people, including Bob. My heart skipped a beat. I had seen most of those people around town, and I had never paid them any attention.

"OK, so what do I need to do?" I had signed up for this madness; I might as well earn my pay.

"You need to start checking all the shelters in town. In other words, you need to start investigating. It's not like humans are going to talk to Bartholomew and me." Constantine was right about that.

"We'll compile a list for you. You should rest. We've got lots of work." Bartholomew was ready to work, all night.

"Are you guys sure about that?"

They both looked at me as if I were crazy.

"OK, fair enough. Good night."

With one last look at the boys, I headed to my new room. I wanted to help, but I was exhausted. On top of that, I had a lot of stuff to process.

Chapter Thirteen

It appeared I didn't have that much to process after all. I lay down on the bed, and I was out before I knew it. Constantine woke me up at 5:30 a.m. for our regular training session. He proceeded to inform me this would be our normal time every day, including weekends. He had lost his mind. Day two on the job, and it was obvious this was interfering with my regular life. I needed to ask Abuelita to change my schedule if possible. I was a morning person, but I still needed at least six hours of sleep to function.

Bartholomew was definitely a night owl. He had left me a nice list of potential places to check out on the kitchen counter. He had even prioritized them based on their hours of operation. Most of the shelters, food kitchens, and service organizations were downtown. Downtown was a ghost town at night, and even during the day, it was fairly deserted. Unfortunately, it didn't have enough residents for one to notice whether people were disappearing. Most of the businesses had moved west following Interstate 30. Many boarded-up buildings and closed-down stores were downtown. The local museum, the Perot Theatre, and funky restaurants were also there. In general, downtown was a bizarre mixture of art district and forgotten town. I totally loved it.

Too bad I couldn't start directly on my list. Before I could leave Reapers, training needed to get done. I was convinced new torture devices had been built in the middle of the night. This morning, we had a set of pull-up bars. I had no upper body strength, so the concept of pull-ups was hysterical to me. Airborne school had been hell, but I had managed to survive it. Constantine's boot camp, on the other hand, was likely to kill me. His first instructions were to dangle from the bars and work on doing high kicks. The cat was nuts. I was a musician, not a gymnast.

After an hour of psychotic pull-up exercises, we moved on to balancing exercises. This area I didn't mind so much; I didn't want to fall off a balcony anytime soon. We practiced some weird routines using Pilates ropes that I was sure Constantine had made up. According to Constantine, I needed to master the art of suspension. I had no idea what he was talking about. Where was I supposed to be suspended from? It was probably a good thing I never got around to asking him, since we moved to cardio for another hour. Constantine was easily offended if you were able to talk during his cardio sessions.

For the second day in a row, I was soaking wet and smelled like hell. I prayed the evil overlord would have mercy on my soul, but no. Last hour, we went underneath the loft next to the vehicle entrance. With Constantine in the lead, I was prepared to enter another medieval torture chamber. I was pleasantly surprised. The room underneath my sleeping chamber was a high-speed firing range.

For a group that is forbidden to kill, they sure had violent devices. I was afraid I was going to be out of practice, but like most things the military teaches, shooting was another muscle-memory activity for me. I was in heaven. It was a sad thing to admit, but I missed having a real gun with me, specifically an M16 rifle. That had been my buddy. Constantine actually had to kick me out of the range. According to Bartholomew's list, I needed to be at Saint Edward's Outreach Center before it closed at noon.

It was past eleven in the morning by the time I hit the shower. The good news was that I could shower in under three minutes—thank you, Uncle Sam. The bad news was that I was starving, and the only thing quick was Constantine's odd shake. I asked what was in those things, and he told me I'd rather not know. I called them Constantine's protein shakes. They tasted like peanut butter shakes. Whatever the secret ingredient was, it was supposed to help me heal and develop muscles.

The reality was that I did not want to know what I was drinking. With my luck lately, I was probably drinking mouse droppings or some other disturbing ingredient. I grabbed the suspicious bottle and ran out the door. I took one last look around and found

Constantine getting ready to nap on the couch. No wonder he was always ready to go—he napped all the time. I wasn't hating on him—just envious I couldn't do the same.

By the time I made it to the outreach center on Ash Street, they were getting ready to close. The outreach was known as the Blue House to its clients. It shared the house with something else that I had no idea about. If I'd gone to church more often, I might have known. The highlight of my day was being able to find it. The outreach was located on the back side of Saint Edward Church. They provided daily lunches to anyone who showed up, Monday through Friday.

Honestly speaking, I had no clue what I was doing. I was not an investigator and had no experience getting information out of people. It wasn't as if I could just ask if anyone had seen a bunch of witches stealing people. Bartholomew's paper said to look around and be sociable. Driving the Whale made me look more like a person in need than like someone looking for a friend. That stupid hole did not help at all.

I climbed the four short steps in front of the house and entered. Inside the outreach, the first thing I saw was a large counter in front of the entrance. There was a small corridor that opened up to a back area. The room was divided by a set of curtains blocking the view to the left—unfortunately not very well, since I saw a work table and pantry shelves in that area.

At the entrance, a pretty blonde, maybe in her early twenties, handed me a plastic bag. The food was set up like an assembly line on the counter. You took a bag and grabbed an item from each stack. It was a pretty efficient system, since they were only open for two and a half hours.

"Please take only one item from each basket. You can get your coffee at the end of the table." She pointed to the coffee station, where a lady in her late sixties with gray hair was pouring cups.

I handed her back her bag and looked around the room. There were only four people, including the pretty blonde. The servers had little name tags that read *Volunteer*. I couldn't find anyone who was actually staff.

"Thank you, ma'am, but I was actually looking for a friend of mine. He's about six feet two inches and maybe two hundred pounds. His name is Bob. He's an army vet. He might be hurt. Have you seen him, by any chance?" I was, technically, looking for Bob, so I could use that angle to start.

The outreach was made up of volunteers of different ages and genders. On a Tuesday morning, most of the people there were probably retired. A handsome man in his sixties moved closer to the serving counter. He had a fabulous head of shining silver-gray hair and a great mustache to match. I was sure he had been a heartbreaker in his youth. Then again, by the look on the faces of some of the older ladies in the room, he probably still was. He just didn't know it.

"On any given day, we normally see between a hundred and a hundred and fifty people. Unless he was a regular, it's hard to say." He had a strong voice to match his confident demeanor. I was hooked—he had my vote for sexy mature man of the year.

"Do you have a last name? Maybe we could ask some of the clients. Bob is a bit generic," the little blonde holding the bags said. Next to the pile of bags, she had a clipboard with names. She looked out of place and way too young next to everyone else. I wondered why she wasn't working or at school.

"Unfortunately, I don't. Maybe I could talk to the people who stopped by, if you guys don't mind." Why hadn't I ever asked Bob his last name? Oh, yeah—because I never thought he would get kidnapped.

"Sure, but most of our clients are gone. We're getting ready to close. They know anything special is passed out early," the last lady in the room said. She was in charge of passing out the entrees. The lady was in her early seventies, maybe older. She had that grandma look that was kind but stern. I had no idea why she was still there. She looked as if she should be home resting.

"That's true. Thank you anyways." I was getting ready to leave when the handsome man spoke up again.

"What happened to your friend, if you don't mind my asking?" He looked as if he was used to being in charge and having people listen to him.

"We think he was abducted. He's been missing since Sunday." I felt a lump in my throat form.

"Oh, Lord help him," I heard the lady by the coffee whisper. The elders did the sign of the cross, but not the blonde. Interesting—a non-Catholic volunteering at a Catholic shelter. That was really unusual for this area.

"Have you checked the library? A lot of our clients hang out there. Maybe somebody has seen him there," the blonde said. She was very helpful and actually looked concerned.

"Thank you. That's a good place to start. I'm sorry to have bothered you all. Have a great day." I walked toward the back door. The flow of the place was one way; you came in one door and left through another. As I said, very efficient.

Outside, I was standing on a ramp at the side of the Blue House. A picnic table was set by a large tree, and a few people were still waiting around. I took a deep breath and headed their way. Their conversation stopped as soon as they saw me. There were three men, ranging from mid-twenties to early fifties; at least that was my best guess. They all looked as if they'd had rough lives and had been exposed to too much sun. Their skins were leathery-looking. As I got closer, I realized they were probably younger.

"Hi. I'm sorry to bother you gentlemen, but could you help me? I'm looking for a friend of mine." The military had done a great job training me in saying *sir* and *ma'am*. A little respect goes a long way, especially if people aren't used to receiving it.

"Yes, young lady. How can I help you?" the oldest of the three, a tall black man, asked. The other two looked at him in shock.

"Who made you king? She said 'gentleman.' She was obviously talking to me," the youngest man, in his twenties, a blond boy with haunted eyes, said.

"I'm the wisest out here," the older man said with a devilish grin.

"Wise, wise my ass. You're just old," the middle one, a Latino guy in his thirties, said.

"Thank you, Juan. You tell him," the blond said.

I was staring at Texarkana's own United Nations. One thing I had learned from the military was that when you stopped looking for differences in people, you were always surprised at how alike everyone truly was. At the end of the day, a poor person was a poor person regardless of race. These three men understood that and embraced it. I wanted to hug them. Instead, I just smiled.

"Don't be jealous. You'll get there one day," the black guy said. By the look of their postures, they were ready to banter all day.

"Sorry. Maybe all three of you could help me. I'm looking for a friend of mine. He's been missing since Sunday."

The three men suddenly got very quiet. They all looked around, worried.

In a hushed voice, the black man told me, "You look like a smart girl. Stop looking around and asking questions. Bad things are happening to those who ask questions. If your friend is missing, I'm sorry, but he's not coming back. Go home and get away from here."

Before I could say anything else, they all got up and left. They headed north toward Seventh Street. I really sucked at this investigation gig.

Chapter Fourteen

It was not meant to be that I would make it to work at a reasonable time this week. The library was a total bust, in more ways than one. The Texarkana Library was on the Texas side of downtown, with the entrance on Third Street. It sat in the center of the block. If you parked on Oak Street, as was my custom, you got to enjoy the unique design. One wall was made of glass, and it curved around itself almost in a semiarch. From Oak Street, you had to walk down a flight of stairs to reach the library. It had parking spaces on almost all sides.

The library was a favorite location for a lot of people, especially those whose resources were low. It had AC and heating all year long, free computer and Internet access, bathrooms, and a drinking faucet. You were out of the elements, and nobody bothered you. As long as you were quiet and stayed in your lane, the staff left you alone. It wasn't a huge library, but the couches were cozy, and, like most southern places, the staff was friendly. I knew the library very well; I was a regular. Remember, it wasn't till the day before that I actually had a real income.

Unlike some of the people around town, I wasn't bothered by the library's location. I was an avid reader. I could afford the ten dollars for the library card rather than hang out at Books-A-Million. I did love Books-A-Million's coffee. If the library ever opened a coffee shop, I would never leave. I was blaming my love for books for my giant disaster.

I spent over two hours at the library. Hey, no need to judge now; the first hour, I conducted business, which translated to scaring the hell out of everyone with all my questions. Bob had never mentioned going to the library. I was pretty sure none of these people had ever seen him there. On top of that, they were doing a reading day at the library. The place was packed with moms and little Mini-Mes. The few people who did talk to me said the same thing: stay away, and don't ask questions.

I was tired, and my cheeks hurt from all my smiling. Trying to look harmless and sweet was a lot harder than I had thought. You have to move slowly, look submissive, and not attract a lot of attention. When you're five feet eight inches and have plenty of lady lumps, as the Black Eyed Peas described them, it's hard to blend in. Even with my baseball cap, I managed to draw lots of stares. I gave up after an hour and decided to take advantage of the trip. I checked the mystery aisle and then the fantasy aisle. I needed to do some research on this magic crap.

I was walking on cloud nine. I had books and plenty of time to change before work. The Whale had no AC, and it was still in the eighties and humid for September. I wasn't complaining too much. I could handle the heat better than the cold. After the short walk back to the parking lot with all my books and movies, I was sweaty and sticky. By the time I reached the Whale, my plans were shattered. Someone had slashed all my tires. Really? Who does that kind of stuff, and especially to a minivan? I could have been a mom with four kids.

Bartholomew had programmed his number into my phone, as well as the Reapers' main line. I called the main line, in case he was still asleep. Constantine picked up, no idea how. I was so mad, I didn't even care to know how he'd done it. I managed to ramble off my disaster without screaming. It was my lucky day. Constantine was bored and had a million questions. After the interrogation was over, he told me to stay put and wait for his buddy to show up. I had to admit, Constantine had connections. In less than twenty-five minutes, a wrecker showed up to fix my tires. Let's be honest. One tire I could have managed on my own. But all four—that wasn't fair. Nobody carried four spares in the trunk in case of emergency.

Two very large men got out of the wrecker and went to work. I was impressed with their speed, but it still took them over forty minutes to change all four tires. By the time they were done and I was able to leave, I had less than forty minutes to get to work. No wonder people thought interns sucked. We were never on time for anything. There was a conspiracy against me. That was my story, and I was sticking to it. The only thing productive I did while I waited was practice my third-eye exercises. I focused on the Kidtopia Park across the street. The park was empty. I wanted to avoid being traumatized by the vision. I was definitely not looking at the guys working on the Whale.

It was 4:10 p.m. by the time I made it to Abuelita's. Abuelita was busy working her magic by the stove. I dropped my keys in their usual place and grabbed my apron. I was still mad.

"Please tell me somebody didn't actually slash all of your tires."

My jaw dropped. "How in God's name do you know that?" Was Abuelita a psychic and nobody had told me?

"Come on, Isis. There are not that many tow-truck companies that a talking cat can do business with. Besides, Reggie is the best in town. Everyone uses him." She didn't even look up. If Reggie was in that damn manual, I was going to shoot somebody.

"He might be the best, but he's not very discreet, by the looks of it." Reggie was not my favorite person right now.

"Oh, Reggie is very discreet. Unfortunately, everyone knows his radio frequency." My looked of pure confusion was enough to have Abuelita translate her statement. "It's like having a police scanner. You just know what places to avoid depending on whether Reggie's heading that way."

"That's totally creepy. Thank you for freaking me out. Next thing, you'll tell me you chase after ambulances. My boss is a creep."

Anybody else would have killed me. Abuelita just thought it was funny. "I'm well informed. But seriously, you've been on the job two days, and your tires have already gotten slashed. Who did you piss off?" Abuelita was right. I was on a roll.

"Besides those witches, nobody." Great. The witches were on the offensive against me. Maybe Bartholomew was right. Since I could see the supernatural world now, that made me a target. I was in serious trouble.

"Isis, I told you, watch your back. I hate training new people, so don't get killed." Words of wisdom from the peanut gallery. Just what I needed.

I left Abuelita to her cooking and got busy with my own work. Even with the regulars getting there at five-ish, I was really behind.

I hadn't swept the outside in a few days. The chairs were still up on the tables, and dishes were in the dishwasher. This was normally a two-person job. I was surprised she hadn't asked Angelito to come in.

I decided to ask on my way to sweep the front of the restaurant. I was feeling nosy, but I needed a distraction from my issues. "Abuelita, where's Angelito?"

A strangled sound came from the back. I heard pots slamming, and Abuelita walked to the bar area with a huge knife in hand. I panicked—let's be honest; she looked dangerous. I didn't want to test how good my new health insurance was. I took a careful step toward the door in case I had to take off in a hurry.

"That little boy had a date with that girl of his. Do you know I still haven't met her? There's something really...oh, what's the word for it?" She was waving her knife in the air like a machete.

"Wrong? Suspicious? Shady? I could go on here. Which word?" I was getting really good at deciphering Abuelita's lingo.

"Yeah, that one. Shady. That's exactly what's going on here."

"Abuelita, you do know in most cultures, people don't meet the family until they're really serious, like marriage material. Angelito goes through girls kind of quickly. It's only been a week, if that." Granted, for Angelito that was probably considered serious—even long term.

"Isis, I know all of his friends and even those loose girls he hangs out with. Why is this one different? I don't like it." She went back to the kitchen before I could respond. She was furious. Thank God I had to clean outside.

Texas didn't have the breathtaking fall colors of New England. Instead, we had a mild version of summer, with a breeze that begged you to nap. I swept the outside quietly, but I was daydreaming of napping. Tuesdays were my lazy day. I normally would be sitting on my little porch reading a book and drinking lemonade. Now I was driving around town like a maniac, chasing crazy witches, and working two jobs. I missed my lazy days.

My daydreaming didn't last long. I had an early customer and had to move. Fortunately, he wanted a to-go order. After he left, I picked up the pace. I couldn't afford to waste time if customers were walking in. I barely finished on time before the place was packed. Gabe and the Joneses were in their usual seats, followed by a group of boys in the opposite corner. My third eye was closed, but I was starting to feel their energies. Gabe felt like sunshine on a summer day at the beach. The Joneses had the feel of a cool breeze before rain. The boys, on the other hand, felt like a hot day in the desert—dry but penetrating.

"So, four flats in one day. That's probably a new record," Gabe said as I refilled his horchata.

"Hey, I'm good at making an impression."

"That is definitely an impression." Gabe's smile was intoxicating. Hard to be mad when the man looked good enough to eat. I had always thought God had lost an angel, but I wasn't expecting it to be true. Who said God doesn't have a sense of humor?

By the time seven rolled around, I was totally dizzy. The stress of the day, my lack of food, and all their energy were making me dizzy. I felt drunk and tired just being around them. The trash was piling up, and most of the customers were gone. I had a few to-go orders, but I could sneak outside and be back in time. I grabbed the bag and headed toward the back door. The Dumpster to the restaurant was at least twenty feet from the building. From that angle, I had a great view of the cars in the parking lot up front. The air felt amazing on my skin. I took a deep breath and felt a shiver all the way down my back. When I turned around, something hard hit me across the head.

I flew across the back lot and landed headfirst on the dirt. The trash bag was to my left, and fortunately, it hadn't busted on me. Everything looked a bit blurry. Someone grabbed me by the hair and pulled me up. The sensation was excruciating. I had never been in a fight before, but I finally understood why girls always put their hair up. My hands reached up, trying to free myself from the attacker. Unfortunately, that left my midsection wide open. I got a swift jab to the ribs followed by a hook to the face. I bit my lips, and I could taste the blood in my mouth.

"You should have listened to the homeless people, little girl. Obviously, you learn lessons the hard way," a muffled female voice said in my ear. I felt the pressure of a knife on my neck as my hair was pulled again. Another female, wearing a Dora the Explorer mask, walked in front of me. These weirdos had some nerve co-opting poor Dora. Thankfully, no children were passing by, or they would have been traumatized. For that matter, I was.

I couldn't scream without the knife digging harder into my neck. I was on my knees and barely had time to see the girl land a kick on me. She was fast. At least I was able to cover my midsection. Death was not around; time had a way of slowing down when she was near. Killing me was not part of their plan. Option two, beating the hell out of me, was. Horrible plan for me. I was truly dizzy and maybe delirious.

Then I heard gunshots very close to my head. Were they going to shoot off my legs, too?

"Get off her, or I will blow your head off." Abuelita had enunciated each one of her words. She radiated cold energy that I could feel from behind. I wasn't sure what was more frightening: Abuelita's voice or the sound of the shotgun as she reloaded. Oh God, please don't let her use it, or I was a goner.

"This isn't your fight, *vieja*. You don't want to get involved," a female voice I hadn't heard before said from my left, with a patronizing tone.

"Funny, you're in my parking lot. You know the rules. This is neutral ground. You want to try this again?" Abuelita had moved into my line of vision. She was an avenging angel, shotgun at the ready, a pair of knives by her side, and a bat tied to her apron behind her.

Without a word, the assault was over, and I was dropped to the ground. Abuelita moved slowly to cover me. I was flat on the ground, and everything hurt. I raised my head just in time to see the Whale blow up. Those psychopaths blew up my minivan, Hollywood style. Stunt coordinators would have died for that shot. The Whale was engulfed in flames, the windows were shattered, and the frame looked as if it had collapsed into itself. I rolled over to stare at Abuelita. Her mouth was wide open in shock.

"I think it would be safer if I stopped working here." I didn't want Abuelita getting hurt because of me.

"Isis, please. We're not going to let some skinny witches run us off. Besides, family doesn't turn on one another when things get tough." Abuelita looked down at me and winked. For an orphan, I had gotten a huge family in a very short time. This was probably how those Chia Pets developed.

"Thank you." I hurt too much to say anything else.

"No need for thanks, but let's get you inside. The police will be here soon, and we have some explaining to do. Don't say a word. I'll handle it. I'll take you home once they're gone."

All I could do was nod. Everything was throbbing. She grabbed me by the arm and took me inside.

Chapter Fifteen

By the time the cops left Abuelita's, it was way past ten. I wasn't sure what Abuelita was saying; it all sounded muffled to me. Every once in a while, they all turned toward me, Abuelita motioned for me to confirm something, and I did. I was a good little soldier when it came to following instructions, at least when the police were involved. Two cops took our statements while hot Smith watched the burning Whale. I saw him from the window, and he still had a fabulous behind.

Reggie was at the scene before the cops were gone. I wasn't sure how he knew. Maybe Abuelita had a panic button somewhere to call him. I had a horrible habit of making emotional attachments to things, especially things given to me. Watching the Whale hauled away, I felt as if I had let my godmother down. How was I going to explain this to her? She knew when I was lying, even over the phone. My poor Whale. It broke my heart.

I didn't remember when Abuelita brought me home. My body was on autopilot. I walked into the loft before I realized where I was.

"Holy crap, what happened to you?" Bartholomew was on his feet, running toward me before he finished his sentence. He cleared the room and walked me over to the couch. I dropped down like a sack of potatoes. Absolutely no grace on that dismount. I dropped my head on the armrest. It hurt so bad everywhere. "Constantine, hurry," Bartholomew yelled across the room.

"Ouch. Please tell me you ran over a tree." It took Constantine less than a minute to cross the room and land on the couch. He, on the other hand, made everything look smooth.

"Sorry, Yoda. Got jumped from behind by our friendly neighborhood witches," I muttered, my head on the little cushion on the couch. I had no idea when the cushion had appeared under my head. "Oh, and those bitches."

"The witches?"

"Yeah, that, too. Thanks, Bart. Those things blew up the Whale." I tried to get up, but everything hurt.

"You mean the Whale looks worse than you? Now, that's a horrible mental image." Bartholomew sounded traumatized.

"Why didn't you put them to sleep instead of letting them beat you?" Constantine sounded mad.

"Put them to sleep? How? With my Jedi mind powers?" When pushed to the limit, my anger takes over.

"If you want to call it that. Every intern gets the power to knock people out. The stronger you are, the longer the spell. Please tell me you read the manual." Constantine was inches from my face. I closed my eyes and felt my cheeks warming up. "Isis, you are going to get yourself killed if you don't take this seriously." Now Constantine was mad. I hated that stupid manual.

"Why didn't you make an audiobook instead? It would make great listening material during your torture sessions." I was whining. How sad. "Besides, it's not as if I have that much free time here."

"Those are excuses. The result is the same—you look like a plane just used you as a landing zone." I didn't know it was possible, but I was sure Constantine took a deep breath to calm himself down. His eyes were glowing red, and he looked as if he were growing in size.

"I'm sorry; you're right. How do I make this power thing work?" When in Rome, resign to their will.

"Each intern's manifestation is different. You're mixing your gifts with Death's blessing. It's our way to avoid unnecessary killing and keep humanity in the dark. Teck had darts that he injected with his own compound." Constantine tried to calm down. His eyes stopped glowing, and he looked his normal size.

"Great. I'm not an alchemist. I barely passed chemistry. I'm a musician, remember?" Maybe I had picked the wrong career path, but God, chemistry sounded so boring to me.

"Isis, magic comes from the soul. All Death did was enhance what was already there. If you tried a spell, you probably would poison them to the ultimate slumber." Constantine waited for his words to sink in.

"You could do like the Pied Piper," Bartholomew said from his chair at the workstation.

"Thanks, Bart. I thought you were on my side. Now you, too, are making fun of me."

"Isis, I think Bartholomew had a great idea." Constantine was staring at me.

"What?" I was staring back and forth between the two of them. They had lost their minds. "OK, guys, the one who got hit in the head was me, remember?"

Constantine rolled his eyes at me; I wasn't sure how. "Isis, please." People were saying that a lot lately. Constantine continued without even blinking an eye. "You've heard the saying 'Where there's smoke, there's fire.' Most of your folktales and stories are based on some truth. Like the religions of old are now your mythologies. Believing in things gives them power. In your case, it's like faith."

"So, you're saying the Pied Piper was real." Why was I even surprised anymore?

"A man who used magic through his music to enchant people, yes. The rest of the story is very iffy. Think of the power music currently has. It makes people want to move, even those who can't dance. Now imagine adding an intent to that. It's powerful." Constantine had a smirk when he finished.

"OK, so maybe I have some hope." I tried to sound positive.

"You have more than hope. We do need to add some martial arts and grappling to your training. You can't be taking any more beatings." Oh God, he was going to kill me.

"Constantine, if magic comes from the soul, what happens when you misuse it?" I needed to change the topic fast.

"Your scientists and religious groups understood this very early on. Your scientists found that for every action, there is an equal and opposite reaction. The religious leaders developed the golden rule—do unto others as you wish to be done to you. The rules are simple. Anything you put out there will come back to you in one way or another."

Bartholomew and I were listening in silence. Neither one of us moved. Bartholomew cleared his throat. "Is that why you are always preaching about intentions?"

"Buddhism has a beautiful saying: cause no harm to any living thing. Every time those witches use their power to kill and destroy, it destroys a part of their soul. Makes them easy marks for demons and the like." Constantine looked sad as he spoke.

"What about those who worship the devil?" Theoretical discussions were not my specialty—way too many variables.

"They know where they're going. They're just trying to get points to have a higher status in the afterlife. Some want to transcend to demons." I had officially heard it all. "OK, enough chitchat. We've got work to do. Bartholomew, go make Isis a bath. You know what to use."

"Yes, sir." Bartholomew flew out of the room faster than I believed possible.

"I can make my own bath." I struggled to sit up.

"No, no you can't. We don't have all night to watch you wobble around. In the fridge there is a shake marked Isis. Grab it on your way to the shower and drink it." Constantine was not leaving any room to argue.

"Do I have to?" I was afraid of drinking any weird potions.

"Girl, don't make me scratch your eyes out. Go to the fridge and then the bath. Sit in the tub for twenty minutes, no more and no less. Move!" He yelled the last part, since I was sitting there with my mouth open.

There was no need to argue. I struggled to my feet and shuffled across the room. By the time I had reached the fridge, Bartholomew was back from my room. He saw me and made a beeline toward me. Without a word he opened the fridge, grabbed my shake, opened the lid, and handed it to me. No words were spoken—just smiles and nods. Bartholomew was wiser than I had ever imagined.

I refused to admit to Constantine that the shake was actually delicious. It was a peanut-butter-and-banana shake, and probably the creamiest I had ever had. It had a hint of vanilla and maybe cinnamon. It was so good; I didn't care what else it had. Yeah, I loved food. By the time I had shuffled to my room, the shake was half-gone. I forced myself to the bathroom instead of stopping by my bed. I would never get up if I sat down.

The bathroom smelled like jasmine, peppermint, and vanilla. Not what I was expecting. I loved all those fragrances. It took me almost three minutes to take off my clothes. I normally could undress in under twenty seconds. I set the alarm on my phone and placed the phone on the outside ledge of the tub. My bathroom had a walk-in shower and a separate tub. The shower and tub were next to each other on the right-hand wall. The tub was a modern piece that looked as if it were carved from the wall. It had a small ledge around it.

The toilet was on the opposite side, and it was inside what looked like a small closet. I had two sinks that formed an L shape, with lots of counter space. The bathroom was awesome. I didn't know how they had done it, but it was made for me. I looked at the alarm and made sure it had twenty minutes on it. I didn't need Constantine coming in to yell at me. . The water was close to boiling levels. I felt like a large lobster, and my skin was slowly cooking.

I was told your body adjusted to baths and they stopped being as hot. Either the tub had a hidden heater, or this water was magically boiling itself—it never cooled off. By the time my alarm went off, I was a giant prune. The room felt cold after I had been boiled for twenty minutes.

Somehow, I never felt clean after a bath. I jumped into the shower and washed off. As I rubbed my stomach, my abs didn't hurt as much. My head wasn't throbbing as much. It was hard to admit, but Constantine's brew worked. I didn't understand how, but I was significantly better.

I walked to my room to get dressed and found a flute case on my bed. I was afraid to move closer, in case it disappeared. My heart was pounding by the time I reached the bed. A note was lying on top of the case.

Dear Isis, your mom asked me to hold this for you. Hope it brings you as much joy as it brought her. Death.

I cried. The last time I had seen this was in the burning vehicle with my parents. It was my mother's flute. I had never liked the flute; I preferred the saxophone. When they died, that was all I wanted to play. I poured my heart out over things a little girl is not meant to understand. Here it was, looking better than ever. I opened the case. Inside was a picture of my parents and me after my first recital. Mom had placed the picture there to remind me to have fun while I played.

I took the picture out and placed it on the nightstand next to the bed. I needed a frame for it, but it was enough for now. I crawled into bed and took the flute with me. Tears rolled down my cheeks, but I played. The most haunting melody came out, full of pain and sorrow. My pain and years of sorrow, anger, and loneliness. I played, and I felt a small pressure release in my heart. I was not an alchemist, but, by God, I was a hell of a musician. I wasn't sure when, but I knew I could make the magic work. I fell asleep in my towel holding the flute.

Chapter Sixteen

It was barely five in the morning, and I was already up and working out. I had no idea what Constantine had put in that shake, but I felt amazing. Yeah, my muscles still ached, but I wasn't bruised from the beating last night. On top of that, I had slept like a baby. Constantine was usually up and ready to roll by the time I got up; this time I beat him. It was going to be a great day.

I was on my fifth pull-up when I noticed the new additions to the gym. True to his word, Constantine had added a punching bag, one of those weird training mannequins you see at martial arts centers. After careful examination of the gym area, I saw that we had some weird ropes hanging from the ceiling, not to mention lots and lots of jump ropes. I was impressed and a bit worried. Constantine had some impressive connections to deliver in the middle of the night. Unfortunately, this meant that my training sessions were going to get even more painful.

"Well, somebody woke up feeling much better today."

I jumped at least four feet off the ground due to Constantine's voice. How did he do it? I knew cats were sneaky, but Constantine was the king of stealth.

"You need a bell or something wrapped around you. You scared me to death." My heart was racing, at least 150 beats per minute now, and it had nothing to do with my workout.

"Not my fault. You should be paying more attention to your surroundings. What if I were the bad guys?" Constantine was too happy with his own skills.

"I'm sure they would have shot me instead of sneaking around trying to scare me. You're just mean." I was at least breathing normally now.

"Oh, please. It wasn't that big a deal. But back to you. How long have you been here?"

I did a quick check of my watch. "Almost an hour. I woke up with tons of energy." I really wanted to knock the teeth out of that crazy witch who'd hit me the night before, so technically, I was pissed.

"I like the motivation. Isis, remember, these witches are good. They're powerful and well prepared. They've been evading us now for over a year. You've been doing this for two days. You need to be careful." Constantine jumped on the bench to have a better look at me. "You're looking better."

"So, you're saying I have no way of beating them?" My hopes were crumbling.

"That's not what I said. Trust me, a few crazy witches are not going to stop us. We just need to be smarter than they are. Unfortunately, they're pretty smart." Constantine had moved over to the punching bag and other weird artifacts as he talked.

"How is it possible they are able to do this? Why can't Death sense it?" I was feeling pretty good. I walked over to one of Constantine's torture machines and started doing inverted sit-ups. The blood quickly rushed down to my head in the odd position.

"That's what we wanted to discuss yesterday. Bartholomew has been running all possible scenarios on his computer. The only thing we could conclude was they're killing them in a place where Death cannot enter."

I stopped mid sit-up, with my body perpendicular to the floor. I had to turn slightly left to look at him. "What does that mean?" It was one thing to be working out for an hour, but I was not awake enough to follow Constantine's theories today.

"Think about it. If a person dies here on earth, Death senses it and appears before the final breath. But what if they were taken outside, to a place where nobody ever dies? Death would have no access or jurisdiction there." Constantine looked at me, waiting for me to make the connection. I was silent for a minute. This wasn't possible.

"Constantine, are you suggesting they are taking them to heaven to kill them?"

"Don't be silly, child. The Big Guy and every angel would have pulverized them. We would have seen a hard-core meteor shower or some other crazy phenomenon. Access to the promised land is guarded very well. No, not heaven, but you're on the right track." That was a lovely mental picture. Thanks, Constantine.

"Oh, no. Not hell." I really didn't want to go to hell, alive or dead.

"Hell is another one. And your own personal favorite, purgatory." Constantine sat on another bench, this time in his sphinx pose. We were both silent for a minute.

"Hell or purgatory—those are our options. Great! Why couldn't they be hiding at the Golden Corral or Walmart? So, what now?" And my day had started so well.

"You want easy? Please! Isis, we work for Death." OK, so Constantine had a point. "First thing we need to do is narrow down locations. We have less than four days, counting today, to find these witches and stop them before they move on."

"How do we know they haven't left yet?" With my luck lately, anything was possible.

"Why waste their time beating you up? Besides, if they've left, they'll need to find another location, and they don't have enough time. And it would be really hard to travel with kidnapped people without drawing attention." Constantine was pensive as he spoke. "Isis, you're going to have to make some house calls. When was the last time you went to church?"

"Church? Like a Catholic church?" Constantine nodded. "I've been to Saint Ed a couple of times."

"That's a great place to start. On Wednesdays, Father Francis holds confession at eleven in the morning, before the Mass. You should stop by. Tell Father Francis that Constantine says to keep it real." Why was I surprised that Constantine knew the priest? Why did anything ever surprise me anymore? Oh yeah—because he was still a damn cat.

"Do I want to know how you know the priest?"

He actually smiled at me. I was not getting an answer out of him.

"So, I need to go to confession. Great." I hadn't been to confession in over a year. It was painful to me.

"Hey, some discussions need to be done under strict parameters. For your protection and Father Francis's as well. We all know the power and binding laws of confessions."

Constantine was right. I didn't want this crazy secret to get out to anyone. Under confession, anything I said to Father Francis could not be discussed with anyone, regardless of who. One of the strongest vows that was ever made. It was the reason people still flocked to confession to clear their conscience and received absolution.

"How is Father Francis going to help us?" I was hoping this would be an easy answer.

"Unlike heaven or hell, purgatory is a transition place. So, nobody is actually guarding it from the other side. Normal points of access to it are Catholic churches." Constantine read the confused look on my face. "Catholics are the only ones who believe in it and created it. Father Francis should be able to tell you if anybody has tried to cross from his gates."

"The job of a priest always seems so lonely and odd. This is not helping their case." On top of watching over congregations filled with all sorts of weird people, they were also responsible for the passage to purgatory. That job was awful.

"It is a calling, not a career; remember that. Now let's discuss your powers. I'm glad you were able to tap into it, but we need you to think lullaby, not suicide."

"What are you talking about? What suicide?" I had obviously missed something.

"Your playing last night. It was haunting, full of pain and sorrow. Bartholomew and I had to put on headphones before we killed ourselves. A bit too powerful." Constantine shook his head like he was trying to clear the memory away.

"Oh my God, I'm so sorry. I didn't realize I was doing it. I just got carried away when I saw my mother's old flute." Last thing I wanted was to hurt either of them.

"Relax, Isis. We were not hurt. But remember, music has power. Your emotions will drive the magic. You need to focus on putting people to sleep, not to death." I didn't like the idea of my feelings translating into actions that could affect others. That could get messy.

"OK, so I need to play a lullaby." I didn't remember the last time I played a lullaby, if I'd ever played one.

"Yeah, like 'Rock-a-Bye Baby.' That kind of stuff." He flicked his paw as he spoke, in a nonchalant sort of a way.

"You do know that ends with baby and cradle falling from the tree." Such an odd song to sing to a sleeping child. I was disturbed.

"It was not my idea to put the cradle in the tree to begin with. Besides, you get the idea. Nothing fancy but sleep-inducing." Constantine was right; I needed something sleep-inducing. I needed to do some research now. "Have you figured out how you are going to use it? I doubt the witches will give you time to pull out your flute, tune it, and then play. It also doesn't make for a very practical weapon."

"Baby steps now. Let's cross that bridge when we get there. Besides, I was a paratrooper band member, not that different." This got more complicated by the minute.

"Yes, my little paratrooper, but you were not jumping out of a plane carrying a musical instrument. If I'm not mistaken—and I know I am not—you dropped down with an M16. Big difference." I really did not want to know how Constantine knew so much.

"Got it; adding it to my list." My to-do list was increasing exponentially. It didn't look like I ever got anything done.

"What time do you have to report to Abuelita's this week?" Constantine brought me back to reality instead of my never-ending list.

"Oh, I don't." I started stretching my arms as I looked at him.

"Did you get fired? Nobody fires an intern, not even Abuelita. I'll make a call and get this sorted out." Constantine was up on all fours, and he looked like a giant fur ball.

"Hey, tiger, slow down now. Nobody got fired. Abuelita gave me the rest of the week off to solve this case. She was afraid I might get killed if we don't fix this soon." I normally talked fast, but those last sentences flew out of my mouth. Constantine unruffled himself and sat back down.

"Well, nice, that was a really good call on her part." Constantine yawned and stretched himself at the same time. "OK, now that you are all warmed up, let's get started."

"Started? I thought I was done." I was going to die. Constantine was a cruel cat.

"Isis, I have seen your fighting moves. Girl, you suck. If you take another beating like you did last night, you will break something important. So, stop whining, and grab the boxing gloves. We need to start with jabs and kicks. Your upper body is weak, but we can work on it." Constantine walked over to the gloves and waited for me. I was not getting out of this so easily. I was pretty sure I did not know how to throw a punch.

Constantine proved my theory. I couldn't throw a punch to save my life. In the military I excelled at the range with my rifle, not hand to hand combat. By the wall near the corner of the building, Constantine had installed one of those suspended punching bags. The types boxers used on TV. They made that look easy. I threw three punches, and the thing almost knocked me down. I had no rhythm when it came to boxing. After an hour of my horrible display of skills, Constantine called it quits.

"I need to find you a partner. This is not working out. Go shower and eat breakfast. We have a long day today. You need to be on time to church." Constantine looked defeated, and I was the one getting beat up by the bags.

"Yes, Drill Sergeant." I snapped to attention, with my legs together and arms at my side, head straight. To add insult to injury, I even saluted him. Constantine glared at me.

"Move. Out." He was not a happy camper. I was sure with his fifteen pounds, he could produce a quick death. I ran toward the loft before he could execute me.

Chapter Seventeen

I was getting old and slow, because my showers were taking longer and longer. By the time I finished getting dressed, I had just enough time to get a shake. Where did the shakes come from? More questions that I was sure Constantine would have a bizarre answer for.

Bartholomew was up checking for more missing people. It didn't take a lot to make a growing boy happy—he had a plate of sausage patties. He was munching while he typed.

With the Whale out of commission, Constantine let me borrow his car. The cat had a car. And not just any car—he had a yellow Camaro. Of course, he had named it Bumblebee. I was pretty sure that name was copyrighted, but I was not discussing that with him. Besides, he was letting me borrow it. I did get a lecture on the proper maintenance and care of Bumblebee. With my luck with vehicles, Constantine had a right to be worried. God, I was worried.

Saint Edward Catholic Church was on the back side of the block from the outreach. While the outreach sat on Ash Street, the church itself was on Beech Street. The church had recently turned one hundred years old, and it was beautiful. It was more in tune with traditional churches up North and not with the stadium-seating style you saw in the megachurches in the South. The church even had stained-glass windows on all sides.

I parked across the street from the church, in front of the church's office. It was a little past eleven in the morning, and I needed to catch Father Francis before he stopped confessions to get ready for Mass. I quickly climbed the steps leading to the main entrance of the church. The church had a small vestibule separating the main entrance from the sanctuary. Like most Catholic churches, holy water was placed by the door to bless yourself with. I dipped my right index finger and did the sign of the cross. I slowly pushed open the next set of doors and walked in.

The interior of the church was beautiful. Churches and places of worship had a sense of calmness to them that was breathtaking. If you found the right one, it felt like coming home. As I walked in the door, I noticed the large crowd. The church could easily hold four hundred people, with sets of pews separated by an aisle in the middle. Most Catholic churches had daily Masses. Normally senior citizens, retirees, or the church staff would attend. In cities with larger Catholic populations, you could have a few dozen show up. I had been to daily Mass at Saint Edward's before, and the number of attendees was fewer than ten.

Today, we had at least 150 people. They were mostly sitting at the back of the church. If they were all waiting for confession, I was screwed. I stood at the entrance looking for a place to sit near the back. In unison, the entire row sitting in the ushers' pew by the wall stared at me. It was a sickening sensation, as if all those eyeballs could see into my soul. I swallowed and tried to look away. A lady in her forties dressed in a long, green dress got up. She beckoned me over. She was the next person in line to enter the confessional.

"Ma'am, you don't have to. I can wait." I couldn't cut in front of all those people in line.

"We have all the time in the world, dear; yours is short." Before I could protest, the confessional's door opened. A young man, maybe in his twenties, walked out. He was wearing a white suit, like John Travolta in *Saturday Night Fever*. "Dear, go in. He's ready for you."

The lady almost pushed me inside. By the time I turned around, she had closed the door.

People in this church were serious about their confessions. Father Francis sat behind the kneeler. Unlike most TV shows, Catholics faced their priest for confessions instead of kneeling behind the weird screen. A chair was in front of Father Francis. He wore his priestly clothes and was holding his Bible. Father Francis was in his late sixties, with salt-and-pepper hair and green eyes.

He had a warm smile that made you want to talk. I guessed that was a good thing in his business.

I took the seat and made the sign of the cross. I looked around the small room, nervous. I noticed—on the wall—the prayer of contrition, the normal prayer people said after confession. It was in Spanish and English. I was impressed. This meant I wasn't the only person who couldn't remember the prayers. Father Francis just smiled at me. I took a deep breath to calm myself.

"Father, this might sound weird, but Constantine said to keep it real."

Father Francis nodded at me, made the sign of the cross, and said, "Tell him to keep it low." Either the priest and that crazy cat were in a gang, or I had just witnessed a challenge and password take place. I might need to explain to Constantine that in order for this to be effective, he should let me know what the password was supposed to be.

"I will do that. By the way, how do you know Constantine?" My curiosity always got the best of me.

"Constantine gets around. He's been busy lately. But I'm sure that's not why you're here. So, what brings you to church, Isis? I haven't seen you in a while." Wow, Father Francis had a way of making you feel welcome and guilty all at once.

"You know my name. Can I assume you know who I work for?" I was not blending in very well.

"A lot of people know your name, child. It's been years since Death has had a Catholic intern. Granted, I doubt that he did that on purpose. Death tends to be fair in his choices." For the priest, Death was a man, which was interesting. No wonder nobody had a clear picture of Death. It was different for everyone.

"Father, I have a horrible feeling Death made a mistake with me. I suck at this. Honestly, I'm completely unqualified for this weird job. I don't even get all this magic stuff." Without fail, every time I went to confession, I started whining. Probably because it was the only place somebody had to listen without judging me.

"God doesn't choose qualified people to serve him. He chooses imperfect people to do extraordinary things."

"That I believe, Father. But God didn't choose me. Death did. Not the same thing."

"You have a valid point, but do you honestly think that if this weren't part of your divine plan, God would have permitted it?" Priests always got you with their theological questions.

"My heart wants to believe this is all part of my destiny, but my brain has a hard time processing it. All I know is people are missing, and I want to help." I was staring at the floor as I spoke.

"In that case, my child, have faith. Know you are exactly where you're supposed to be."

I felt the pressure in my chest lessen. Deep down, I was looking for validation that I wasn't crazy.

"Thank you, Father. Now, have you seen anything weird around the church?" I sounded childish, but Constantine hadn't prepped me on how to broach the subject.

"Everything around the church has been quiet. The souls, on the other hand, have been restless. They've been coming in more often. Something is bothering them; I can feel it."

My mouth dropped.

"You can see them?" Father Francis sounded astonished.

I nodded slowly. "You can't?"

He shook his head. This was way too creepy for me.

"Father, if you are correct, your church is currently filled with the souls of purgatory."

"Priests are not blessed with that gift. We're responsible for praying for the souls to move to the next life. I didn't realize interns could see them."

"No offense, Father, but I don't consider seeing dead people a gift." I took a breath to calm myself. I needed to get focused again. "So, nobody—alive, I mean—has been around here asking questions? Or trying to use the property?"

"You're the first one, Isis. We're a small congregation in comparison to other churches, but our members are active. The other two associate priests and I live next door. Hard to sneak around when you have priests walking the grounds at all hours." Father had a really good point there.

"Thank you, Father, for your time. I'm sorry to have bothered you." I tried to get up, but Father Francis grabbed my hand.

"Wait. I have something for you." He pulled a rosary and a small bottle of water from his pocket.

"Were you expecting me?" How had he known I was coming today?

"I knew you would eventually come. It never hurts to be prepared." He handed me the items and smiled. "They're already blessed. You might not believe it yet, but there is a reason for you to be here. Don't lose yourself trying to figure it out."

"Thank you, Father." I didn't know what else to say. I tried to get up again, but he held my hand.

"How about a real confession now?"

I dropped my head in defeat. I had thought I was going to get out of this without too much soul-searching. I was so wrong.

It took me a while to get started, but once I did, I couldn't stop. Father Francis listened without questions or judgment. Ten minutes later, I was finally out of the confessional. Confessions were painful, but I felt lighter after they were done. It was the first time I had spoken about the accident to another human being; talking to Death was not the same thing. The shame and horror of it had been destroying my soul. I felt better. A small peace was creeping inside of me.

The souls were gone; only a few people were sitting in pews at the front of the church. I walked over to one of the closest pews in the back and knelt for my penance. Father Francis had given me ten Hail Marys and told me to pray for the souls in purgatory. For the first time in my life, it actually made sense to do that.

Someone sat next to me. I felt her more than anything, since I had my head bowed down.

"Please help the lost people. What those people are doing is not right. Nobody deserves to be destroyed." It was the voice of the lady in green at the confessional.

By the time I looked up, she was gone. Why couldn't people just tell me what was going on? Maybe God could send me a text or an email. I didn't take hints very well.

I took another deep breath and went back to praying; at least I could manage that much. My day was pretty packed, but I hadn't been to Mass in a while. I decided to stay for the daily Mass. Unlike a weekend Mass, the daily Masses took only thirty minutes, but you still received communion. At the rate I was going, I would need all the divine help I could find.

Father Francis left the confessional and walked to the end of the aisle. For weekday Masses, he started his procession inside the sanctuary by the last rows of pews. The Mass had only seven people in attendance, and I was one of them. Father Francis walked slowly up to the front, singing a hymn. He smiled at me as he walked. I was sure by his look that he was praying for my soul.

Chapter Eighteen

Daily Masses were probably my favorite. Maybe it was the small crowd or just the speed of Mass. Either way, I felt better. I didn't have any clues besides knowing that Saint Edward's wasn't the entrance the witches were using, and I could see dead people. The last part I wouldn't mind forgetting. I still had Bartholomew's list, so I decided to check out a few more places. Downtown was not very big, but it was closer to start from Saint Edward's than Reapers. Bartholomew had provided some suggestions. He recommended I start at Randy Sam's. At this hour most of their clients would be out—typical shelter policy.

Randy Sam's exterior looked like a metal warehouse. From Bartholomew's info, I knew they housed about a hundred people. They took men and women but no children. The Salvation Army was the place for families with kids. I had taken for granted the number of homeless people each community truly had. The shelters were always located in some remote part of town. The themes across America appeared to be, *We care for the afflicted just as long as they're not next door to us.*

The drive from Saint Edward's to Randy Sam's took less than four minutes. The downtown traffic at this hour consisted of people either heading to one of the hospitals or the court system. It was almost like New York City's financial district at the southern tip of the island. On the weekend, the place was a ghost town. Few shops were open at this time. It was a shame because the downtown was so quaint. I'd dreamed of living down there when I'd first arrived. I just couldn't afford it.

According to Bartholomew's notes, Randy Sam's should have been deserted at this hour. He was sadly mistaken. The place was packed. I parked in their visitors' lot, in front of the building. I had passed the building hundreds of times, but I had never been inside. I wasn't sure why; when I'd first moved to town, I slept in the Whale. Maybe I was as elitist as those I criticized. But I would need to postpone that reflection for another time. It was Wednesday, and we were running out of time.

I locked Bumblebee and walked to the main entrance. A small reception area was set up outside the sleeping area. According to Bartholomew, a lot of the staff there were mainly unpaid volunteers. That was also the case with the outreach and most of the centers in town. A lot of people donated their time and money. Maybe I was a cynic.

A cute blonde in her late teens sat at the reception desk. She had curly hair, almost like Shirley Temple's. She'd probably gotten teased a lot growing up. Nobody should be that cute at that age.

"Hi. How can I help out?" The blonde even had a childlike voice. That was a little freaky.

"Hi. I was looking for a friend of mine and was wondering if maybe you've seen him. I haven't seen him in a few days." That was partly true; I was still looking for Bob. Technically, that was not a lie, unless you asked my godmother. Another reason I avoided lying was that my godmother was a walking lie detector. It was a waste of time lying to her.

"What's your friend's name?" The blonde pulled out a ledger with at least fifty names.

"Bob. I don't know his last name." I sounded so lame. As soon as I found Bob, this name thing was getting corrected.

"Bob? Not Robert? Just Bob? I don't have any Bob on the records. Maybe if you had a last name." I was sure she was trying to be helpful, but her tone infuriated me.

"Yeah, sorry, we just met. Would it be possible for me to look around?"

"Sorry, I can't let you. Not our policy to let strangers walk around. We have to protect our clients' privacy. Especially now."

It had been worth a try, but I hadn't thought she would agree.

"What do you mean?"

"The director has decided to let the clients stay in the center all day. It seems a couple of the regular clients have not returned, and some of the others are restless." She looked over her shoulder, concerned. She looked as if something or someone was ready to jump at her.

"Have you seen anything strange around here?"

"That's the thing. Nobody has seen anything. It's been business as usual, so I have no idea what's going on. But I'm only a volunteer. I'm a social-work student at A&M." Only in the South did people volunteer that much personal information to total strangers.

"Thanks anyway. Do you mind if I just walk around outside? Maybe I'll see my friend there."

The blonde looked around, concerned, probably not sure if that was part of the policy. "OK, but please don't look creepy. I don't want to get in trouble."

"Thanks. I won't wander long." For an unpaid volunteer, she was sure worried about getting fired.

I left the blonde, with her Shirley Temple haircut, at the desk and walked the perimeter of the building. The back of Randy Sam's looked like a combination exercise yard and picnic area. Unfortunately, the chain-link fence around it gave it a prison look. I wasn't sure whether they were trying to keep the clients in or the nuts out. Either way, it looked pretty intense. I made it to the end of the building, but nobody made eye contact with me. The clients knew people were being kidnapped, and they were not taking any chances.

"Hey, girlie, over here." Across the street stood a brunette in her late twenties or maybe early thirties. It was hard to say; she looked as if she'd had a rough life.

She waved me over, trying to be discreet. She was standing by a tree, looking more suspicious than anything. I wasn't sure if I should explain the concept of camouflage to her. What did I have to lose at this point in the day? I was batting zero on my investigation, so I crossed the street.

"Hi there. Can I help you?" What else was I supposed to say? *What's up, shady lady by the tree?*

"I heard you. They took my boyfriend, so they probably took your friend, too. This place is haunted. I'm going to find him. He's all I got. I'm probably next, and so are you for asking questions." I thought I spoke fast, but this lady beat me. I wasn't sure when she took a breath, but everything was coming out at once. She started crying out of the blue.

"Ma'am, I'm sorry. Do you know who took your boyfriend?" I wanted to hug her, but I was afraid I would spook her even more.

"Those biker bitches. They started coming at night, offering food and shelter to anyone who would work for them. A few guys went, but they never came back. After that, nobody wanted to go, and people started going missing. My boyfriend followed them, looking for his friend, and he never came back." The last sentence was hard to follow because she was crying so hard.

"Did he tell you where he was going?" Maybe she knew something more. I had heard this version before. Don't ask questions was the theme.

"Not really. He just said to wait for him by the bridge for Mass." The girl looked over her shoulder and panicked. "I have to go."

The little blonde was standing by the side of the building looking at us. Great. Now she was going to report me for disturbing the guests.

"Wait, please. Let me give you my number. If you find anything out, please let me know. I want to help." I scrambled through my pockets to find something to write on. I had a light denim jacket. In the pockets I found a stack of business cards. They were actually mine, which was weird. I glanced quickly at the number and handed one to the girl. She pocketed it and left without a word.

The blonde was still watching me, so I waved. She turned around and probably went back to her desk to report me. I was sure I was getting banned. Oh well, another dead end unless the little girl called me.

I glanced at the stack of business cards in my hand. Black paper with white letters, all in italics that simply said, *Isis Black, Reapers Incorporated* and my phone number. Three little lines, and I was official. When did that crazy cat have time to make me business cards? I wasn't sure which one was sneakier, Constantine or Bartholomew.

I decided to head back to Bumblebee. If the tires on that baby got slashed, Constantine would have my hide. I was pretty sure he liked me, but I had a horrible feeling that he loved the car more. I tried to walk quickly back without looking too suspicious. It wasn't as if I were talking to shady characters by street corners—that wasn't suspicious at all. The front desk was empty, thank the Lord. I didn't need Little Blondie to give me any more stares. I was feeling guilty already.

I pulled Bumblebee out of the parking lot and headed toward the library. I wasn't planning to leave the car, in case any more drive-by slashers came my way. There was something off about Randy Sam's, and I just wanted to watch. Of course, it wasn't as if I were blending in, in a yellow Camaro.

I parked near the front of the library, close enough to see the shelter.

After an hour of watching, I was bored to death. I changed Constantine's Sirius channels at least ten times. I played with every button in the car that I could find. My stomach grumbled. My supershake had worn off, and I was actually hungry. I blamed Constantine's horrible exercise routine. I was not used to all this work.

My phone rang, and I almost jumped out of my skin. Nobody ever called me besides my godmother, but that was only on Sundays. I fumbled in my pockets, looking for the infernal device.

"Hello." The caller ID read *Reapers*. I was nervous and wasn't sure what to expect.

"Did you find your lunch?"

I shook my head. Constantine didn't believe in introductions or preliminaries. "Hi, Constantine. Now, what are you talking about? What lunch?"

"Woman, did you not check the backseat? What kind of soldier are you? There could have been a bomb back there, and you would be gone."

Why was he so dramatic? I leaned between the seats and spotted a little cooler behind the driver's seat. It was at an odd angle, and I struggled to get it out.

"OK, I got the cooler. What's in it?"

"Just open the darn thing." Constantine was not amused.

"After that whole speech about bombs, this could be a trick." Constantine had a way of making me paranoid.

"*Now* you want to be careful. Just eat your lunch, and don't die. Did you find anything?" Constantine waited patiently.

I opened the cooler and found an iced tea, still cold, and a tomato, cheese, and avocado sandwich on a gluten-free bun. I ripped the waxed paper off and took a bite.

"Found nothing good. Oh, wow, this is delicious." I was so rude talking with my mouth full, but I couldn't help it. I was starving.

"Yeah, yeah. Bartholomew made it for you before he went to bed. He said you probably would not have time to eat, with all the places on your list. He's a good kid." I had a feeling Constantine wasn't so sure how good I was.

"I've got one more place to go before heading back. Do I need to pick up anything?" I could suck up to Constantine as well.

"Are you sucking up to me?"

"Me? Of course not." Damn, he was good. So not fair.

"Right...just be careful, and don't harm Bumblebee. Bartholomew is searching for empty lots where they could be hiding the people before the ceremony date."

"Will do. Thanks."

Just like that, he hung up. He didn't say hello or goodbye. We really needed to work on his manners. What did he mean by hiding the people? They were not taking them to the other place right away? This was getting worse by the minute.

Bless Bartholomew; he was my hero. He had even given me an apple. I was planning to finish my lunch before I headed to the Friendship Center. The last thing I needed was to walk in there with my stomach grumbling. I needed info, not food.

Chapter Nineteen

I walked over to the Friendship Center. The place was one block down from Randy Sam's and across from the library. I knew very little about the center or their mission. According to Bartholomew's handy little notes, they were more than just a soup kitchen. The center provided training for those who wanted to get back into the job market, as well as after-school programs. I realized I knew very little about Texarkana. The city had a lot of support for people in need, if you knew where to look. I guessed it was the same way in most major cities.

Unfortunately, by the time I got there, the center was closed. Maybe I should have checked them out sooner instead of spying on Randy Sam's. If the blonde was coming out looking around, I didn't need for her to call the cops. If people were missing, the last thing I needed was to get locked up for suspicious behavior. She did look more credible than I did. I was the one outside her business asking weird questions.

I crossed the Friendship Center off and decided to head to the Salvation Army.

I admitted to myself, all these places were pretty close to one another. All were within a five-minute drive or a ten-to-fifteen-minute walk from the others—a good way to make resources easily available to the needy, or a good way to keep them all segregated to one location. OK, I had no idea where I stood on the matter of the homeless in America. I had a hard time understanding how the greatest nation in this world had this much poverty. I guessed I should add that subject to my list of reflections.

I had never been to the Salvation Army either. I was feeling like a bad member of society. I wasn't volunteering or aiding people in any way. At the same time, when you were struggling from paycheck to paycheck, it was hard to look out for the needy. If I didn't die in this case, maybe I could actually help somewhere.

The Salvation Army comprised two large buildings sitting at Fourth Street and Hazel. I was pretty sure I had passed it on my way to Randy Sam's from Saint Ed's. Maybe Constantine was right and I was losing my touch at paying attention to my surroundings. I had developed tunnel vision and was missing details. I had no idea where I was going, so I tried the first building with open doors. An older man sat behind the reception desk.

"Hi, Miss. How can I help you?" He had a friendly smile and a hint of a southern accent. Anytime I lived in a place for a while, I stopped hearing people's accents. So, his must have been really pronounced for me to notice.

"Good afternoon, sir. I was looking for my friend and wondered if you had seen him. His name is Bob, and he's about six feet tall and maybe two hundred pounds." Next time I was getting a picture of Bob. This was ridiculous.

"Sorry, ma'am, we don't have any Bobs at this time. Weird, it's such a common name. But things have been weird lately." He stared at the door pensively. I looked over my shoulder, wondering what I was missing.

"Are you OK, sir?" Why beat around the bush?

"Texarkana is a midpoint. People pass through this town all the time. We normally get people with no place to stay who are heading west to Dallas, leaving Shreveport, or going in any other direction. Lately, nobody new has come in. It's like people are staying away on purpose. You're the first new person I've seen in two weeks." He stared at me with deep-brown eyes. He looked worried and a bit scared.

"Has that ever happened before?"

"No. Some of our regulars have stopped coming. Even one of our volunteers quit. He said that something evil was around here."

"That is really odd. Well, I guess I will be leaving." No reason to stay with the creepy old man at the Salvation Army. "Bye." It was still the South; you had to be polite.

"Miss, you should check out the Church under the Bridge. They have Masses Saturdays at 9:00 a.m., rain or shine. If you don't find your friend by then, maybe he goes there. A lot of the homeless take Mass there and have a warm breakfast."

"Thank you very much." I had stopped at the door. He smiled kindly but sadly.

"Goodbye, Miss, come again. Hope you find your friend." He waved a lazy hand at me and went back to staring out the window.

It appeared the word was getting out that Texarkana was not safe for the transient population. That was a blessing, fewer people to worry about. I got in Bumblebee and pulled out of the parking space. I had a horrible habit of checking my mirrors at least five times. As I pulled up to the intersection, a black car pulled out of the end of the street. I hadn't seen anyone sitting in any of the cars parked. Call me paranoid, but my week was kind of sucking, and I did not want to be followed.

If they were following me, they were going to have to work for it. I drove around downtown making crazy turns without using my turn signal. Something that drove me nuts when others did it. The black car was still behind me. It was a few car lengths behind but still there. Not something that I enjoyed. I drove toward Saint Edward's, then back to the library. I made several loops hoping to lose them, but they were right behind me.

I took a quick turned onto Broad Street. My goal was to head down toward Texas Boulevard and then head home. I was going way past the speed limit when I saw flashing lights behind me. I wasn't sure if this was a blessing or a curse. I pulled over and saw the black car drive by. The windows were tinted, so I couldn't see who was driving. Fortunately for me, they couldn't see my face, either.

I glanced behind me, and the cop was getting out of his car. It was none other than Officer Sexy-Butt. Great, kept getting better and better. That man probably thought I was a menace on wheels.

"Ma'am, do you know how fast you were going?" Officer Sexy-Butt was not smiling and kept looking over Bumblebee.

"Fast enough for you to stop me, Officer. I'm sorry." Being followed by random cars made people distracted.

"That is not the only reason I stopped you. We received several calls of a yellow Camaro driving around downtown very suspiciously. You are not good at blending, are you?" He took off his sunglasses and was staring at me. "Ms. Black, you seem to be in all the wrong places. Let me guess; you were looking for your friend, right?" Wow, he looked menacing when he was mad. He radiated energy like a little microwave; I was sure I was getting dizzy.

"I didn't know there was a law against looking for people or driving around downtown." He was not going to intimidate me.

"You are right; there is not a law, but you are making people nervous. It doesn't help that your minivan mysteriously got blown up. Now you are driving a flashy brand-new Camaro. Can I see your license, insurance, and registration, please?" He'd said *please* as an afterthought.

I prayed Constantine kept his information in the glove compartment. I opened the door, and for the mercy of God, everything was there. Actually, it was the cleanest compartment I had ever seen. Constantine was pretty anal about his car. I handed Officer Cranky Pants the papers and my license. If I got Constantine's Bumblebee impounded, he was going to kill me.

He took the papers and headed back to his cruiser. I couldn't see what he was doing, but he came back five minutes later.

"So, you work for Reapers, interesting. Everything is cleared; here you go." He handed me back all my documents.

"That's it? You're not even going to give me a warning?" What was wrong with me? Did I really want a ticket? I was losing my mind, asking an angry cop stupid questions.

"Why? I already gave you a warning, and you didn't listen to it. So, here you are again, racing down my streets. Would you like to fill me in on what's going on?"

Ouch. He did have a point.

"Would you believe me if I said it was a top-secret mission and that I was innocent?"

The look he gave me said no. He was not believing a word I said.

"Can you at least tell me who blew up your van?" No, he didn't buy it.

"I'm guessing the same people who slashed my tires. I have a winning personality." My charm was not working. Not that I had that much to begin with.

"You do know how to make friends. Let me explain something. I don't like being in the dark. This is my city, and if something is going on, I expect to know." Sexy Pants had that evil glare again.

"I don't know what you're talking about." Yeah, like I was confessing to this cop that I was chasing witches in downtown Texarkana. I might as well put on a straitjacket and save the authorities the trouble.

"That's what I thought. You're all the same. Tell Constantine I'll be there in the morning." He turned around and walked off. Constantine? He had called Constantine instead of his dispatcher.

I was totally confused. Who was this cop, and how did he know Constantine? I was sure I was missing something. What did he mean, he would see him tomorrow? My life was getting more and more complicated. There were too many people involved in this supernatural stuff to keep up. I still had no idea where these witches were hiding or who they were. We were running out of time and places to look. On top of that, now I had an angry cop after me. This was not a good day.

I needed cheering up, so I decided to stop by Taste and See on my way home. The owners were locals and very nice people. They had the best gelato in town. Actually, they had the only gelato store in town. I also wanted to say thank you to Bartholomew for lunch. I wasn't sure what his favorite flavor was, so I got him salted caramel. It was one of their classics, and you could never go wrong with that. I got an espresso flavor for Constantine. He looked like the caffeine type. For me, I got a double scoop of tiramisu and cookies and cream. Hey, I didn't have gluten intolerance. I could indulge. Happy with my delicious surprises, I headed back to Reapers. Who said I didn't know how to bribe people?

Chapter Twenty

By the time I pulled into Reapers, I was exhausted. I was slowly making myself more upset over that crazy cop. Did he know I was an intern? If he did, didn't he know the rules? What did he mean, we were all the same? I had more questions than answers. I parked Bumblebee in its designated spot by the Deathmobile. It was such an odd combination of cars. I shook my head.

I struggled to balance all the desserts. I had taken mine out earlier instead of leaving everything inside the nice packing job the girls at the store had done. Some things were hard to resist. Doors were a bit more challenging. I managed to make it to the kitchen table in the loft without spilling anything. Bartholomew was at his command center, and Constantine was napping on the top of the sofa. From my angle, it looked as if Bartholomew was actually playing a game.

"Hi, Isis. Welcome back," Bartholomew said, barely looking up at me.

"Hi, Bart. I got you some gelato, if you can take a break." I was expecting complaints or grumbling. Instead, I got both Bartholomew and Constantine at the table in less than two seconds flat. I swore Bartholomew dropped his controller and ran over. Constantine snapped his eyes open at the word "gelato," and he was across the room before I could finish.

"Did I get one, too?" For a five-thousand-year-old cat, Constantine was looking like a kitten right now.

"Of course, you did. Espresso for you, and salted caramel for Bart." I placed bowls in front of them.

Bartholomew pulled two chairs out, and they took their respective places. Constantine licked his without much preamble. "This is delicious. Thank you. I could sing, because I'm happy."

I laughed. Constantine was amazing at impersonations. Pharrell was in trouble.

"Yes, thank you, Isis. What made you decide to get us gelato?" Bartholomew barely stopped eating as he spoke.

"Bad day. I figured we all needed a break."

"Emotional eating. Bad sign. We might need to add more run time to help you burn some emotions and calories." I couldn't tell if Constantine was serious or not.

"He's just messing with you," Bartholomew said, reading the worried looked on my face.

Constantine winked at me with a devious grin. Yeah, he was good.

"What did you get?" Like most cats, he was also extremely curious and nosy.

"I got tiramisu and cookies and cream."

"Wow, you are having a bad day. What happened?" Constantine actually looked concerned for me.

"Nothing. That's the problem. I found out nothing. Father Francis hasn't seen any strangers around his church, but the spirits are anxious. Did you know I can see dead people?"

"Uh, don't say that phrase around Death. She's still mad about the intern who helped with that weird film. But, technically, you see souls. Remember, we are in the soul business. Comes with Death's gifts." Constantine was back in his teacher mode.

"Great. I'm not happy. Souls talked to me and even touched me. How is that possible?"

"Because Death can talk to and touch the souls. In case of a horrible major disaster, interns can function as Death's representative in ushering the souls. You need the gift." I was pretty sure Constantine enjoyed lecturing me.

"Do I want to know what kind of major disasters?"

Constantine and Bartholomew shook their heads in unison. When the boys were synchronized, the answer was not a good one. I decided to drop it.

"Did you go anywhere else? You were gone a really long time." Constantine was back to business.

"Did you like your lunch?" Oh, wow, I had totally forgotten to thank Bartholomew when I came in.

"Yes. Thank you so much. That was so sweet of you. I was going to tell you it wasn't necessary, but I was starving. Thank you."

"Any time. You're always running late, so I figured I could help." Bartholomew was smiling in between mouthfuls. All I could do was smile back.

Constantine cleared his throat.

"Oh, sorry. I went to Randy Sam's and made a little volunteer girl paranoid. People are staying inside during the day. At least nobody will try to kidnap them while they're in groups." I stopped to eat my last spoonful of gelato. I should have bought more. "On my way, I stopped by the Salvation Army and met another creepy volunteer. The volunteers in this town are a bit weird."

"You were busy." Bartholomew was trying to be supportive.

"Oh, it gets better. I was followed by a car leaving the Salvation Army and then got pulled over by the same cop, Officer Smith. I think that man hates me. By the way, why is he coming over tomorrow?"

"To be your partner for our hand-to-hand combat training." Constantine had a way of delivering bad news with very little feeling. I was going to kill him.

"Please tell me you're kidding." At least I managed not to sound too bewildered. But it was hard to contain the surprise on my face.

"He's a wizard. He's also the one who's been making the shakes. Pretty good cop, too."

Now I was truly speechless. Why was every guy I found hot, something out of this world?

"Constantine, I don't think that's a good idea. The man hates me." If not hate, he really despised me.

"Stop being so judgmental. He might surprise you. So, be ready bright and early. He'll be here by six."

Thanks, Constantine, for the great news. Now I was never going to sleep.

"By the way, Isis, you have a message. That boy from Abuelita's stopped by today. He left this for you." Bartholomew passed me an envelope with my name on it.

The only boy from Abuelita's who came to mind was Angelito. I wasn't sure why Angelito would be leaving me notes. He had my cell phone. Why didn't he just text me? By the time I opened the damn letter, I was worried. This could be really bad. I decided to read the letter out loud, for the boys' sake.

"Hey, Isis, the girls who jumped you will be at Shooters tonight. Be careful. They're a bunch of biker chicks—very dangerous." That was the whole note.

"Why is he telling you this?" Bartholomew had read my mind. "Something's not right about this. Why didn't he just call you?"

"I have no idea, Bart. Maybe I could follow them and find Bob and the rest of the people."

"Isis, Bartholomew is right. This could be a trap." Constantine was still as he spoke, and every word was precise.

"Why would Angelito be working with the witches?" Angelito was not a bad guy, clueless about girls.

"Boys do dumb things for girls. Trust me; I've seen it through the centuries." That one I truly believed. Constantine was right, and Angelito was notorious for poor decisions when it came to girls.

"Unless you have a better idea, guess I'll be going out tonight." I dropped my cup and spoon in the trash can. Bartholomew and Constantine just watched me and said nothing. I went directly to my room.

I was very confused about the note. Angelito had never sent me a note before. None of it made sense. I sat down on my bed, contemplating the note again. I lay down and debated texting Angelito for more info. I was more tired than I thought, because I passed out. It was eight thirty in the evening when I woke up. I wasn't sure what time the witches would be at Shooters, but I needed to hurry. I took a quick shower and grabbed a pair of pants and a shirt. Normally, I avoided makeup at all costs. Today, I added mascara and eyeliner to my face. I didn't want to attract too much attention while I was there. I finished dressing and headed back out toward the kitchen door.

"How was your nap? You look refreshed," Bart said from across the room.

"Who are you supposed to be?" Constantine was still at the kitchen table, this time staring at me.

"What do you mean?" What was he talking about?

"Dressed like that. You look like Lil Wayne or that other guy. What's his name?" Constantine looked over at Bartholomew.

"Tony Hawk," Bart said.

"Yes, thank you, Bartholomew. That's the one. Isis, why are you dressed like a skater kid?"

Did I really look like a skater?

"This was what I wore when I went to clubs in New York City." Nobody was complaining up north.

"Girl, those were hip-hop clubs. Besides, it was New York. Here, you need to dress to fit in. Like a girl, not a twelve-year-old boy."

I had boobs. I did not look like a twelve-year-old boy. Constantine was a horrible career counselor.

"I like what I'm wearing. No need to get all sorts of mean about it." I was whining, but I didn't care.

"Isis, don't be silly. You're in Texarkana. Please put some on tight-fitting clothes, like most girls in this area. Remember, recon operation. Don't draw any more attention to yourself."

Constantine had a point. I needed to blend in. "Bart, do I really look that bad?"

He paused for a second. "You look really cool but definitely skater boy." I dropped my head, defeated. "You won't blend in at all."

"Fine. I'll go change. But I'm going on the record: this was not my idea."

Being girlie was hard. Everything was always so complicated, from the hair to the clothes. Normally, it took me less than ten minutes to get ready. I had been staring at the open door for almost thirty minutes. This was not going well. I hated dressing up, and this was a massacre. I found a pair of black leather pants I had bought for a Halloween party one year. I also found a tank top with patterns and jewelry. It was one of the few presents my godmother had given me that I didn't hate. The combination was not bad at all. But I felt very self-conscious. I didn't like tight clothes at all.

I stepped out of my room, this time with a little less confidence than before. I was sure I looked ridiculous. Why had I listened to those two?

"Much better. What took you so long?" Constantine was tough.

"It was pretty hard to put clothes on that make me look fifteen." I was so self-conscious.

"Don't be so dramatic. You at least look like a normal girl going to a normal human bar." Constantine was placing a lot of emphasis on *normal*.

"Fine. I'll take it. As long as they let me in." It would suck to drive all the way there and not be able to get in.

"You will now. If I'm not mistaken, Wednesday is karaoke night there."

I was staring at Constantine in shock. "How did you know that? Actually, never mind. I don't want to know." I walked over to Bartholomew, who was sitting in his computer area. "Hey, Bart, I need some help."

"Sure thing. What do you need?" He paused his game and turned around.

"What are you playing?" I had been wondering this for a while.

"He's actually training, thank you very much." Constantine had slid back onto the back of the couch when I wasn't looking.

"Training? In what?" Bartholomew's training looked a lot more fun than mine.

"Multitasking, among other things. The boy's a hacker. He must be at his best game as well."

I couldn't argue with Constantine's logic, even if it didn't make any sense. "Fair enough. Why can't I do this?" My training sucked.

"Probably because you're out in the field doing legwork. Happy now?" Constantine was not good at taking criticism.

"OK, fine." I knew when to surrender. "Bart, I need some supplies." I handed him a list I had made up that morning.

"Really? All of this? Impressive." His eyebrows were arched as he read the list.

"Can you do it?" I had no idea what kind of resources Bartholomew had.

"Of course, I can. Some might not be legal."

I hadn't thought about that. I didn't want to go to jail, but I needed to be better equipped.

"Do your magic, Bart. Thank you."

Constantine had moved over to the computer table and was reading with Bartholomew. He looked impressed.

"Always. By the way, here's your earpiece. That way we can keep up with you, in case something goes wrong." He handed me a little device that looked like a high-level hearing aid. I wasn't sure why we needed it, so I just ran with it. Bartholomew helped me get the hearing aid in my ear. The piece blended in extremely well.

"We'll do a comm check when you get out of the building. Be careful, now." Bartholomew sounded more like my big brother, if I'd had one.

"Isis, don't get killed now. We kind of like you." Constantine was back in teacher mode.

"Well, thank you. I kind of like you two as well. OK, I'm off. Wish me luck." This was getting way too sappy. I needed to get going before I missed the biker gang of evil witches.

Chapter Twenty-One

I wasn't much of a drinker, so sports bars were not my thing. I also didn't care too much for watching sports on TV, regardless how big the screen was. With all that said, it shouldn't have been a big shock that I had never been to Shooters. I had passed it plenty of times on my way to the VA. They both sat on Frontage Road, parallel to Highway 30. The easiest way to get there was to take 30 to the state line exit and then stay on the service road. Normally the drive would be less than ten minutes, but I was dragging my feet.

For a Wednesday night, this place was pretty packed. Shooters sat in the middle of the lot, with parking spaces all around. I parked in the last row closest to the road. I wasn't sure what to expect, but I didn't want to draw attention to myself. The plan was simple—find the witches and, hopefully, follow them to the victims. I wasn't happy about being there, but we didn't have that many options. I turned Bumblebee off and slowly climbed out. Keys, my license, and cash were in my front pocket. My cell was in my back one. The fewer things in my hands, the better.

I made my way slowly to the front of the building. From my right side, I saw a figure coming my way. My pulse increased, and I considered running back to Bumblebee. He was wearing jeans and a hoodie, with the hood over his head.

"Looking good, Isis."

I exhaled slowly. "Why are you hiding in the dark, Angelito? Hasn't anyone told you how shady you look?" What was wrong with this boy?

"Hey, I'm not supposed to be helping you. So, pretend you don't know me." Angelito bent over to tie his right shoe or whatever he was pretending to do.

I pulled my cell phone out. "That's not that hard to do. You look creepy. But what do you mean, you're not supposed to be helping me?" I was trying not to look so obvious and to blend in.

"Look, my girl is friends with the chicks who jumped you. She's not like them, but they're still friends. I figured you might want some payback. That was pretty shitty, what they did to you." He switched legs and started working on his left. "Be careful, Isis. They're crazy. They're hanging out by the pool tables."

Without another word, Angelito got up and headed inside. That was all I'd gotten—I got, crazy girls by the pool tables. Angelito was in over his head. I doubt his little girlfriend was as innocent as he believed. I didn't have time to worry about Angelito's love life right now. Somehow, I needed to figure out where the pool tables were located in this place. Since nothing else was holding me back, I made my way toward the door.

A very tall and very muscular bouncer stood at the door. I smiled at him, but he just nodded back. The man was focused. Inside the door, there were girls standing behind a desk checking IDs. I walked to the right and handed one of the girls cash and my ID. I hadn't realized they had a cover charge. I paid and made my way inside.

Shooters was divided into two sections. To the left they had a stage area, with a dance floor and tables around it. To the right they had pool tables. No wonder Angelito's instructions were vague. You couldn't miss the pool tables. There were at least seven on that side of the room. The two areas were separated by a bar in the middle. That way the bartenders could serve both sides without missing a beat. I liked the layout.

The witches were on the right side, by the far wall—at least five of them. They were flirting with a group of guys. I made my way in the opposite direction. I found a space by the bar that would provide enough cover and concealment for this weird expedition. I ordered a strawberry daiquiri from the bartender. He even added whipped cream. I couldn't complain too much; the daiquiri was pretty good. I could see the witches from across the bar but not very clearly.

On the stage, a couple of girls were singing karaoke. I hoped that was their intent. They'd had too much to drink, and they were completely out of tune. I've never understood the obsession with going onstage to make a fool of yourself. That poor Katy Perry song was getting destroyed. I gave the stage one last look and turned to face the bar. Across the room, the biker witches were having a great time. I didn't recognize any of them. I needed to get closer. Unfortunately, there was no way for me to blend in on that side of the room.

Once again, I hated to admit it, but Constantine was right. My previous outfit would have been a horrible choice for this place. I barely looked as if I belonged now. There was a special attitude most of the girls in this bar had—they knew they belonged there. I screamed, "Angry girl—get the hell away!" Not the best vibe when you were trying to fit in. As I considered my options, two of the witches headed to the door. This was my only chance.

The witches went out and took a right. I didn't want to be suspicious, any more than I already was, so I headed straight. I walked around the parking lot, trying not to draw too much attention. They took another right and headed toward the rear of the building. This was such a bad idea, but I was out of good ones. I followed at a distance.

By the time I reached the back lot, the witches were gone. It wasn't as if they were moving that fast. On top of that, I didn't hear a car moving. I walked a little farther down, toward the apartment complex. At the last row of cars, I saw a body on the ground. A smart person would have turned around and called for help. Crazy intern went alone to investigate. I found a young man lying on the ground facedown. I rushed to his side.

"Oh, please tell me you are not that dumb." The female voice was over me, and I knew the hard cylinder on my head was a gun without even looking.

"What can I say? A girl can pray for a little luck." I needed a lot more than luck.

The guy rolled over and smiled at me. Dark-brown hair with big brown eyes, probably in his twenties. He moved with a grace I hadn't seen in many guys my age. He jumped up and joined the girl behind me.

"Thank you, sweetie. I can take it from here," the girl with the gun purred to the guy.

"My pleasure, baby."

I wasn't sure who gave whom the kiss, since I was still on my knees facing the pavement. I heard footsteps leaving. I was going to kill Angelito.

"Raise your hands nice and slow. I would hate to accidentally shoot you."

Accidentally my ass. I raised my hands. "Now, do I just sit here and wait for further instructions, or what? If I don't make it home soon, my guardian will be really mad." I really was hoping Bartholomew and Constantine were listening. I had no other way to use the panic word "guardian" without sounding crazy.

"Oh, you poor little thing. No, you can stay right there. You're starting to be a real pain in the ass." I heard another set of footsteps.

"The van is on its way," another female voice said from behind me.

"Good. We can tie this little girl up and throw her in the river. Pump her up with meth, and nobody will ever question a thing." Wow, the first girl was ruthless. She was going to drug and drown me. Wasn't that overkill?

"You're going to do all that just for me? You shouldn't have." I was terrified. My voice sounded a little shaky, so I knew she wasn't fooled.

"Isis, hold on. Backup should be there in twenty seconds." I almost screamed when Constantine's voice came through my little earpiece. I really hoped I had twenty seconds.

"Are you at least going to tell me why you're doing this? How much did you pay Angelito to set me up?"

"Child, you watch too much TV. We are not going to tell you shit. If you haven't figured it out by now, you're not very good at your job," the first girl said very arrogantly. If only she knew this was only my third day on the job, and I sucked at it. "Besides, poor Angelito is too much in love to know what's going on. I was surprised he had any sense left to even tell you."

"At least tell me why Texarkana." I needed only a few more seconds. I could ramble with the best of them.

"Border towns are so much fun. What's that noise?"

Oh Lord, I was praying Constantine was sending me a squad of Navy SEALs or special forces. At this point, I would have settled for dangerously armed Boy Scouts.

I heard scraping all around me, but it was too dark to see anything. My arms were getting tired, and the rocks were digging into my knees. A loud hiss came from my left, and then another from my right. I wasn't sure if a tiger was on the loose or a rattlesnake.

"What's that sound?" The second girl sounded scared. Oh, good. At least I knew they could be spooked.

"Probably some straight. Keep an eye out for the van. We need to get out of here." The first girl was not worried at all. "Don't get any strange ideas now, little girl." She shoved the gun at my head to make sure I was paying attention.

My arms were going into muscle failure. I was ready to drop them when something flew over my head.

"Ahhh, what the hell?" The girl with the gun was screaming. I glanced over my shoulder, and I was speechless. She was being attacked by a cat. Before she could rip the cat off, two more jumped at her and her friend.

"Isis, run. Now."

I didn't need Constantine's instructions. I was on my feet and running straight back to the apartment area.

"No! Get that bitch!" The first girl fired the gun at the same time she was screaming. I wasn't sure where they were coming from, but more cats kept appearing.

"Constantine, cats! Really! They're going to get hurt."

"Isis, on such short notice, just be thankful. They're as stealthy as they get. Besides, they have to catch them first to hurt them. Get to the street, and hurry." Constantine was right. They were stealthy, and they moved faster than anything I had ever seen.

Between the screams of the witches, the hissing of the cats, and the gunshots, the parking lot of Shooters had become a battle zone. I kept low among the cars, trying to avoid attention.

"She's over there. Get her." Too loud to avoid attention, the girl with the gun yelled orders in my direction. That evil van had made it around the corner and was heading straight at me. I was going to get run over. I was too far from Bumblebee to get away.

I ran between cars, heading to the service road. The passenger in the van was halfway out the window. She threw something at me. Fortunately, I slipped, and it went over my head. Whatever it was, it hit the Ford F-150 on the side and left a huge hole. I struggled to my feet and started running again. I was so dead.

The two witches from the back had joined the chase. I was out of breath. I wasn't paying attention to where I was going and almost got run over by a dirt bike. I stopped dead in my tracks. The driver lifted his shield. "Isis, hop on. Now." I was hallucinating. I had to be. There was no way Bartholomew was driving a dirt bike.

"Isis, hurry!" he screamed at me.

I hopped on the bike. I had no idea where he had learned to drive, but Bartholomew was handling the bike like a pro.

"Package recovered," I heard Bartholomew say through my earpiece.

"Nicely done. Bring her home." Constantine sounded relieved, and I was exhausted.

Bartholomew did a U-turn and headed up the street going the wrong way. I heard the witches scream. I closed my eyes and let Bartholomew take us home.

Chapter Twenty-Two

After an hour of tossing around in my bed, I decided to get up. It wasn't even six in the morning, and I had had less than five hours of sleep again. I couldn't sleep. I couldn't shut my mind off, either. We had less than two days, and we knew nothing besides the fact that these witches were tough and arrogant. Not a lot of information. Bob was still missing. People were still disappearing, and I kept getting beaten up. After last night, I was overwhelmed and lost. I got dressed and headed to the training area. Maybe I could take some of my aggression out on the punching bags.

I guessed I wasn't the only one who couldn't sleep. Constantine and Bartholomew were already on the first floor. Unfortunately, they were not alone. I had forgotten Sexy-Butt was coming over. A large practice mat was set up in the middle of the floor. It looked like a martial arts ring. Bartholomew was wearing shorts and a T-shirt and no shoes, and he was facing Sexy-Butt in the center of the ring. Sexy-Butt, on the other hand, had loose sweats on with a long-sleeve workout shirt. Constantine was sitting on a chair on the outside of the ring. They all stopped when I approached.

"I was planning to let you rest through Bartholomew's session before calling you up." Constantine was being nice. Now I was worried.

"Couldn't sleep. I can come back if you'd like." I guessed I could always go back upstairs and watch TV.

"Don't be silly. You're here; let's get busy. I assume you both have met, based on the number of warnings." Constantine looked between Officer Sexy-Butt and me.

"Yeah, I guess." That was a way to put it.

"Good. We can skip the introductions. Eric is our resident martial arts expert and local wizard." Great. He was a martial arts expert on top of being a wizard.

"Wait. Why can't you stop those lunatics?" I was pissed. All this time I had been running around, and he had been doing nothing.

"First, I'm a police officer above all. I cannot act on behalf of the order and be a cop. Those two things should never cross. And since nobody has made a public report about those psychos, I can't even enforce the law. So, thank you!" He was actually mad at me. As if this were my fault.

"Hey, this is not my fault. What was I supposed to do? File a report that witches are taking people in Texarkana? I already filed one for Bob, and you see how well that turned out. Have you found my friend yet?" I was ready for a fight, and sexy, little Eric made for a great target.

"Enough, you two. This is childish. We all know these witches are dangerous and somehow are always ahead of us. Fighting each other is not going to solve this mess. Stop it." Constantine didn't raise his voice when he spoke. He looked like a king on his throne. "Now, let's review what we know calmly. There are at least five witches in town and at least half a dozen missing people. What else?" Constantine had taken his teacher voice again.

"They have a way of making men do whatever they want." I was not happy about that.

"Most women have that effect on men, Isis." Constantine was not amused.

"Not like that. It's something different. The one holding the gun on me said she was surprised that Angelito had any sense left." I walked over to the edge of the mat and sat down. Bartholomew started stretching in the middle of the mat while Sexy Eric did push-ups. I could hit him.

"Could be a love potion or a mind-control spell." How was he talking so normally in between push-ups? He wasn't even winded. I refused to stare, but he was at twenty in less than thirty seconds.

"We got mind control, kidnapped people, and a coven on the loose in town." Constantine was talking out loud.

"And very powerful. The last spell they threw left a hole the size of a basketball on a truck," Bartholomew said, finally joining the conversation.

"OK, I know nothing about witches and spells, but doesn't it take time to become so powerful? These witches looked like they were in their teens or maybe early twenties."

Constantine and Sexy-Butt Eric stopped and looked at each other.

"OK, what am I missing?"

"Is it possible?" Eric asked Constantine, uncertain.

"Is what possible? What's going on?" Oh, thank you, Bartholomew. At least I wasn't the only lost one.

"They're stealing the years out of people." Constantine looked devious when he said it.

"Yeah, still lost. What does that mean?" It was way too early for all this cryptic madness.

"Oh, wow. That explains why the bodies we found did not match their ages when they died." Even Bartholomew had figured this out. But it didn't make sense. That wasn't possible.

"Please tell me you're kidding. They're not making themselves younger by stealing people's souls. Are they?" My stomach was turning in knots. I wanted to throw up.

"Not just younger. They're making themselves immortal. Humankind's greatest fear is death. They found a way to cheat Death and not age." We all stood in silence, staring at Constantine. "Death is going to be mad when she finds out."

"Oh, great. Now what do we do?" My job really sucked.

"We still need to find them before the equinox. Their powers will be greater on that day. With all the witches celebrating around the world, the energy will be easy to tap." Thank you, Constantine, for stating the obvious. "Right now, you need to train. You suck at hand-to-hand combat."

He was so evil. I groaned in protest. "Thank you for reminding me. I'm sorry about Bumblebee." Before I could finish my sentence, I looked over my shoulder. Bumblebee was parked in its usual spot. "How did you get it back?"

"I got people," Constantine said very smoothly.

"Do your people ever sleep?" When did they get it there?

"Isis, dear, I can't reveal all my secrets." Of course not. There was no way Constantine was ever going to spill the beans.

"Can we start now? I need to check some things out at work." I had totally forgotten Sexy-Butt was always on duty. I wondered why he wasn't a detective. Maybe that was against some witch code.

"Yes, we're wasting time. Bartholomew, start going through your drills with Eric. Isis, warm up on the rower and then the punching bags." Constantine was back in drill-sergeant mode, so there was no way to argue.

I was fully awake and decided to jump on the treadmill first. Five minutes of brisk walking had my blood pumping. My warm-up went fairly quickly. By the time Bartholomew was done with his drills, I had completed a full circuit of push-ups, pull-ups, and squats. I had been told it took the body less than two weeks to start toning. After years of conditioning, exercises were another form of muscle memory. I was slowly finding my rhythm again. It probably helped that I was drinking those weird shakes as well.

Bartholomew and I switched places. He went to work on the bike, and I walked to the mat. Hand-to-hand combat was the one thing I had avoided in the military. Sexy Eric was bouncing on the balls of his feet. He looked strong but flexible. I was going to die.

"We're going to start with some self-defense, OK?" Eric sounded just like Constantine, with that teacher's tone. "I'm going to throw a few punches; you need to block them." He looked at me, and I nodded.

Eric threw a couple of fast punches and a jab. I managed to get hit each time and didn't block a single one.

"Oh, wow. You are really bad at this." He actually sounded sorry for me. "Weren't you in the army?"

"Yes, but I was in the band. Why does everyone keep forgetting that I'm a musician?"

Eric stopped and actually looked at me. It was as if he had never noticed me before. "I though all of Death's interns were notorious killing machines."

Great. I was making the interns look bad.

"Sorry to disappoint you. But this is day four for me, and no, I'm not some crazy assassin. God, I still haven't read the manual." I sounded so pitiful.

Eric gave me the strangest look. "You are not what I expected." That was a common phrase lately for me. "How about we start from the basics and work our way up?"

I had no idea what that meant, but it sounded better than getting beaten up. "Please, let's do that." I was too lost to care. I needed help, and it seemed Sexy Eric was our new kung fu master.

Two hours later, I was sore in places I didn't know I had muscles in. Eric showed me the correct way to throw a punch, the proper stances for kicks, and how to block. I spent most of my time on the defensive, dodging and backing up. We went through drills of kicking and punching over and over. I had underestimated the amount of energy and concentration it took to fight. At one point, he had me in a headlock with the intent of teaching me how to get away. I managed to knock us both on the floor, but I was still trapped. Constantine was very proud of my progress. I wasn't sure what he was talking about; I still couldn't block fast enough.

By the time Constantine walked Eric out, I was on the floor, staring at the ceiling. My clothes were covered in sweat, and I couldn't move a muscle. I looked like a hot mess. I heard Constantine thank Eric and mention something about seeing him Saturday. I hoped it wasn't this Saturday. I doubted I would be able to walk by then.

I was still staring at the ceiling when Constantine came over and glared down at me. Trust me—it will scare the hell out of you to have a talking cat three inches from your eyeballs.

"Wake up."

I couldn't help it. I jumped. He was way too close not to be scary. I sat up, staring down at him. Constantine looked as if he were smiling at me. The nerve of that cat. He was devious.

"I'm up. No need to yell."

"Who said I was yelling? Good job today, Isis. In a few weeks, you'll be able to defend yourself in a fight." Constantine sounded really sure of himself.

"Sure, if those witches don't kill me first." At the rate they were going, that could happen sooner rather than later.

"Stop being so dramatic."

"Constantine, you know I'm right. If Bartholomew hadn't showed up last night, they probably would have killed me."

"But he did show up. What's your point?" Constantine sat down next to me and did his sphinx pose.

"He could have been hurt." I didn't want anyone else to get hurt.

"We're in this together, remember?" Bartholomew had walked over from his practice area.

"This is really dangerous." I was pleading, but they just looked at each other.

"We work for Death. It comes with the territory. Good news—your order is here." Bartholomew looked like a kid on Christmas morning. He enjoyed changing the topic.

"See, things are looking up. You got presents. I need to make a few calls. You need to stop by the Cave tonight."

I had no idea what Constantine was talking about. This Cave thing sounded sketchy.

Constantine headed upstairs without an explanation while Bartholomew and I headed toward the shooting range. Three large crates were lined up against the wall. Bartholomew made his way toward the first one and popped the lid. A couple of new M16s were inside the crate, with sights and extra magazines. I really didn't want to kill anyone, but I was really tired of getting beaten up.

"Are you sure you're not an arms dealer?" It was hard not to smile at Bartholomew.

He took a bow and smiled.

"Nice job."

"Thank you. I got extra ammo. If these witches are as strong as we think they are, bullets might not stop them. At least the effort will take its toll, especially if shot from multiple angles."

I had asked Bartholomew to research special ammo. I wasn't sure what damage this would do, but we needed all the help we could get. Bartholomew proceeded to show me the rest of the goods. He was good.

Chapter Twenty-Three

The morning flew by, and I wasn't sure what we had gotten done. I tested every weapon Bartholomew had ordered. I ensured the sights for all the guns were accurate and that I could handle each one. I was out of my league with spells and one-on-one combat, but at least I knew I could handle an assault rifle. I was tired of bringing knives to gun fights, as they said in Texas. To make things legit, Bartholomew sent the paperwork for my concealed gun permit. While everyone in Texas had guns, I didn't want to go to jail for hiding mine.

After my intense weapons session, Bartholomew and I went over maps of Texarkana. For a small town, this place was really spread out. There were too many weird buildings to hide people and just odd locations. We didn't have time to go door-to-door. Downtown was looking like the best setting, out of the way and with some abandoned locations. I was not too happy about searching any of them alone. Bartholomew suggested asking Sexy-Butt, a.k.a. Officer Eric, for help. At this rate, I would take any help I could get.

Constantine was working his magic to get me into the Cave. I still had no idea what that was, but I wanted to find Angelito before I headed out. Thursdays at Abuelita's was still the weekday special, and we served only dinner. Doors were opened at 4:00 p.m., so I knew Abuelita would be at the shop already. Angelito normally showed up by three thirty. I had at least an hour to get some info from Abuelita before he showed up, and then I could nail that lazy bum. I couldn't believe he had set me up.

I pulled up to Abuelita's, and this time I parked in the back. I didn't want anyone seeing Bumblebee. I also didn't want anyone blowing it up. I was sure Constantine would turn me into Swiss cheese if something happened to his ride. Life was not fair when a cat had a better car than I did. I was not normally an angry person, but every time I thought about the Whale, fantasies of vengeance filled my mind. I really wanted to shake the hell out of those witches.

"Hi, Abuelita!" I shouted even before I walked into the building. I wasn't scheduled to work, so I didn't want to scare her to death. Or worse, have her shoot me.

"Oh, Isis, what are you doing here?" Yeah, huge blessing I yelled. Abuelita was pointing the shotgun directly at me.

"I was looking for Angelito and wanted to check up on you. Are you OK?"

Abuelita was like a rock—nothing could disturb her strength. Today, she looked haggard. Older than ever, and even her normally tight hair was out of place. Not messy but with hair falling out of the bun.

She took a deep breath and looked around. "Well, when you see him, you tell him I need to talk to him."

"You haven't seen him? Abuelita, you live in the same house with that boy. How is that possible?" I had never been to their house, so I had no idea if you could miss a person in the same space. With Abuelita being so overly protective, I figured she would be in his room checking on him.

"Isis, I have no idea what's going on. He's gone by the time I come in or comes back after the time I fall asleep. I hardly see him. Today, he texted me again, saying that he has things going on and can't come in. Something is not right." Abuelita was crying. A very intimidating thing to do when you're holding a shotgun with one hand and a large metal spoon with the other.

I walked slowly over to her. I had no idea what to say, so I did the only thing I could think of. I hugged her.

"I'm sorry, Abuelita. I'm sure he's OK." I wanted him to be OK. I hoped that counted as the truth.

"Isis, you're a horrible liar. But thank you, dear. I needed that." With another pat on the back, she let me go. Abuelita put the shotgun down and started mixing her pot.

I took a deep breath and dropped my head. "I think Angelito is messing around with the witches." I blurted it out before I could stop myself.

Abuelita stopped and stared at me. That was a lot of eye contact to handle from one intense lady. "Are you sure?"

"Kind of. He mentioned that his girl hangs out with the biker gang in town. It just so happens that our sweet local coven is a biker gang. I don't know how involved he is."

I was worried about Abuelita's reaction, but she squared her shoulders and looked focused. "Well, that explains things better. I should have known something wasn't normal. That boy doesn't fall that hard for anyone. He's way too selfish for that. We might need to fix this." I had no idea what "fix this" meant, but I felt bad for the witches. Abuelita's look promised it wasn't going to be pretty.

"Do I want to know what you're planning to do?"

"Nothing to worry about, dear. Nothing dangerous—not yet. I do need to go home and pick up a few things of his. Do you mind watching the restaurant? My cousin is coming in to help out, but not till four o'clock. I'll be right back." That was a rhetorical question, since she was heading toward the door before I had time to agree. Abuelita gave me one last wink, and she was out the door.

Great. Now I was stuck at work. I wasn't dressed in my normal Abuelita's clothes. I had khaki cargo pants and a gray T-shirt. If Abuelita was jumpy, I was paranoid. I had pepper spray, a Taser, two pairs of butterfly knives, and keys in my pants pocket. If someone was jumping me today, they were going down hard. I refused to unload anything from my pockets, but I couldn't just sit there doing nothing. My hair was in a ponytail, so I decided to at least wrap it in a messy bun.

Nothing was set up for the dinner crowd. Chairs had to be taken down from the tables. Silverware needed to be wrapped in napkins and plates pulled out from the dishwasher. In other words, everything needed to be set up quickly. I was praying that her cousin would show up soon, but I wasn't holding my breath for that one. Abuelita's family members were never on time for anything. They would be the ones to be late to their own funeral.

Abuelita was true to her word. She was back in less than forty minutes. I was still busy setting up the place when she entered the kitchen with an armful of stuff. I gave her a quick glance, and I was sure she had a teddy bear under her arm. I hoped she wasn't planning on sacrificing the poor thing.

"Isis, my cousin called. She's running late. Do you mind covering till she gets here?"

"Sure thing, Abuelita. I just need to be home early, but I can cover." No need to get mad; I should have seen this coming. Between the nieces, the cousin, and Angelito, no wonder Abuelita thought I was amazing. They made me look good—they were totally irresponsible. That was the reason they never worked the weekend shift.

My body went on autopilot as I thought about Abuelita this weekend. I was feeling guilty for leaving her alone. Unfortunately, if I didn't do my main job, a lot of people were going to end up dead. It had been a while since the result of my job was death. It was an odd feeling. I wasn't sure whether I was happy about it or disturbed. By the time 4:00 p.m. rolled around, I was completely depressed with my own thoughts.

I went over to the kitchen to check on Abuelita before opening the restaurant. On the far stove, she had a small pot boiling. It actually looked like a small cauldron. I had no idea what she was doing, but she was whispering who knows what into the cauldron.

I cleared my throat for her benefit. "Abuelita, are we ready to open?"

"Yes, dear. Please get the door. Beans are ready to set in the front area." Abuelita's voice was distant, almost muffled with a weird accent. Not Spanish but almost Cajun. Her loose hairs were starting to flow in their own invisible air current. That was way too much for me. I did a quick U-turn and headed back to the dining area.

The last thing I needed was for Abuelita to go all *Exorcist* on me. If her head started spinning, I was out that door so fast, I could break Olympic records. I was not as brave as I hoped. I almost ran to the door to get away. I was totally distracted, because I missed Gabe standing on the other side. By the time I noticed, I had jumped five feet off the ground in pure horror. Abuelita didn't even notice.

"Isis, I'm so sorry. I thought you saw me." Gabe was holding my arms, trying to steady me.

"No, it's my fault, Gabe. I'm totally spacing out. Please come in."

Gabe was still holding me when I flipped the door sign to *Open*. "Are you sure you're OK?" He was examining me very carefully. I probably looked pale.

"Yeah, I'm good. Thanks."

"OK, then." Gabe stepped away from me and was heading toward his seat at the bar when a thought crossed my mind.

"Hey, Gabe, could I ask you a quick question? I'm not sure if you could answer me. You wouldn't happen to know where Bob is located?" I was hoping he was getting my meaning.

"We see and hear things."

I might as well ask. "Could you help me?"

"We're not allowed to intervene in the affairs of man. We watch and report. We preserve free will." Well, so much for divine intervention.

"Great. Love free will." I knew I sounded sarcastic. "Could you at least tell me if they're in heaven?"

"I can at least give you that one. Nope, they are not. Watch your back, Isis. They're dangerous, with complete disregard for others." Gabe smiled and patted my arm.

"Thanks, Gabe." At least he wasn't trying to kill me. I needed all the help I could get. Too bad the only ones playing fair were the angels. Too bad the witches didn't mind influencing people. By the way Abuelita was acting, she knew exactly what was going on.

Well, at least I had tried. Gabe took his seat, and I went about my business. By the time Abuelita's cousin showed up, it was close to seven o'clock. I was tired and smelled like Mexican food again. The place was running smoothly, and my guilt was gone. She could close up for Abuelita.

I needed a shower and a new set of clothes before heading out to this Cave place. I hoped Constantine was ready to give me more details. Good deed for the day done. I had no idea what Abuelita was brewing in the back, and I was too chickenshit to ask. I planned to check back with her later.

Chapter Twenty-Four

It was not a good sign that Constantine had let me dress myself tonight. Neither he nor Bartholomew said much about my outfit. I definitely looked like a skater kid. The only thing I wasn't wearing was a hoodie, but I had braided my hair. No need to pretend and fake being anything else; I was heading toward the Cave. The Cave, no other than the devil's club. Not just any devil or demon, but the Prince of Deception himself. I was going to Lucifer's club. Great. From angel to the devil—this day was getting better and better.

I had a million questions running through my head. The only one Constantine answered was that the devil owned clubs. The cave was one of many. It was technically not in Texarkana, but a door was opening there tonight. Constantine had pulled some strings to get me an audience with the prince himself. Wow, what a guy. Constantine needed to stop doing me favors. Favors like that were going to get me stuck in hell, literally. The good news was that according to Constantine, the Cave was not in hell, so I could leave. Who needs enemies when you have Constantine around?

The Cave was by invitation only. Only those who knew where to go could find it, and only those with permission could get in. Constantine's instructions said the entrance was at the Broad Street Park. I had been to this park before, and it wasn't technically a park. It was in the middle of downtown on Broad Street. One of the old buildings had collapsed, so they gutted the space, left a semi-storefront entrance, planted a few trees, put in a small brick stage and great landscaping with picnic tables, and called it a park. The space had no roof and was open at both ends.

To make things even more interesting, the park was less than a block from the county's correctional facility.

Either the devil had a sick sense of humor, or this club was really small. I was to walk in, head toward the back of the park, and give my card to the bouncer at the door. On a Thursday night in September, downtown Texarkana should be pretty calm. The Perot Theater was not having a show, so I found a parking space right in front of the park. Constantine had said to take no weapons. I left everything in Bumblebee, including my wallet. All I took was my lip gloss.

I had Constantine's reference card in my hand. The park was dead, but according to Constantine, I was looking for a bouncer in the back. I walked in as if I belonged and headed toward the back. The little park was not that long, and I reached the back in less than a minute. I stood ten steps from the back entrance and waited. September nights were getting cool, so I was glad I was wearing a long-sleeve shirt under my T-shirt. I crossed my arms, trying to be patient. Without a word, a six-foot-tall black guy materialized from the shadows. I saw him out of the corner of my eye. Even knowing he would show up, it was creepy. The man was handsome, with great definition everywhere.

"I was wondering if I missed the party." I stepped up to the bouncer and handed him my card. I was pretty sure I was holding a black square on both sides, but when he flipped it over, it had a gold paw in the middle. I didn't know if the bouncer was impressed, but I was. Constantine had skills.

"The guardian sent you. Interesting. Hope you don't mind, but I'm going to need to search you." The bouncer put the card in his front pocket and signaled for me to turn around. I was always the poor victim at the airport who got searched, so I knew the drill.

I extended my arms and spread my legs wide. For a big guy, the bouncer was quick and light on his feet. The search took less than thirty seconds. He inspected my lip gloss very carefully. He looked disappointed when he realized it was only lip gloss. What was he expecting, a blade in there?

"I don't need to remind you this is a business establishment, and we don't want any trouble." Sure, he didn't. The look in his eyes was murderous. He was ready for me to start something.

"Of course. I'm just here to talk."

He gave me a look almost like the Rock before a wrestling match. I wasn't sure if I was going to make it out alive.

The bouncer inclined his chin. He walked over to the wall on his right and pulled over a velvety curtain. This was where I walked in faith. My rational mind kept telling me I was going to smack my face into a wall. My intuition said to trust Constantine. If I died, Constantine was going down. Without looking back, I stepped through the velvety curtain and went through the wall. The place was pitch black.

"Watch your step, and hold on to the rail while going down the stairs." Those were the last words I heard the bouncer say as the curtain fell back in place. So, down the dark stairs it was. I went down twelve, maybe thirteen steps before I reached another velvety curtain. Before my eyes could adjust, the curtain was pulled open for me. I stood frozen in place. I wasn't sure what to expect, but this was not it.

The Cave was definitely underground, but it was not a Cave. It was a cross between Ricky Martin's club in "Living la Vida Loca," the Jennifer Lopez and Pitbull club scene from "On the Floor," and Cirque du Soleil, all in one. Crystal chandeliers hung strategically around the club. On a stage at the far wall, a full band was playing their hearts out. Balconies were filled with people on either side of the stage, with a pit in front of the band. Dancers were suspended from cages, cables, and even small platforms scattered through the club. If the United Nations needed a postcard, this place had everyone represented.

"Good evening, intern. Should I escort you? He's expecting you."

Wow. I was betting the devil recruited at *GQ* for his staff. The bouncer next to me was breathtaking, just like the first one. I had to swallow a few times to get my thoughts in order.

"Yes, thank you. That would be great."

GQ smiled at me and led the way. "First time? Don't worry; you get used to it." I wasn't sure how, but GQ's voice sounded like a purr in my ear. It was crystal clear even with the music pounding. I had to admit, the devil had a killer DJ.

I wasn't sure if the bouncer did it on purpose, but it appeared we were taking the scenic route. Everyone stared at me as I passed. I was hoping it was because I was the only one fully dressed.

If Shooters had tons of half-naked girls, in this place they were just naked. They even had full samba dancers in their full outfits. Nobody needed beer goggles in this place; these people were beautiful.

GQ led us up a staircase to the left of the stage to an empty balcony. At least it looked empty as I approached.

At the top of the circular staircase, I got a full view of the balcony. Unlike most theater balconies, this one was set up to look at the whole club, not just the stage. To the left, a pair of Victorian-looking chairs were facing the stage. To the right, a very black leather couch was by a wall, facing the opposite way. I was sure it was custom made, and it was huge.

"Your Highness, she is here," GQ said to a man on the couch. He was dimly lit, and I wasn't sure what to expect.

"Thank you, Adam. You can leave us."

Adam gave me one last look that screamed *I'm watching you*, and then he walked back downstairs. Honestly. As if I could kill the devil.

"Well, well, this is a pleasant surprise. Normally, it takes interns at least a few months before they venture down my path."

I was speechless and probably drooling. I got a full view of the devil as he walked around the couch. The devil was hot. OK, not just hot. We're talking Brad Pitt in *Interview with the Vampire* sexy hot. He was blond with piercing blue eyes, and he was wearing the best Armani suit I had ever seen a man pull off. This was not happening to me. How was this possible?

"Has anyone ever told you it's not polite to stare?"

"Are you serious? I mean, I'm sorry. OK, I think I'm lost. Who are you again?" I was sure Constantine had given me the wrong directions. Where were his horns, red skin, and tail? This was not my idea of the Devil.

He actually laughed at me. He even had a sexy laugh. No wonder Christianity was losing the recruitment battle. Jesus was portrayed with sandals and messy hair, and here was the devil, straight out of *Cosmo*. That wasn't fair.

"Now, Isis, do you really not know?" He walked over to one of the chairs and sat down, drink in hand.

"You're not what I was expecting." That was the honest truth. Was he really the devil?

"Blunt and brutally honest. I like that. But you're right. I guess I'm not, considering your boss is whatever people have envisioned. I can see why you're surprised. I'm a little vainer. The horns and flames got old after a while. Besides, horrible for business. Nobody wants any of that." A capitalist devil. My day was getting better by the minute.

"I can only imagine. But I won't take too much of your time. I just have a few questions." This place was a sensory overload, and I needed to get out before I did something stupid. Like actually want to stay.

"Of course, you do, dear. What are you going to give me in return?"

"Give you? Give you...like what?" I was going to strangle Constantine for not explaining this better.

"Knowledge is power, and you know people tend to die for power." He was caressing his drink as he spoke.

"Sorry, death is out of the question. House rule. I can't kill anyone, and I'm sure that includes me." I was definitely not making a deal with the devil.

"Oh, really? You might need to share that rule with some of your peeps. But no, I was thinking something more enjoyable." The devil's eyes ran down the length of my body. I was sure I was blushing, but I was not going to look away. I could do arrogant with the best of them.

"What do you have in mind?" I crossed my arms over my chest and waited. I was not going to volunteer for anything. Constantine had said to let him spell things out. Don't fill in blanks, or I would not get a straight answer.

"Defiant. Death made an interesting choice with you. Some entertainment. How about a dance-off? It is a club, after all." The devil was playing with me. Great. A dance-off didn't sound so bad.

"Fine." I hadn't gone all the way down there for nothing.

"That's the spirit, dear. On the main stage, of course. Oh, be careful with the competition. They fight dirty." He sounded mischievous.

I walked back down the staircase and headed to the main stage without looking back. I was met by a pair of tough-looking chicks at the edge of the stage.

"Song?" a bad chick with crazy, spiky, pink hair asked me. Her twin had spiky, blue hair. At least they were wearing clothes, even if they were see-through. Oh, I got to pick my own funeral anthem. Great.

"Chris Brown's 'Look at Me Now.'" If I was going to die, I was to do it my way.

They both smiled and walked to the DJ. I made my way up on the stage. Of course, like every horrible dream most people had, the entire place was dead, and still everyone was staring at me. The devil leaned down over his balcony and smiled as Chris's lyrics started: "You can't hate from outside the club. You can't even get in." I figured he would appreciate the reference. He did.

The music started, and I let the beat and the flow take me. The acoustics in this place were mind-blowing. I closed my eyes and went down my own routine. I moved from shoulder rolls to butterflies to Chris's own moves. I had been twerking before Miley knew the meaning of the word. It didn't hurt that I had spent months memorizing the routine to this song. I could have given Chris Brown a run for his money here. Of course, shaking my ass and flaunting my moves was too easy—dancing came natural to me. To make things interesting, the devil added a few sword-waving, dancing ninjas. I hated ninjas.

"Poles!" I yelled at the DJ. With a wink, I had stripper poles rise from the floor. My upper-body strength might have sucked, but I had a hell of a roundhouse. Only in a place like this would the stage have been stocked with stripper poles ready for the calling.

This was my show, and I wasn't going down that easily. I timed my moves to Busta Rhymes's lyrics and slammed my opponents with a kick to the chest. The crowd went wild. I slid to the left and then back to the right, ending with a *Matrix* bend to avoid the blade over my head. I just needed to survive this song—all four minutes of it. I was doing great at avoiding the swords, sliding down the poles, and throwing kicks. My boy Lil Wayne came on, so it was time to shut this mess down. I moon danced to the side and grabbed one of the silk ropes from the ceiling. I wrapped my arms around the silk, took a leap off the stage, spun around, and kicked one of the ninjas in the face. I wasn't planning to kill anyone, but I was winning this contest. I released the silk, did a quick roll back to the center, and twerked the rest of the song off. I was sweating to death, but I was still standing.

Why weren't those witches challenging me to a dance-off? I got this! The crowd was going nuts, and the devil was smiling. I wasn't sure if that was a good thing or not. He gave me a bow, and I hopped off the stage. I wasn't planning to push my luck. I took the stairs two at a time.

"Impressive. I did not see that coming." The devil was smiling a very dangerous smile. He handed me a drink, which I really wanted since I was parched.

"No, thank you, sir." Constantine had said not to drink from any open container.

"Of course. I'm sure Constantine gave you the warning." I just smiled. "How about a bottle of water? Not open." Could you trust the devil? He probably read the look on my face. "I'm still a business owner. If people can't trust the water, they'll stop coming." He was a true capitalist.

"I'll take the water. So, what should I call you?"

He handed me a bottle and gave me the most innocent smile. "Call me Jake."

I almost spit my water. "So, Jake. Jake? Really?"

"I've always liked the name Jacob. So much history behind it." Oh yeah, he was arrogant to the core.

"Fair enough. So, tell me, Jake, are the witches working for you?" I was too tired to play any more games.

"Sorry, Isis. Not mine."

"What?" All that work for nothing. "Are you sure?" If they weren't his, who were they working for it?

"They're independent." Was he reading my mind? "Besides, killing a bunch of people in my name doesn't get me anything. Those souls would go straight to heaven, most of them as martyrs. Do I look like I want to help the competition?" He was definitely all about business.

"Are they killing in hell?" I was praying they weren't. I really didn't want to go there.

"I wish they were. We have a score to settle. I don't enjoy losing souls to wannabes. Half of their victims were coming to me anyway. Not anymore."

Oh, I had totally forgot about that part. He was not a happy camper.

"You know, you could have sent Constantine a text instead of making me do all that work." This was truly a waste of my time.

"I could have. But I wanted to meet you. Besides, now you've earned your own right to be here. That's a huge thing. Not everyone can come to one of my clubs. And as long as you're not blowing up the place, you're welcome—both for business and pleasure." He handed me a black card. Unlike the paw Constantine's had, mine had stick figures dancing. That was too cool, because they moved as you moved the card. I couldn't help but smile.

"Thanks, I think. Not sure when my boss will give me time."

"You do have a very jealous boss. I would hate to incur the wrath of Death." The wrath of Death—I had never thought about that before. "Come back soon, Isis."

"Hopefully, not too soon." I waved at Jake and took off. That was way too much for one night for me. I needed to leave before somebody else tried to challenge me. Jake gave me another devious smile before I walked away.

Chapter Twenty-Five

There was a heavy pressure on my chest, and I was struggling to breathe. My eyelids flew open when a wet thing touched my nose. A pair of huge eyeballs was inches from my face.

"Holy Jesus Christ! What is going on?" I screamed.

"It's six a.m., and you're late for practice." He sat back on his back legs and looked down at me, very king-like—which meant he was not happy.

"I had a long day. Remember, you sent me to see the devil." I tried to cover my mouth as I yawned. It was way too early for this. I wanted more sleep.

"That was yesterday. Today is Friday, and we have things to do. Get. Up." Constantine was an evil overlord. Why didn't anyone believe me?

"OK, OK. Just remember, if I fall down, I warned you." I was sure if I fell down, the only thing Constantine was going to do was laugh at me.

"You've got five minutes. Eric is already downstairs." Constantine hopped off the bed and was heading out before I could speak. I had thought Eric was not supposed to be back till next week. Great. Another beating, before breakfast.

Sleep was out of the question after Constantine had scared me to death. My heart was still racing, and I was wide awake. I really wanted to skip practice, but I doubted I had an option. I forced myself out of bed and shuffled to the bathroom. After quickly brushing my teeth, I got dressed in a pair of yoga pants and a tank top. My hair was a hot mess, so I pulled it up into a quick bun. It wasn't as if I could impress Sexy-Butt downstairs. He was turning more into Sour-Face.

By the time I made it to the gym area, I was ready to battle. I was expecting Bartholomew to be doing his drills with Eric and Constantine giving orders. Instead, all three were gathered around one of the bench tables. Bartholomew was sitting on the floor, Constantine on the bench, and Eric was in a squat. I shook my head. He could even do those well. That boy really sucked. I sneaked behind them to find them staring at a laptop.

"What are you three looking at?" I was praying it wasn't porn and I would have to kill Eric and Constantine.

"You! Nice moves, Isis. I didn't know you had it in you."

I had no idea what Constantine was talking about till I focused on the screen. By God, I wished they were watching porn now. It was a video feed of me doing last night's dance-off.

"Ouch, that looked painful. Nice roundhouse, Isis." Bartholomew looked very impressed.

"I'm actually impressed. An intern who got information without killing anyone. How did you know the Devil would have poles at the club?" Eric had stood up and was giving me his undivided attention. I was sure I liked it better when he ignored me. His intensity was overwhelming.

"He's the Devil. If he didn't have stripper poles, nobody else should. How did you get a copy of that?"

"It's all over YouTube." Bartholomew's matter-of-fact voice was scarier than Constantine's.

"Oh God. That's out there for the whole world to see?" I prayed I would get hit by lightning.

"Only for the supernatural world. This is a private channel." Bartholomew was still not helping.

"That's a relief. At least my godmother won't see it." I was pretty sure they had missed my sarcasm, since they all looked way too happy. "That was not helpful. The supernatural community, from what I've seen, is huge. Did I mention huge? And I don't even know who's in it."

"Stop overreacting, Isis. It wasn't like you made a fool of yourself. If you had lost, that would have been embarrassing. All you needed was to drop the mic." That was the first compliment Eric had ever given me.

"Thanks, but after all that, I didn't get anything."

"What do you mean?" I had Constantine's full attention. "Did the Devil not talk to you?"

"Oh, he talked to me. He just didn't say anything useful. And he goes by Jake."

"Imagine that. He has always been an arrogant one." At least I knew Constantine was not a fan, or he didn't like competition in the arrogant department. "Let's hear it."

I took a deep breath before starting. "The witches are not his. In his terms—and I quote—they are wannabes. They are also not working out of hell."

"That's really good news. We really don't want to go to hell. Well done, Isis."

Was I missing something, or had Constantine also given me a compliment? "OK, what's going on? Why are you two being so nice to me?"

"I'm nice," Bartholomew said, almost offended.

"You're always nice, Bart. These two, not so much. What's the deal?" I crossed my arms and faced them. I had my angry face on.

"Nothing's going on. We're just glad everything went well." Constantine was way too quick for that to be the truth.

"I didn't get much."

"It's like science. We're eliminating everything that is not it so we can find what it is."

I tilted my head and stared at Constantine. Was he rambling? "We have no time for trial and error now. And thank you for destroying my illusions about science." Great. Even science was failing me.

"Why do you think they call it practicing? Obviously, doctors have not perfected their craft." Constantine was on a roll. I was never going to see a doctor the same way again.

"Constantine, stop playing with her. Just tell her. Most people try to outsmart the Devil and end up losing their souls. Why didn't you try to bargain with him?" Eric was calm as he spoke, but he was curious.

"Bargain with him? Was that even a choice? What could I possibly have that the Devil might want?" The boys were officially losing their minds.

"You could owe him a favor for information." Eric turned to face the screen again.

"A favor?" I was outraged. "If I had to owe him a favor for the crap he gave me, I probably would have killed him. Besides, it's not like you could ever beat the Devil at being cunning and deceiving." I was young, but I was not stupid.

"That's a very good insight. Not bad at all, Isis." Constantine spoke with a hint of a smile and pride in his voice. They had not thought I would survive the trip.

"OK, if you were so worried, I would lose my soul yesterday, why didn't you tell me?" I crossed my arms over my chest.

"He's a client. Every intern has to learn how to work with him. You managed pretty well and didn't blow up the club. This is great for business." Constantine was definitely proud.

"We need to work on our reputation. People are convinced I'm the plague. Or worse, a crusader." I really didn't want to get strip-searched everywhere I went.

"That's a pretty accurate description. Interns have a tendency for preemptive strikes and overkill." Eric looked kind of bashful as he spoke.

"Basically, we're a bunch of homicidal maniacs." All three nodded in unison. "Great. That is just great. That explains why even the Devil's people were worried around me."

"Everyone, let's start practicing. I think we've been going at this all wrong. Instead of trying to fix your weaknesses, we need to maximize your strengths. Let's skip the punches and make those kicks of yours killer." Eric was a little too happy about that. I glanced at Constantine and Eric, and they both looked wicked. This was going to be painful.

"I love it. Bartholomew, start warming up. Isis, hit the mat." All Constantine needed was a cigar, and he could be a mini-Hannibal from the A-Team.

Resistance was futile with these boys. A week at this job, and I really missed my old life. Anyone who complained about having a boring life should have taken over mine. I watched Eric do a few warm-up stretches before stepping onto the mat. He was as limber as a gymnast. I had no idea how a person could be so graceful and hit so hard. While Eric was bent into a table pose, I stretched my thighs and calves.

"Is that all you're stretching?" How did he notice from his side of the mat? Not only was he a contortionist, but now the boy had eyes in the back of his head.

"Yeah. No need to overtire my muscles before starting. Whenever you're ready." Besides, I was going to get a beating regardless of how much I stretched. So, why delay the inevitable?

At least I was not disappointed in the training. Eric's sympathy level didn't last long, and he proceeded to train me like a madman. I informed the overzealous, crazy man that I was not training for the Olympics—just survival. I was not very concerned with form but pure effectiveness.

After forty-five minutes of pure hell, my legs were shaky, and I was sure I was going to collapse. I had no grace, and I just limped off the mat. My legs were jelly. Between last night and this morning's torture session, I was going to need Epsom salts and a bath.

"You look like hell, Isis," Bartholomew casually said as he handed me a bottle of water on his way to the mat. To add insult to injury, Eric didn't even look tired. I really hated that boy.

"I love you, too, Bart." It was hard to be mad at Bartholomew. He was too damn cute. He was at that age right before boys hit puberty, when they still look sweet and innocent. Too bad they grow.

I was stretching on the floor when an idea hit me. "Hey, Bart, is this your computer?"

Bartholomew was stretching his calves and looked over his shoulder. "Yeah. Do you need it?"

"Does it have a recording feature?"

"From Audacity to Wave Horizon are installed. Anything you need should be in there."

Of course, they would be. This was Bartholomew we were talking about. "Awesome. Do you mind if I borrow it this morning?" I was eyeing his computer like a kid in a candy store.

"Sure thing. Let me know if you like it, and I'll order you one this afternoon." The look of shock must have been pretty obvious on my face. "I'm sure it's in the budget." He smiled and turned around to face Eric for his lesson.

"What are you thinking about, Isis?" Constantine had walked over to me and was eyeing me very suspiciously.

"Music and how to capture it." I was still staring at the computer.

Constantine glanced at the computer and then back at me. "Your gift." He raised an eyebrow, or whatever the equivalent was for cats, and gave me an evil grin.

"You're right, Constantine. I can't walk around with a flute and ask people to wait while I play. I need something readily available." I needed to start thinking like a soldier—working smarter and not harder. Trial and error was going to get me killed if I wasn't careful. "Do you think it would work?"

"Musical recordings have been causing people to kill themselves for years. I'm sure you can put a few to sleep without a problem."

"How long does the gift normally last?" I needed a time frame to work with.

"It depends on the intern and the strength of your desire." Constantine had his philosophical teacher face on.

"Perfect." Maybe things were finally looking up for us.

"Perfect? What does that mean?" Constantine did not enjoy being puzzled.

"I only need to pour my soul into it for two minutes, tops. Then I can create a loop of it. As long as it plays, the people will sleep." I loved technology.

"Not bad, Isis. You're finally thinking like an intern." Constantine was actually smiling. "You're going to be like the Pussycat Dolls in their video with Timbaland. 'Wait a Minute, Girl.'" How did he do that? Constantine's imitation skills were amazing. I shook my head.

"Imagine you liking a group named Pussycat." Constantine smiled at me. "I'm going to finish my workout and then head upstairs. I still need to check out Sacred Heart today." Constantine agreed and headed back to watch Bartholomew, shaking his tail. I was amazed he was still singing to himself. He even moved in sync. Unbelievable.

I wasn't sure how long it was going to take me to do the recording and then the editing. The sooner I started, the safer I would feel. I also needed a few disposable players—I wasn't planning to leave my phone everywhere. This whole business made me nervous. I wasn't that crazy about a soundtrack, especially one that was going to knock people out.

Chapter Twenty-Six

The next time I decide to pass out my business cards to people, I really should ask for names. I got a text from an Ana, who claimed to have info. First of all, who was Ana, and why didn't Ana have a last name? I had enough issues with no-last-name Bob; I really didn't want to add another to that list. Ana was an early riser, since the message had been left at 7:00 a.m. By the time I finished trying to track down Ana, it was almost 10:00 a.m. Ana was scared and irrational. After lots of pleading, she agreed to meet.

I felt as if I were back in the army. I was doing a lot of "hurry up and wait." I rushed my shower to meet Ana at the Salvation Army by 10:30 a.m. I was praying nobody would stop me. Bumblebee was packed like a small military convoy. After my last adventure, I was not taking any chances. I really didn't want to kill anyone, but I had no issue seriously injuring people. Thoughts like that were probably the reason interns had such a bad reputation.

Downtown was pretty slow. I wasn't sure where I was supposed to meet this Ana. She hadn't stated whether this meeting was on the street, inside the Salvation Army, or at a nearby building. Her directions were sketchy at best. I parked Bumblebee on the opposite side of the street and walked over. My stomach was growling so loudly, I was sure the dogs could hear it. I had forgotten to grab food again. I walked slowly toward the entrance; hopefully, the scary volunteer wasn't on duty today.

"Pssst—over here."

Anytime you hear a *pssst*, you know it's not a good sign. I stopped short of the door and turned around.

The mystery Ana with no last name was the girl from Randy Sam's with the missing boyfriend. She was looking really rough.

She was wearing the same clothes I had seen her in, but they were dirtier and ripped. Her hair looked as if she'd gotten hit by a weed eater. I was starting to think I would be safer with the crazy volunteer. This was how being stuck on a horrible blind date felt. It was the moment after you realize you're stuck and can't run away.

"Hi, Ana. Are you OK?" That was the understatement of the century. But what else could I say? *Hey there, you look like shit.*

"There is a door. We need to avoid it."

Oh, wow. This was going from bad to worse very quickly. What in the world was she talking about?

"I'm sorry; what door?" This was nuts, but at least I sounded really sweet and nice.

Ana was looking over her shoulder. "The ghosts—they told me. Avoid the door. They're coming for me." OK, at least that explained why she looked like hell. I would look like death rolled over if ghosts were talking to me and Constantine wasn't there to explain it. "You think I'm crazy, don't you?"

"Oh no, sweetie. Trust me. After the week I'm having, I totally believe ghosts are talking to you. But there are a lot of doors around here. You might need to be more specific." It would be really nice if they could give exact locations or better descriptions now. If they were going to get involved, the least they could do was be helpful and not just annoying.

"The golden door is coming at the lines crossing." It was official: ghosts sucked.

"What does that mean?" I had a horrible feeling this was as much as I was going to get from little Ana.

"Oh, no. They're here." Ana was staring over my shoulder as if Death were walking behind me. I wasn't sure what to do, so I slowly turned around. The last thing I needed was to get jumped again. There was nobody there, and by the time I looked back, Ana was running away.

For a fragile, crazed person, she could really haul ass. I had no idea what motivated me to do it, but I took off after her. I was probably safer in front of the building by Bumblebee. At least I was carrying the mace and Taser. Anything that came my way was going to be sorry.

Ana took a quick left at the end of the block. I was amazed her skinny legs could move so fast.

I pushed to a sprint and reached the end of the block just in time to see Ana get abducted by my favorite black van. I wasn't sure whether Ana tripped into the van or they pulled her in. Ana was so occupied getting away from me that she didn't even notice the people in front of her. The van didn't even stop. They were rolling before the doors were closed.

"Dammit." This was becoming a horrible pattern. I really wanted to choke the shit out of those witches. There was no sense in trying to chase them—by the time I reached Bumblebee, I would never find their trail. How could you hide a black van in Texarkana? There were not that many of those stupid things running around. An F-150—that was a different story. But a sixteen passenger van? No way.

Time was running out. I headed back to Bumblebee. Another trip downtown that was a total waste of time and demoralizing. I was so consumed with self-loathing that I almost missed the man sitting on the hood of Bumblebee till it was too late. Bob's friend from Beverly Park was having a picnic on Bumblebee. I placed my hand in my pocket, in case I needed to use the Taser.

"Comfy?" I was skipping this part of my report to Constantine.

"Not a bad place to be for a Friday morning in September." The man wasn't even looking at me. He looked pretty defiant. He was peeling an orange and dropping the skins on the street.

"That's lovely." I forced myself to calm down. It was not his fault I'd lost Ana. But he was still sitting on Bumblebee.

"There's a big price for info on your pretty self, Ms. Isis."

I froze. I realized he wasn't drunk today. I gave him my undivided attention.

"Is that why you're here? To make some money?" If the underground community of Texarkana as well as the supernatural one was spying on me, I was screwed.

"Hell no, girl. Those crazy bitches took Bob, and more are missing. We're not cattle. They can't push us around." The man was pissed. He spit the seeds of his orange for pure emphasis.

"Why are you here?" I was a little nervous.

"Payback."

I wasn't expecting that answer. "You want payback? Really? You came to me." He obviously had not seen me fight.

"You're friends with Bob, and you had some really gangster issues with those bitches. We heard they'd been beating you up, and here you are, still asking questions." The little man was eyeing me up and down. If Constantine had been there, he would have approved. "You have guts, little girl."

"That or I'm just dumb." Honestly speaking, this wasn't about the job anymore. I really hated those witches.

"This is our town. We refuse to be run off." The man noticed my confused look. "The underground citizens of Texarkana stay out of trouble, and the community is good to us. We're planning to keep it that way."

"That's a good plan. So, why are you here?" It was way too early to have philosophy discussions about Texarkana. We needed to get to the point.

"You need help." He said that with a smile, as if it should answer all the world's problems. Maybe I needed to start doing drugs, because some people made no sense to me.

"OK, continue." Why did I always had to pry the information out of people?

"Ms. Isis, you need eyes and ears in this town. I'm your man."

"You're here to offer your services, no questions asked? I could be a cop or some crazy nut on a vendetta." People were not this trusting.

"I confirmed you're friends with Bob. Bob is a good man. He helped others and never let anyone be abused. You bring Bob back, we can be square. A friend of Bob's is my friend." He looked sad as he mentioned Bob's name. He didn't believe there was any hope for Bob.

"We'll bring him back. We just need to find these witches by tomorrow at sunset. Can you help me with that?" We had a common goal.

"With pleasure." A devious smile spread over his face.

"What do I call you? Unless you're cool with *Bob's friend*."

"Shorty." Well, that was fitting. And again, no last name. The underground community could all be pop stars with this one-name thing.

"OK, Shorty, you know I need help. What do you know about this group?" I was ready to test this new informant thing.

"They got money and connections all over the city. They have infiltrated most nonprofits to get info on the underground." Shorty started cleaning his nails with a pocketknife.

"That explains why they can find people and pick the ones nobody notices." Damn, they were organized and smart. No wonder ninja intern hadn't found them. He had underestimated them.

"They also move all the time. They're never at one location for more than a night, maybe two. They have big muscles with them."

"Shorty, are you sure you want to get involved? Everyone who talks to me goes missing. You said it yourself about Bob." I really didn't want to add Shorty to this list.

"Ms. Isis, nobody's safe anymore. A gypsy came from New York yesterday. The same thing happened there. All they found were dried-up bones. He left town." Wow, I really had underestimated the underground community. They had a better communication system than the gossips on Facebook.

"That's right. Nobody's safe, Shorty." We stood in silence, staring at the Salvation Army. "Shorty, do you have a phone?"

"Obamacare, baby." Shorty pulled a cell phone from his pocket. Blessings for government programs. If Bob had a phone, we could have used the GPS to track him. But no, he had to be a paranoid vet. I was going to strangle that man.

"Good. Here's my number." I handed him a card. "Save it in your phone, then burn the card. We don't need anyone finding it on you."

"Oh, nice. This is very *Mission Impossible*-like." Shorty was easily amused.

"I would love for this to be simple." I reached for my wallet. Shorty looked malnourished.

"Whatever you say, boss." He was already busy programming his phone.

"Shorty, when was the last time you ate? Besides the orange."

"I eat all the time."

I was sure it wasn't anything healthy, or even enough. "Here, Shorty, go get some food, and maybe take some of your peeps with you. I normally work at Abuelita's on the weekend. Come and see me sometime." I handed him a stack of twenties. I didn't care how he spent the money. I didn't want to disrespect him, but I knew what it was like to be hungry.

"You don't have to pay me."

Now that I had a job that paid over the top, giving away $200 didn't hurt. I was glad I had made an ATM run on Wednesday. I needed to do another one today.

"I'm not. Just buying you lunch."

"Where? At Tao?"

I had to smile. I had never been a blessing to others. I hated receiving charity, but I always welcomed a meal. Shorty was the same way.

"If that's what you like, why not? My boss pays me well. I'm sure she would appreciate me buying lunch for our friends. We are friends, right?" I didn't want to insult him.

"Yes, ma'am, we are." He pocketed the cash and smiled brightly.

"Good. Now get off the car. Don't you ever dare tell a soul you were sitting on Bumblebee, or the owner will kill you."

Shorty's eyes got really wide, and he hopped off the car. "This is not your car? Why didn't you say something?" He was actually polishing poor Bumblebee.

"I wish it was. Those witches blew up my minivan." My poor Whale.

"They did you a favor with that one." Shorty was shaking his head at me.

"Thanks, Shorty." I was glaring at him. The nerve of the man, and he was walking. "Don't you have to get to work now? Be careful, and try not to get kidnapped."

"Leaving, boss." With that, he turned around and headed down Hazel Street toward the train tracks. He looked like a man without a care in the world.

Maybe my day wasn't a total loss. I watched Shorty for a minute and then got in Bumblebee. Now that I knew the world was watching, there was no point in hiding. I was hungry and had music to make. I decided to make a few more stops before heading back to Reapers.

Chapter Twenty-Seven

Sacred Heart Catholic Church was not far from downtown, less than ten minutes away. I decided to make a quick trip to the church before heading back. Hopefully, my stomach would not growl. Lunchtime was a horrible time to be driving around State Line, but it was the most direct path—drive north on State Line to Texas Boulevard, and then a quick right on Elizabeth Street. I didn't know the church schedule, but I was sure I could find somebody in the church's office. If I was lucky, maybe a priest.

I made really good time and got there in less than seven minutes. I had to force myself to drive past the smoothie shop, which was a test of dedication today. When I pulled into the parking lot, only a few cars were there. I parked to the farthest left, overlooking the cemetery. I had learned living in Texarkana that both Catholic churches had cemeteries. The one at Saint Edward's was not attached to the church, like this one. Graves and cemeteries always creeped me out. The irony was not lost on me. Of all the places to work, I worked for Death. I got out, with a quick prayer that this would be a short trip.

"Isis."

I looked around for the person calling me. It was almost a whisper, but I swore I had heard my name. I had a really unusual name; nobody was going to say it by accident—unless they were talking about the terrorist group, but somehow, I doubted it.

"Isis."

There it was again. This time it sounded like multiple people saying my name. Almost as if the words were carried by the wind. "Isis." The voices were coming from the cemetery.

"Damn the devil to hell. Why me?" I couldn't help it. Was I really going to go in there?

"Isis."

My job sucked. Obviously, the voices were not going to give up. I took a steadying breath and marched forward. Ever since I had taken this job, all I had done was take deep breaths.

It didn't take long for that cold feeling cemeteries gave me to kick in. I barely managed to cross the threshold, and it was there. The way this day was going, all I needed was a fog to come in, and the sinister effect would be complete.

"Isis." Those stupid voices were still calling my name. I was surprised at the number of people wandering around the cemetery. There were at least a dozen or so around the place. There were not that many cars in the parking lot for all these people. Had they all carpooled?

I was told people at cemeteries wanted solitude and privacy. I made it a point not to look anyone in the eye and to move quietly around the tombs. It took me a minute to realize I was literally walking around on the tombs, not on the little trail. Before I could change course, I saw a priest kneeling by one of the graves. I had a choice: wander around till I found the boogeyman calling my name or talk to the priest. I hated interrupting his prayers, but I really needed to get out of there. Trying not to step on any more graves, I hurried forward.

"Excuse me, Father." I was so happy priests wore uniforms, or else I would have never seen him.

He made the sign of the cross and looked at me. "Good morning—or is it good afternoon?" He was an older priest, maybe in his late sixties, with a fabulous head of white hair. If he grew a beard, he could pass for Santa Claus. He even had dimples on his cheeks.

"I don't think it matters, Father." He just smiled at me. He had a contagious smile, and I smiled back.

"Oh, good. It's been years since I wore a watch. Telling time by the sun is really hard." He looked at the sky, and I followed. This poor priest needed a cell phone or maybe a better secretary.

"I bet, Father."

"How can I help you, dear? I'm sure you're not here to indulge an old man in his fancies."

Oh, good. At least he was direct. Now, how to explain this. I doubted that Constantine had sent him my info.

"Father, my name is Isis, and I have a few questions for you. They might sound odd." *Odd* was probably an underestimation as well.

"Isis, my dear, we've been expecting you." I didn't think it was possible for his smile to get any bigger. It was so brilliant. He could have passed for a human flashlight.

"You were? Why?" Honestly, that was creepy. I had never been to this church. How did he know who I was?

"Father Francis mentioned you might be coming."

"Oh, thank God for Father Francis. So, you know who I am and why I'm here?"

"Yes, dear, I do." He was still smiling, but not as brightly. I really liked Father Francis. This just made my life so much easier.

"Great, 'cause we're running out of time. Father, have you seen anyone around here?"

"You look a little flushed, dear. How about we stand under a tree and get out of this hot sun?"

"Sure thing. Thanks." I was starting to sweat. The Texas sun was no joke, even in late September. The weird thing was, the priest wasn't sweating. He was probably used to wearing so many layers already. "I'm sorry; I didn't catch your name."

"Sorry, dear. I'm Father George." He extended his hand.

"A pleasure, Father." His hand was freezing. Father George probably needed the sun.

"We had some strangers stop by a few months ago. They were wandering the grounds during the day and came back at night. This church is my place of duty, and I will protect it above all else." He looked over the grounds with a sad smile on his face.

"Did they come back?"

"No, dear. Once they realized I was here, they stopped coming." He directed his sad gaze at me.

"So, if both the Catholic churches are secure, there's no way they can get into purgatory, right?" Purgatory was very confusing to me, and I was Catholic. At least I could use the excuse that I hadn't been a Catholic all my life.

"I wish, dear. The gates to purgatory are always open at the churches, but you can force a hole to it at any other location." He was very matter of fact.

"How is that possible?" Between the dogmas of the church, other religions, and now the supernatural world, it appeared my education was very limited.

"Think of a house. It is always easier for a thief to break in through a window or door. What happens when all those are secure and well watched? What would a thief do?"

"If he wanted something bad enough, blow a wall up or dig a tunnel. I guess like those bank robbers in movies." That would be extreme. I would just rob a different house.

"With enough energy, and the boundaries between the worlds thin, you could do almost anything."

I slapped my hand on my forehead. Father George just smiled.

"Of course. Hence, the equinox." I really hated those witches.

"Remember, Isis, faith makes the impossible possible. Hence, purgatory. This equinox is especially dangerous because it falls on a Saturday."

"How could they use that to their advantage?" Why did it matter at all?

"Not only are the Wiccan communities celebrating the equinox, but Catholics and Jews hold their services at that time on Saturdays. They will be tapping into the collective power of the universe." Father George was looking thoughtful again.

"Great. No pressure at all now." I was so screwed.

"No pressure, Isis. They're going to be even more dangerous once they've tapped in to all that energy. Please be careful."

"Thank you, Father. How do you know all this? Father Francis wasn't this helpful." No offense to Father Francis. I really liked my priest.

"I've been around longer. Nowadays, people just talk to me outside confession. I don't have the same vows to keep, and I can share information more freely." Who would be dumb enough to give that much information to one person—even a priest?

"Thank you again, Father. I really appreciate it." I wasn't too excited about shaking hands with him again.

Father George saved me the discomfort. He raised both of his hands over my head and did a silent prayer instead.

"Go in peace, my child." With those last words, he walked away. He headed across the cemetery toward a couple who were crying by a tomb. I felt creepy watching, so I left.

The voices, mercifully, had stopped. They could start calling somebody else.

I headed outside the cemetery, and a light breeze picked up. It was as if time had stopped, and the only thing I could feel was the sun. For some strange reason, my heart was racing. I was staring at the ground when I almost ran into a lady on the sidewalk.

"I'm so sorry. I didn't see you there." This was the second time in less than two hours that I had been surprised by people because I was lost in my thoughts. According to the army, complacency kills. They should add absentmindedness to that list.

"It's OK, dear. Are you OK? You look upset."

I had never met my grandmother, but I imagined she looked like this lady. Short with white hair and full of compassion. She was wearing a pair of stylish capris, sandals, and a pink shirt. She made the whole outfit look good and even age-appropriate. I was so jealous. Maybe style came with age.

"I'm good, ma'am. I just finished talking to Father George, and he gave me more than I could handle."

Before I was finished, she was doing the sign of the cross and looking pretty pale. "Child, bless your soul. Father George has been dead for over a decade."

I dropped my chin to my chest. Of course, he was. Only the dead and the hoboes talked to me.

"Do you need me to take you inside, sweetie?" I knew grandma was not being patronizing. It was the South, and everyone around wanted to be helpful.

"No, I'm good. I probably didn't hear him correctly." How could I say this without sounding crazy or wild?

"Sweetie, you probably did see Father George."

OK, now I was really confused. "You don't think I'm crazy?" Because I was starting to question my sanity at times.

"I don't think you're crazy. There are too many unexplainable things going on. If you said you spoke with Father George, I believe you. You're not the first one to say that." She looked at the cemetery with hope.

"You think he's stuck here on earth as a punishment?" Why would any soul want to stay in this place after passing?

"I believe his calling was so strong, he's still serving after his death. Now run home, dear. None of our priests are in. You've already experienced enough for one day."

In agreement, my stomached growled. I was so embarrassed. "Thank you, ma'am. Have a good day."

She patted my cheeks and sent me on my way.

I rushed to Bumblebee and climbed in. Constantine needed to explain how to tell the difference between the dead and the living to me. I couldn't be having conversations with dead people and not know it. Those things were helpful to know so I wouldn't share things with the wrong person. It appeared the dead were a lot more helpful to me than the living.

My stomach did one more loud protest, and I headed for food.

Chapter Twenty-Eight

I was having lunch at my favorite place in Texarkana, Big Jake's on New Boston Road. I had no idea whatever possessed me to start going there. For someone who didn't eat meat, a BBQ place was almost sacrilegious. The smell of cooked meat never bothered me; the taste, on the other hand, made me sick. Another reason I was weird. Someone who didn't eat meat in Texas: I was an endangered species.

I remembered the first time I had gone in. It was a Saturday night, raining, and I was starving. I prayed they would have some side dishes I could eat. To my surprise, their baked potatoes and chili potatoes were to die for. I was hooked. To make the addiction complete, this place was like Cheers, where everybody knew your name. Big Jake's was pretty busy for lunch, but most people didn't stick around too long, so finding a table wasn't hard.

I walked in, and I immediately relaxed. It was probably the only normal thing I had done all week. I was fourth in line, but I didn't care. After my crazy day, I was going to indulge in a fried pie. It was like an oversize empanada with fruit filling and deep fried. Nobody could ever say Texans didn't know how to eat. I learned that in Texas, they fried everything. This included veggies. Amazing taste, but I was sure my arteries were collapsing.

The people in front of me were obviously new in town, because they had been staring at the menu for over five minutes. Thankfully, the staff at Big Jake's were the happiest people I had ever met. They actually loved their jobs, and I later learned they got paid really well. Maybe I should have looked harder for work before settling on Abuelita's. Not that I was complaining—I loved working at Abuelita's, and her hours were more my style.

It felt as if I were in line forever, probably because I was starving.

"Hi, Isis. The usual?" My day had just gotten ten times better. My favorite Big Jake's staff member was on the register, T. J. T. J. was at least six feet tall, with brown hair, hazel eyes, and a mocha complexion. I was sure he was mixed, but I had no idea with what.

"Make it a large and a pie."

"Wow, you're living dangerously today." T. J. laughed at me. For the last three months, I had always ordered the small chili fries. On most nights, I barely finished my order.

"It's been a long day and an even longer week." Normally, I could stare at T. J.'s eyes for hours. Today, they had a different hint to them. There were specks of gold I had never noticed before and an intensity that was a bit overwhelming. I had to look away.

"Isis, you OK?" I had a horrible poker face, and most people could easily interpret my moods.

"Yeah. Sorry, T. J. Just hungry and tired." At least that much was true.

"You're having a hard week."

I handed T. J. a twenty and tried to smile. He handed me my change and a cup. "Here you go, girl. Grab a seat. I'll bring you your food in a minute."

"Thank you so much." I was so hungry, I was sure I looked pitiful, because T. J. just shook his head.

I walked over to the drink area. Between the drink area and the register, they had a barbecue-sauce-and-baked-beans bar. I filled my cup with ice and sweet tea. Only in the South would I ever drink sweet tea. Some things do not make the crossover well across the country. It was like asking for clam chowder in Texas. You were looking to be disappointed. Then I grabbed some baked beans. They were free if you dined in. I made it a point to pay attention to scooping my beans; I had once made the horrible mistake of grabbing some of the sausage that was cooked with the beans. Not pretty when I took a bite of it.

Customers were making their way out. Big Jake's wasn't too big—just the right size for a small joint. Two rows of tables and booths ran the length of the place. With enough aisle space so people could move comfortably around, the place always felt homey and inviting. I was also a sucker for locally-owned establishments.

"Here you go, dear." I was barely seated at one of the booths by the window when T. J. brought my plate to the table. "I really would like to see you finish all that today."

"Have some faith, Grasshopper. I got this."

"Right." With one last smile, T. J. walked back to his register. Normally, T. J. was either smoking the meat or preparing the plates. Very rarely, was he at the register, but they all rotated stations. Guess today was his turn.

My fries were perfect—golden brown and covered in melted cheese. I took three at a time and popped them into my mouth. I was in heaven, and my tummy was finally happy. I took a spoonful of my beans and for a few minutes forgot all the worries of the world. No wonder we were addicted to food in this country—food was connected to so many emotions. As I enjoyed my lunch, I wondered where Shorty had decided to grab lunch today.

"Hi, Isis. Please don't kill me." For a moment I thought I was going to choke on a fry. Of all the people to drop in on my table, Angelito was not on my list.

"You have some nerve showing up here. Are you following me? Are your little friends planning to beat me up again?" It was a blessing we were in public, because I wanted to reach over the table and choke Angelito with my fries. Instead, I popped a few more into my mouth before I gave him a piece of my mind.

"Isis, those girls are not my friends. I had no idea what happened till this morning when I overheard them talking."

He looked pretty miserable, but I wasn't buying it. "So, you didn't set me up? They just happened to be prepared for me to show up. Do you really think I'm stupid? Just tell me if your girl made you do it." I was pointing at him with a fry. I was trying to keep my voice down so as not to draw attention. I was probably failing, since T. J. looked as if he was ready to leap over the counter and kill Angelito for me. Another deep breath. Why not? Deep breathing was becoming my favorite hobby lately.

"Trust me. She's not like that. She's sweet and loving. It's not her fault her sister is the leader of those nuts."

Oh, great. So, it was a family affair. Even better. I shook my head. "Angelito, there is no way she is not involved if her sister is running things. Wake up. You're in serious danger. Stay away from them." I was wasting my time. He wasn't listening to me. He looked almost high. "Are you on something?"

"Of course not. Abuelita would kill me." He looked worried when he said her name.

"Speaking of Abuelita, when are you going back to work?"

Angelito was getting nervous and looking over his shoulder a lot. I had a clear view of both doors, since my back was toward the bathrooms.

"I'll be there tonight. I'm worried about her." That was ironic. He was worried about his grandmother.

"If you spent more time around her, you would know she's worried sick about you. Are you avoiding her?"

Angelito wouldn't answer my question or even meet my eyes.

"Angelito, what's going on?"

"Isis, I have no idea. I heard those girls talking about Abuelita and using me to get to her. What does that mean? Why would anyone want to hurt my grandma? Everyone loves her." Angelito looked as if he wanted to cry. He was blaming himself for this. Oh God, what was I supposed to say now?

"Are you sure that's what you heard? Maybe it was because she stopped them from beating me up the day they blew up the Whale." Or maybe it was because Abuelita was a badass at whatever it was she did. I knew I didn't want to make her mad or be on the receiving end of her wrath.

"You think so?" He wanted to believe something.

"Probably. You know they're crazy, right?"

He was staring at his hands. He had them folded on his lap. I grabbed another fry, hoping he would talk.

"I'm planning to stay with Abuelita at the restaurant and then make sure she's secure at home. I can't take any chances. I need to get Lily out of that group." So, mystery girlfriend had a name: Lily. Too bad she wasn't as sweet as her name.

"Do I even want to know what you have in mind?" I really didn't want to, but I was afraid it was coming.

"I heard them talking about squatting at the Grim tonight. I'm going to get her out after I'm done with Abuelita. I can't leave her there."

"How do you know she wants to leave? Angelito, please don't do anything stupid." I shook my head. This whole thing was stupid. "Why are you telling me this?"

"Because Abuelita trusts you. Isis, if something happens, please tell her I love her. I'm just trying to do the right thing." He tried to smile but never made it.

"Oh God, that sounds so morbid. Please don't get killed, or Abuelita will lose it." He wasn't listening to me.

"I'll be careful. I promise." I didn't believe that. "By the way, if you're trying to hide, you need a less flashy car. Driving the only yellow Camaro in town makes you stand out. I saw you a mile away." With that, he got out of the booth. He grabbed one of my fries and headed out the door. He winked on his way out. Angelito was an idiot, but he was loyal. I just couldn't trust whatever influence he was under.

"You should be careful with that one, Isis. Something's not right about him." T. J. was probably working on his stealth moves, because I never heard him approach me.

"Too many things are not right lately, T. J. Angelito is just the icing on my problems." I was watching Angelito climb into his F-150 truck. Something was seriously wrong with him.

"Oh, I didn't know you were dating him."

I had made the fatal mistake of popping a fry into my mouth when T. J. was speaking. I was choking on it.

"Isis, are you OK?" He was gently tapping my back. I prayed he wouldn't try to give me the Heimlich.

I took a big gulp of my tea. "God help me, no. He's the grandson of my boss. Nothing more, thank God."

"Oh, sorry. No need to die over it." He was still smiling at me. "But still, stay away from him. Whatever he's on, it's pretty strong." T. J. walked away with a rag in his hand. He started wiping down tables. I could see him watching me out of the corner of his eye.

I was sure whatever Angelito was on could not be purchased at any normal market. I needed to do something, but I wasn't sure what exactly. This could be another trap. Anytime Angelito was involved, it was hard to guess. I also needed to head back home and work on that recording. The one thing I was pretty sure of was that Saturday was going to be a huge day. And T. J. was right—I had barely finished half of my plate. I devoured my pie. I was feeling a little guilty for having lunch and not checking if the boys had any. I walked over to the counter to order them something.

"T. J., could I order two plates to go, please?"

He looked at me, very confused. "Wow, that's a first. You barely finished your lunch."

"I got roommates now—my stepbrother and a cat. I forgot to check with them before ordering." Bartholomew could be my stepbrother, and Constantine was still a cat. A talking cat, but a cat nevertheless. So, I wasn't lying, not too much.

T. J. just smiled. "Wow. No wonder your week has been crazy. Do they eat meat?"

I nodded as I stared at the menu, confused. I was feeling like a newbie.

"Let me help. How about brisket plate with beans and potato salad? A house favorite. Not sure what you should feed a cat."

"Just give me another brisket plate with everything."

"For a cat?" T. J. was giving me an incredulous look.

"Hey, he comes from a very spoiled household. I'm not taking any chances for a mutiny now." I tried to smile.

"Whatever you say, Isis. You are the greatest roommate ever. Where were you when I was looking for mine?"

"Thank you; you're my hero." Fortunately for me, T. J. dropped the conversation.

T. J. smiled, and this time I swore his eyes were sparkling. I paid him and was out of Big Jake's in less than ten minutes. After all my food, I wanted a nap. How was I going to write music about napping when I was falling asleep? I would probably knock myself out in the process.

Chapter Twenty-Nine

The lights on the first floor were all on. Nobody was in the gym area, so I wasn't sure what was going on. I parked Bumblebee next to the Deathmobile and walked around to grab the food from the backseat. Constantine and Bartholomew were coming out of the shooting area. They were deep in conversation.

"What are you two talking about? You look very suspicious." I struggled to close the door while holding the food and drinks.

Bartholomew looked up and ran over to help me. "What are you carrying?" He closed the door and grabbed the drinks.

"Lunch. I wasn't sure if you two had eaten already." Bartholomew and I started heading toward the stairs. Constantine was smelling the air as he followed us.

"Nope. We got a new shipment in, and we were taking inventory." Bartholomew was eyeing the bag as carefully as Constantine. Food was going to be their downfall.

"The missiles are missing, but at least all the smoke grenades got here on time."

I tripped on a step. I looked at Constantine in shock. "Missiles? Grenades? I thought we couldn't kill anyone."

Bartholomew and Constantine were up the stairs and heading inside by the time I recovered.

"We can't—unless it's self-defense, of course. Unfortunately, this is war. They attacked you first. Repercussions are in in order." Constantine was scary when he was mad.

"No wonder the world fears us. When provoked, we're ruthless." This was serious stuff going on.

"We'll never start anything. As long as people don't interfere with our job, we leave things alone. The moment the line is crossed, we will destroy them." Bartholomew put the drinks on the table. I knew it was irrational, but I felt sorry for those witches.

"What's for lunch?" Thank God for Bartholomew. At least he was focused on the present.

"Brisket with beans and potato salad."

They both were staring at me, mouths wide open.

"Isis, are you feeling OK?" Constantine jumped on the table to get a closer look at me.

"Yeah, Isis, are you all right? When did you start eating meat?" Bartholomew was ready to take my temperature.

I laughed. "It's not for me, you silly boys. I already had lunch."

"Oh, wow. You were scaring us." Constantine sat on the table, relieved.

I shook my head, still amused, and placed the food in front of them. I grabbed a bowl with water for Constantine. We all settled into our respective seats. Like most people, once we claimed a seat, we continued to sit in the same spot—Constantine at the head; Bartholomew to the left, closest to the computer; and me on the opposite side, closer to the kitchen.

Bartholomew took the first bite. "Wow, this is really good." He was all smiles. Constantine was purring from his side of the table.

"Great food, and it's gluten-free."

Barbecue was going to be an easy go-to from now on. They were loving it.

"What made you go to a barbecue place when you don't eat meat?" Bartholomew was trying to talk in between bites.

I was sipping my tea. "Big Jake's has great chili fries, and they're cheap. When you're broke, you find the places with the biggest servings for the least amount of money. It's a plus when the food is great."

They both agreed.

"How did it go? You were gone for a while." Constantine was back in business mode.

"Good and bad. Which one you want first?"

"Bad. At least we can end on a happy note." Bartholomew was awesome and so positive.

"Found Ana, and then she was kidnapped." That pretty much explained the whole thing.

Bartholomew and Constantine were staring at me. Constantine was in midbite, and Bartholomew had his fork in the air.

"Isis, that's not bad news. That's actually horrible. We need to work on your definitions." Bartholomew's happy mood had vanished, and he placed his fork back on his plate.

"Did she at least tell you something?" Constantine licked his paw.

"She mentioned seeing ghosts, and they told her something about a golden door coming."

"Do you believe her?" Bartholomew was not buying it.

"She looked like hell. She believed she was seeing ghosts. Who am I to argue? Besides, I see dead people all the time, as I found out today."

"You are Death's intern. You don't count. What soul did you run into now?" Constantine never took my ghost issues seriously.

"Father George at Sacred Heart."

"Oh, great. How is Father George?" Why was I not surprised Constantine knew him?

"I guess he's OK, considering the man is dead and hanging out at a cemetery. I don't get it. Is he in purgatory?" I had figured it would be rude to ask the dead guy. I had no issues asking Constantine.

"Girl, please. He's actually a unique client. Death delivered him to heaven. Once there, he spoke with Saint Peter and asked to come back. Saint Peter agreed. Death brought him back, and he's been watching over that church and flock ever since."

I was so happy Bartholomew was looking at Constantine, as confused as I felt.

"I thought you said he was dead. What do you mean, Death brought him back?" Bartholomew said exactly what I was thinking.

Constantine looked at both of us as if we were stupid. "Of course, he's dead. Death delivered his soul to his new home. Remember, we deliver souls. How else was he going to get there? Granted, it was a little unconventional." Constantine ate another piece of his brisket before going on. "She left him her card, so anytime he gets tired, she'll take him home. In ten years, he has never called. Dedication, I'm telling you. They don't make souls like that anymore."

"That's crazy. I don't think I would have done that." I was honest enough with myself to know that.

"You're also not a priest who gave up sex for your god. Different career path." That was a valid point. Constantine was right—very different paths.

"So, what is the good news? The way this conversation is going, I'm afraid to ask." Bartholomew was hiding his face behind his cup.

"Thanks, Bart. Well, we now have an informant." I gave them both a huge smile.

"You do know we work for D-E-A-T-H, not D-E-A. What kind of informant do we have?" Constantine was a little too proud of his wittiness.

"Constantine, you are not funny."

"Yes, I am. Stop changing the subject. Talk, little girl." Constantine would have made a great mob boss.

"Bob's friend, Shorty. It seems the witches have put a bounty on me. Shorty wants to even the playing field."

"Wait. You got someone in the underground to work for us?"

I nodded.

"Now I'm impressed. That is really good news."

"Technically, he volunteered. Word is traveling around the country about New York. The underground and the souls are nervous."

"When are you supposed to hear back from this Shorty?" Constantine had finished eating and was in his military general mode.

"He knows our time frame. As soon as he hears something, we'll know."

"Not bad at all. We've been trying to infiltrate their communication network for years, but it's almost impossible. They don't trust outsiders. I'm surprised he talked to you, especially with your track record."

"Don't remind me, Constantine. I already feel awful. He's doing it for Bob."

"Good deal. What about Father George?"

"The church is protected, but that won't stop the witches. Based on what Father told me, with enough power the witches can blast a hole into purgatory from anywhere."

"Not anywhere, Isis. Locations are just as powerful as spells. We need to find a place in Texarkana where the walls are weak enough." Constantine had a far-off stare, as if he were seeing a map in his head.

"Constantine, are you going to eat your beans?" Bartholomew said, bringing Constantine back to reality.

Constantine looked down at his plate. "Not at all, Bartholomew. I prefer meat."

"This is perfect. Isis doesn't eat meat, so you can have her share. You don't eat the sides, so I can have your share. I love it."

Constantine and I just stared at Bartholomew. For a boy genius, at times, I forgot he was just a kid.

"That's a great way to look at it." He did have a valid point. I just smiled.

"Oh, I also ran into Angelito at Big Jake's."

That stopped all food eating and conversation.

"Did you kick him?" Words of wisdom from the eleven-year-old.

"No, I didn't, but homicidal thoughts did cross my mind. According to him, the witches are at the Grim. At least for tonight. Shorty said they moved locations all the time."

"Isis, please tell me you don't trust that boy. He already set you up once." Bartholomew was not happy.

"I don't know what to think when it comes to Angelito. He didn't actually ask me anything. He's supposed to be heading that way after work. I would like to check it out before he gets there. If the prisoners are there, maybe I can get them out."

"Isis, that place is going to be guarded pretty tightly. Bartholomew is right. It could be another trap." Constantine was probably right.

"I know, but we don't have a lot of options. The old hotel is condemned. Worst-case scenario, I check it out and find nothing. Can't hurt to look."

Bartholomew and Constantine were not buying it.

"OK, but this time you go prepared. No more of this wandering around half-blind." General Constantine was back in charge.

"I can handle that." The more protection I could take, the better I would feel.

"We have the armory pretty well stocked. We just got in a pair of very stylish night-vision glasses, heat sensors, and, of course, gas bombs." Bartholomew had been busy shopping.

"Do I want to know where you get all this stuff?" By the look on Bartholomew's face, I really didn't. "Never mind."

"We'll load you up." Constantine was way too excited for my taste.

"I'm glad you both enjoyed the lunch. I have work to do before I head out tonight."

"Thank you, Isis. It was delicious. You're very thoughtful."

"My pleasure, Constantine. I don't want you two starving to death. Or eating any more of that cardboard-tasting cereal." That stuff was awful.

"Thanks, Isis. I do appreciate that." Bartholomew smiled. He had cleared his plate and was almost done with Constantine's.

"Anytime, Bart. Constantine, I do have a question."

"Sure thing. What's on your mind?"

"If I can see and touch dead people, how am I supposed to tell the difference between the dead and the living? Father George looked pretty real to me."

"Easy. Their body temperature." Constantine said that with a smile.

"Excuse me. Do you want me to touch every person I see?"

"It's either touching or using your sight. I wouldn't recommend the sight." Constantine was right. The sight would be awful. "Not that hard, Isis. Just shake hands when you first meet them. The souls don't generate body heat, so they'll feel cold to the touch. Besides, it'll make their day. Most haven't touched another human being in ages." That explained Father George's reactions that morning.

"OK, I guess." Shaking hands didn't sound too bad.

"What are you working on?" I was heading toward the door when Bartholomew asked.

"My lullaby. So, cover your ears." The last thing I needed was to knock my own people out.

"No need. I'm heading into a food coma, and by the looks of Bartholomew, he is, too." Constantine was yawning. I was jealous. I wanted a nap myself.

"That's a good idea. I want a nap." Bartholomew was not fighting sleep too hard. "If you need us, we'll be over there, passed out." With that, they headed to the couch to sleep. Life was not fair.

It was midafternoon. I had a few hours to work on my song and get ready for my recon mission. I was tired of not being prepared. If we could at least get the prisoners back, maybe that would slow them down. I was afraid. If we didn't stop them, they would just move to another city and start all over.

Chapter Thirty

My plan was simple: go to the Grim and wait for Angelito. I would follow him in and recon the area. Be back home before anyone noticed, then go back with backup. Why couldn't my plans ever go smoothly? Instead, I got a rambling call from Abuelita around eight that evening. Angelito never showed up, and he wasn't answering her calls. She was going to look for him. I had the horrible feeling that was exactly what the witches wanted. After ten minutes of pleading and begging, I persuaded her to stay put. I needed Abuelita safe.

Instead of her walking into the arms of danger, I volunteered to do it. I had lost my ever-loving mind. What was wrong with me? In less than a week, my normal little life was turned upside down. I barely had enough to time to finish my recording. I never got around to making the loop, forget copying it to any device. Bartholomew felt sorry for me and agreed to finish it.

The boys were not kidding when they said they were prepping me for battle. They ordered custom-made military fatigues. These were all black and coated against spells. Constantine had contacted a witch in Salem who specialized in the extreme. To neutralize the regular thugs' combatants, I got issued a light Kevlar vest. According to Bartholomew, it could sustain any number of rounds. I believed the vest could, but I was afraid my ribs would be shattered just from the impact.

If the clothes were impressive, the accessories were to die for, no pun intended. The night-vision goggles looked more like a pair of Ray-Ban aviator glasses. The black leather boots had trigger-activated spikes, and my belt doubled as a whip. They strapped a machete to my left leg, a 9mm to my right, and my

M16 across my chest. I was a cross between Trinity from *The Matrix*, Rambo, and Batman. I had more firepower than most army squads in the middle of Baghdad. Constantine took revenge very seriously. My earpiece was in place, and by the time I left, I wasn't sure whether I was going on a recon or an execution mission.

I drove downtown very carefully. The last thing I needed was to get pulled over. I refused to strap the grenades to my belt, so they were sitting on the passenger seat. Bartholomew decided to put them in a basket. I was not playing Little Red Riding Hood today. If the witches had spies looking for me, Bumblebee was going to be a problem. It was also Friday night, and some areas of downtown actually had business going.

The Grim Hotel was located on State Line, down the street from the post office and right before you got to the correctional facility. Why didn't these witches just take over the police department? They were fearless. I needed to find a place to park without driving by the hotel. The hotel sat at the end of its block, but it had windows on all sides. To make things worse, the damn thing was seven stories high. That stupid building was actually in the center of downtown. I couldn't afford to walk around downtown with all my gear. I needed a place to park that was close by but would, I hoped, provide me with some cover.

"Bart, any suggestions on parking?" The boys were monitoring both sound and visuals.

"Safest bet, in front of the TRAHC building at Fourth and Texas Boulevard. Then hike up the next two blocks. Everywhere else, they can see you from the rooftop."

"Thanks, Bart. TRAHC it is."

"Be careful, Isis. I haven't seen any movement from that area, but it doesn't mean they aren't using magic. I'm taking care of the cameras."

"I'll do my best. Keep me posted."

I parked the car in the darkest area I could find. Once I got out of the car, my blood started pumping. I wasn't sure if it was the gear or just having the rifle in my hand, but I was more alert. The first thing the army teaches is this: be a soldier. The marines joked that there was no such thing as a retired marine, just one not serving. I guessed it was the same for the army. For the first time in months, I had a purpose, and I was a soldier. I made my way through downtown Texarkana almost like a ghost in the night. By the time I reached the hotel, I wasn't even winded.

"Isis, did you know the Grim is haunted?"

I had found a loose board in the back of the building when Bartholomew's voice came in. I stopped and looked around. "What?" This was not the time for this.

"According to the Internet, seven people died in a fire back in the fifties. So, be careful." Bartholomew sounded worried.

"What do you mean 'be careful?'" I was trying to whisper.

"Isis, there are times when a soul refuses to move on. When that happens, it's stuck in place, haunting it," Constantine said.

I looked around at the extremely creepy building. "Why doesn't Death just drag them away?"

"Remember free will. Depending on the way they die, they won't leave. In those cases, Death leaves them her number to contact her when they're ready. Isis, some never leave. Watch out!" Constantine had a way of making my day so much better.

"OK, from now on, you two are not allowed to nap before a big mission. Got it! This information could have helped before I left the house." If I got out of there alive, we were having a come-to-Jesus meeting, as they said in the South.

"Sorry, Isis." Bartholomew sounded so pitiful.

"Yeah, Isis, sorry. But do not engage them. They could get violent." Constantine was full of good news now.

"Got it. Anything else before I step into the fifth door of hell now?" They were both silent. "Good. Going in."

I passed a few signs on the outside of the building that stated a redevelopment plan was in progress for the Grim. Why would anyone name a building Grim? Why would they want to fix it? By the time I slid inside, I realized why the Grim was still standing. Like most of the old buildings downtown, the Grim was beautiful. It was built back in the 1910s and 1920s, when architecture and aesthetics were the key. Yes, the poor thing was falling apart now, but it still held some of that greater elegance. They didn't build hotels like this anymore. A touch of an era long gone. Now it was being desecrated by those witches.

I was scared but needed to get moving. My boots did not make a sound on the tile floor. The night-vision glasses were amazing as I made my way through the building. I heard voices, and I followed the sound. I was heading to what appeared to be the main lobby when I was pulled back by a pair of hands. It took everything in my power not to scream. I slowly turned my head, afraid of what was holding me.

"Shhh. They'll see you." A woman in her thirties dressed in 1950s clothes was standing next to me. She was beautiful, at least the parts of her face that weren't burned. I didn't need to touch her skin to know she was dead.

"Holy crap!" Bartholomew screamed for me. "Isis!"

"Hi." My voice sounded weak, even to me.

"Come this way," the lady whispered, and she started to move away.

"Isis, don't go." Bartholomew was pleading. I took one look over my shoulder and followed the ghost.

"When in Rome, do as the Romans do. It's a haunted house. Do I have much choice?"

"Isis, at least the souls won't lie," Constantine said, but even he sounded worried.

"Got it."

The woman was moving pretty fast down corridors and passages. We passed a pair of teenage boys, also badly burned. They watched us go, but the woman made them stay quiet.

"Go; keep them busy."

At her words the boys ran off. I watched them vanish through walls. That was when the wailing started.

We took a few more turns and entered a small room. It looked like the back of the reception area in the lobby. The woman pointed at a broken door. I peeked through the cracks. The witches were there—more than I expected. I counted nine, and two of them looked very familiar. One was the volunteer from Randy Sam's, and the other the outreach volunteer. It figured. Angelito was standing by a wall, but I couldn't tell with the glasses what was wrong with him. The place was lit by candles. I took my night-vision glasses off, but it was too dark without them. I put them back on and checked the rest of the room. They had at least five really large guys with them. Horrible odds.

"Get them out," the woman whispered behind me.

"Trust me; I would love to. But I'm a bit outnumbered. Do they have anyone else here?"

"No. The men are new. Normally, it's just the women. They keep coming and torment us." She looked evil when she spoke. That was not good; I was sure Death had a rule against tormenting the dead. "Shhhh." I wasn't sure why she had shushed me; I wasn't talking. She pointed at the crowd behind the door. I leaned in and listened.

"My dear sister, if you won't keep better control of your pet, we are going to have to put him down," the Randy Sam's volunteer said. Great. So, little blonde was the leader.

"Oh, please. You wanted him here. Here he is, Rose. Come, Angelito."

Her sister, a.k.a. Angelito's Rose, was my favorite outreach volunteer.

Angelito moved like a drunk man. There was nothing normal about him.

"Kneel, boy."

He actually did. I was in shock. I hoped Bartholomew was recording this. I had blackmail on him for life.

"Yes, dear, I see that. I wanted his sorcerer of a grandmother, not this useless boy." Blondie grabbed Angelito's face. I was sure she was digging her nails into him.

"She will come for him. Trust me."

"Ahhh!" Oops—I screamed. I couldn't help it. The most disfigured, scary ghost appeared out of the wall carrying an ax. Trust me; that would scare the hell out of anybody. Unfortunately, the witches heard me.

"What was that?" Blondie was looking around in my direction.

"Probably one of those stupid ghosts. What else?" one of the other witches said. Her voice was the same as the one who had held the gun to my head.

"That sounded too human, Natalie. You two go and check it out." She sent two of the really large muscle guys my way.

I had just a few seconds. "I need your help. Can they see you guys?" The dead woman looked terrifying.

"They will now." She nodded at her partner, and she headed straight through the door. Ax Man was right behind her.

"Boys, no prisoners here besides Angelito. I need to get him out."

"Isis, get him if you can. If not, get out as soon as possible," General Constantine said.

"Holy shit!" I heard one of the men scream. The other squealed worse than I had. It made me feel better knowing I wasn't the only one screaming. The feeling went away when they started shooting in my direction to get the ghost. I hit the floor.

Fourteen to one was not the best odds. If they were controlling Angelito, that would make things fifteen to one. I was sure Abuelita would not mind an injured Angelito instead of a dead one. I took a face mask from my cargo pocket and covered all the important parts. I grabbed a tear-gas grenade from Bartholomew's basket. Once the breathing seal was secure and I was sure I could breathe, I kicked open the door and released the tear-gas grenade.

"What the...?" The group started coughing and cursing up a storm.

The smoke was everywhere. The witches were moving around toward the back of the room. A gust of wind hit me, and I had to hold on to the counter not to be knocked down. Little Blondie was standing in the middle of the room. She had cleared the gas, but not before taking a good hit. She looked like hell. It was a small consolation for this week.

"Who in damnation did that?" Her glare landed on me. Feeling devious, I waved at her. "You!" Who knew one word could hold so much hate?

She created a large ball of energy and threw it at me. I barely had time to duck. The light was so bright it was blinding. I took my mask off and rolled to my stomach. In less than two seconds, I had the safety off the M16. Before anyone could throw any more spells at me, I opened fire. The witches scattered like roaches, but I was sure I had hit at least one.

"Do you honestly think you will get out here alive?" Blondie was taunting me.

"I was planning to take a few of you with me. Great way to get my boss here." Dying was not part of the plan. I moved around the desk for better coverage. I saw Ax Man pointing straight down. "Really, dude, do something." That was the worst thing to say to an angry ghost with an ax. He unleashed hell on the world.

Ax Man was swinging as if he were still trying to get out of the fire. He connected with three of the guys, and they dropped like sacks of potatoes. The teenage boys appeared behind the witches, swinging sticks. Everyone was screaming, and spells were thrown everywhere. I couldn't get close enough to grab Angelito. In the distance, I heard police sirens coming.

"Shit, the cops. Let's get out of here. Bring the boy." Blondie was giving orders.

"Hurry. You must leave." My favorite dead tour guide was pulling me away.

"They have my friend." I tried to fight, but she was pretty strong for a ghost.

We were heading down the corridor when I was hit in the head. I heard Natalie yell "Bitch!" and then I was out.

Chapter Thirty-One

I woke up a bit disoriented. I was in my bed, under my covers. I lifted my sheets, and I had PJs on. Had I dreamed everything?

"Hi, Isis." Nope, I had not. Death was sitting in my room again, so it had all been real. I reached over and turned on my night-light. The movement made my head explode.

"Ouch. Hi, Death. What got me?" I rubbed the back of my head, and it was tender.

"A two-by-four."

"That explains it. In battle, a two-by-four is always going to win against a head."

Death smiled. She was wearing a red suit tailored to fit her, and she looked amazing.

"Nice suit."

"A Valentino special." She brushed her skirt, which was immaculate.

"Very nice. So, what happened? I didn't realize I'd killed anyone." I tried to get comfortable on my bed and not slouch on the pillow. Big mistake. My head was pounding.

Death got up and came over. "Let me help." She arranged my pillow and helped me sit up. She sat on the bed next to me and brushed her fingers on my forehead. "Better?" Like magic, the pain was gone.

"Wow, much better. I can see straight again." I rubbed the back of my head. I had a huge lump. Thank God, now it hurt only when I touched it. I wasn't planning to touch it again.

"You made quite an impression. You can imagine how surprised I was to receive a call from the Grim after all this time."

"Are the souls OK?" I didn't want them to suffer more because of me.

"Funny. You asked about the dead and not the living." She was smiling—the smile a mother gives an infant when the infant is learning to crawl.

"The dead weren't trying to kill me like the living." That was the honest truth.

"So I heard. Somehow, they were very protective of you. She gouged the witch's eyes out after the witch hit you."

"Oh God, that's horrible. What's going to happen to her?" OK, I was glad to be alive, but that was extreme. Mental note: never piss off a ghost.

"Isis, she's dead already. No more punishment is needed. Besides, she did it to save your life. I would have preferred other methods."

"Did she kill her?" I was praying she hadn't. Even for a dead woman, that would be a lot to carry.

"No. Her friends took her before I arrived. Some of their puppets did die. After I delivered the residents of the Grim home, I dropped them off as well. You had a busy night." She didn't sound mad, just very matter-of-fact.

"Death, I can explain."

"You can?" There was humor in her voice.

I had to think about that for a second. "Actually, no. No, I can't. We're at war. I guess those are casualties." I sounded cruel but also matter-of-fact.

"I think you've been hanging around Constantine too long." She was smiling.

"You are so right. I sound just like him."

"Not just. You're still not as arrogant as he is. But he's right. This needs to stop tomorrow. I hate looking bad, Isis." The smile was gone, and Death was cold and calculating. I was sure the temperature of my room had dropped. "You have company waiting outside. It's not polite to keep people waiting. I'll let you change." Death got up and headed toward the door.

"Death, thank you." I didn't know what else to say.

"It was in their best interests not to kill you. Be careful in purgatory; they won't hold back." She fixed her suit one more time when she reached my bedroom door. "You're not doing so badly for your first week. Try not to get killed, now." She winked and was out the door.

I rolled out of bed and prayed that Death was the one who had dressed me. It would be really embarrassing for either of the boys to be involved in that process. I walked to the bathroom, and for the first time since meeting those witches, I didn't look like hell. I wanted to do a happy dance for myself. Instead, I quickly used the facilities and got dressed. Company could mean only one person, and that meant I was in trouble.

By the time I reached the kitchen entrance, I could hear the boys talking to Eric. Whatever it was they were discussing had them all agitated. I went straight for the fridge and grabbed the milk. I was thirsty, and for some reason, milk sounded amazing.

"Isis, you are up?" Bartholomew was Captain Obvious today.

"I was told we had company, so here I am."

All three of them looked confused.

Constantine was the first one to ask. "Who told you?"

"Death. Who else?" I poured the milk and started drinking, not waiting for their reply.

"From anybody else, that answer would guarantee a trip to the loony bin." Eric was at least honest.

"She said goodbye hours ago. We thought she was gone." Bartholomew looked really sad.

"Maybe she came back to make sure I didn't have a concussion. It would probably be bad for recruitment to lose two interns in less than six months."

"That's never stopped her before." Constantine had a way of crushing my dreams.

I glared at him. "I hope we're not practicing today. I don't think my head can take it." I took a seat at the kitchen table and watched the boys. I wasn't moving closer to them, so they all migrated to me.

"What happened at the Grim?" Eric almost yelled at me. Bartholomew and Constantine took their usual chairs, and that left the last one for Eric. He paced behind the chair for a bit before sitting down.

"I got hit with a two-by-four, according to Death." I knew I wasn't making this easy for him. I didn't care. If he was going to be a cop, then I had no choice but to be difficult. It was irrational, but I had a concussion. Who could blame me?

"Ouch. We had no idea. We heard the bang, and then you were out. The screams after your fall were horrifying." Bartholomew made an awful face. He looked like a kid who had eaten something sour.

"Death said our dear tour-guide ghost gouged the eyes out of the witch who hit me." I was already past the traumatized stage, so my mind was numb.

"Well, that explains the bloodcurdling screams and curses." Constantine was not fazed. I was assuming that after five thousand years, blood and guts were nothing to him.

"That also explains the eyeballs in the hallway." Eric was looking pale. He had found the aftermath of that; no wonder he was edgy. "Isis, did you hit those men with an ax?"

"Nope, no ax for me. I had a machete and an M16." I wondered where my gear was. I looked around the room, hoping to spot it.

"That's not funny." Eric stood up, angry.

"It's in the armory," Bartholomew whispered from across the table. He knew exactly what I was looking for. I winked at him and mouthed back *Thank you.*

"I wasn't being funny. The dead burned guy did that part."

"What burned guy? We didn't find any burned guy." It seemed that Eric really thought I was making everything up.

"That guy was terrifying," Bartholomew said.

"The placed was haunted. The dead people kind of helped." That was an easy way to explain it.

"Are you serious? What part did you play in the small battlefield?" Eric was glaring at me. "Isis, are you sure you're not part of the terrorist group? 'Cause every time you're around, things mysteriously explode. We've had reports of explosions, gunshots, smoke, gas, screams, howls, and horrifying screeches. Our phones were going off like crazy." Eric took a breath and sat back down.

"I can only claim some of the gunshots and the gas. The rest was not me." I tried to look as innocent as possible.

Eric tilted his head in shock. He was not happy. "Only...only those things. You are truly a weapon of mass destruction. We got three dead, two barely alive, and a pair of eyeballs. How do you explain that?"

"Do the three dead have gunshots in them?" I had been aiming for their legs. I prayed I was not that out of practice.

"That's the weird part. They have gunshot-like wounds but no bullets. We couldn't even find the casings. People heard gunshots."

I hadn't taken the casings; why was he giving me that look? "Can I be impressed by the great police work?"

"No. Isis, you claim the gunshots but not the ax? Those men were bashed in the skull. The ax that was left at the scene. Why?"

"I don't think Saint Peter allows axes in heaven." That was my best guess.

"What?" He threw his hands in the air and then slammed his head on the table. That really looked painful. Constantine, Bartholomew, and I just stared. Eric stayed that way, and the three of us went back to talking.

"So, Death took them home. It was about time." Constantine didn't need much explanation.

"I guess when my new ghost friend couldn't drag me out, and after gouging Natalie's eyes out, she made the call."

"No wonder Eric couldn't find you," Bartholomew said. "We called him as soon as you started shooting. We were hoping for him to get you out before the cops showed up."

"You actually went in looking for me?"

Eric had his head in his hands. He looked like a little kid. "Yeah. I went ahead of my partner straight to where Bartholomew said you were. I ran into the eyeballs instead. I almost puked on the scene. By the time I got myself collected again, Bartholomew called, saying you were home." Eric started yawning. I just realized he had been up all night and was exhausted.

"I don't think an ax-wielding ghost is going to hold up in court," I said.

Poor thing was not amused.

"We have a picture if you want to see it," Bartholomew said.

I had totally forgotten about the video. "I don't recommend it." I was shaking my head.

Unfortunately, Bartholomew was already out of his seat and at his control station.

Before I could protest, Eric was beside him. "I almost stepped in eyeballs. I'm sure I can take your little ghost."

Bartholomew played the video for Eric. Constantine and I waited by the table, watching each other and shaking our heads.

"Holy shit. That thing was there. Please tell me this is fake." Nobody ever listened to me.

"I tried to warn you." I felt a little bad for him. He looked even worse. "The good news is, he's not there anymore. Everyone is safe to continue the investigation." I looked at Constantine, who was agreeing with me.

"Please tell me: Are we going to find anything connecting you to this?" Eric was back at the table, staring down at me.

"Well, Officer Eric, I can't believe you care." I gave him my most fake brilliant smile and even batted my eyes. Constantine started laughing.

"No! I just need to figure out what I'm going to say when they ask me why I'm hanging out with a crazy murderer."

Ouch. He could have at least played it off. I sank lower in my chair. Constantine, on the other hand, was rolling.

"Oh, thanks for the support." I waved my hand at him. "I'm pretty sure if Death took care of the bullet casings, you won't find anything placing me there. Besides, I was wearing gloves and a cap. Unless you can trace droplets of my spit, I'm sure I'm clear."

The boy actually looked relieved. I wanted to kick him.

"Not even on the ax?" He was really hung up on that ax.

"Never touched it. It wasn't mine. I doubt you'll be able to match the prints you find. I don't think you have fingerprints from the fifties." Technology was good, but it couldn't work miracles.

"Great. So now we have a triple homicide nobody can explain." When he put it that way; it was depressing.

"You can always blame it on gangs," Bartholomew said from his workstation.

"True. If only we had a gang problem in Texarkana."

"You do now," Constantine said.

Eric was ready to kill us. Totally uncalled for. Bartholomew, Constantine, and I sensed his tension and waited for him to calm down. We didn't need an edgy cop on the premises. Eric paced a few times and tried to take deep breaths. I felt so much better watching someone else do it.

"Eric, let the investigation unfold on its own. Go home, shower, and take a nap. It will work itself out." Constantine was back in his

Yoda mode. I was impressed with his advice. It was making Eric feel better.

"Fine. I'm going home."

"Bye, Eric," Bartholomew and I said together. We were afraid to spook him any further.

Eric headed out the door and down the stairs.

"Is he going to be OK?" Bartholomew asked.

"He's afraid of the ramifications of the investigation. He's young and doesn't understand that humans will always find a rational explanation for events. Witches, ghosts, and magic will never be part of it. Now I need a nap as well." Constantine hopped down from the table and headed out.

"I'm beat, too. I left your recording, your new devices, and your laptop on the couch. Good night, Isis." Bartholomew walked behind me and kissed my head. He had never done that before. He was really tired. "I'm glad you're OK."

"Am I the only one who sleeps?" I felt really guilty.

"You were unconscious. I wouldn't call that sleeping. Besides, it's barely five a.m. You should take a nap, too. It's going to be a crazy day." With one last smile, he left the room.

My body rhythm was off. I walked over to the couch. Bartholomew had left me a brand-new computer, with a bow and everything. I flopped down on the couch and got comfy with my new toys. Bartholomew had created a loop of my lullaby and stored it on three different MP3 players. At least something good was happening for once.

Chapter Thirty-Two

A nap was not part of my master plan for the morning. Unfortunately, once again Morpheus won, and I was out. I was having another fabulous dreamless night. One of the major benefits of Reapers was the lack of dreams. I wasn't sure whether it was the wards on the building or just having some of Death's blessing, but ever since I had moved in, I hadn't dreamed. The nightmares had stopped, and I was resting. Sleep was a friend, something that I had never known before. I enjoyed going to bed and hated getting up. In a strange way, I finally felt somewhat normal in that area.

I was sure I was in REM when I was, sadly, interrupted by a call from Shorty. I was afraid I had created a monster. The man truly believed he was an informant for the CIA, or maybe the FBI. I barely managed to say hello in a sleepy, comatose stage. He delivered this message: "Boss, Church under the Bridge, nine o'clock. See you there." Then he hung up. I was too dumbfounded to think. It took me at least five minutes to process the situation. According to the phone, it was 8:17 a.m. If I needed to be downtown, I had to leave by 8:45 a.m. That wasn't a lot of time to shower and get ready. For a person obsessed with time, I was always running late.

I was tired of quick showers. My godmother would never believe this. One of my favorite things was to take long showers and let my mind wander. I never managed to do that anymore. This job was really affecting my life. I was out the door with a toaster strudel in less than twenty-five minutes. I wasn't expecting to find parking near the bridge, so I wanted to have plenty of time to walk to the Mass. It was a blessing I did. I managed to hit every red light between Reapers and the service. I was starting to believe this was a test.

By the time I arrived at South State Line's Bridge on Broad Street, the service had started. I was fairly impressed. The Church under the Bridge had over a hundred people truly worshipping. They had a band that was really good. A small lectern where a man with long, Jesus-like hair watched the band in delight. He was a handsome guy, maybe in his mid-thirties, with a nicely groomed goatee. I made my way to the crowd right as he started to minister. A small sound system was set up to one side.

The man's voice was electrifying. There was a passion and a love in his speech that had the crowd transfixed. The crowd was even more impressive. All races, all colors, all religious beliefs were represented. Rich and poor stood side by side, caring for the Lord. The cynic in me wasn't sure what to think. Instead of analyzing it too much, I looked for Shorty. If he was trying to find a busy public place, he had definitely found one. How was I supposed to find that goofy man in this crowd?

After I had done couple of laps around the outside of the crowd, Shorty was nowhere to be found, and I was getting tired. I stopped to listen to the sermon. The pastor was talking about love, hope, and knowing we were children of God. Knowing we were meant for greater things and that our first calling was to care for one another. I wasn't sure if I was moved to action, but his words hit a core in my soul. Before I could think of the message, I felt more than saw a person walking behind me.

"Boss, don't look my way. We don't want to attract attention." Shorty was extremely paranoid and delusional. I was praying it was not a horrible idea getting him as an informant.

"Of course not. I would hate to look shady."

"Everyone is suspicious around here. Now listen, before they see us together for too long. It's going down tonight. They plan to have the packages to the other side by six p.m." He took a sip from his cup. By the smell, it was really strong coffee.

"Are you sure?" That was not a lot of time.

"According to my sources that heard them speaking, they need to be on the other side before the sunset and the packages prepped."

"Sunset at this time of year is around seven o'clock. That's cutting it close, if they only need an hour."

"They kept talking about crossroads. Something to do with major street crossings at a central location." Shorty was sipping his coffee as he spoke.

"Anything else, Shorty?"

"The place is somewhere downtown. That's all we heard."

OK, so downtown and probably in between the two Catholic churches. I needed a map. Hopefully, Bartholomew would be up by the time I got home.

"Nice job, Shorty. Is there any way you could get word to the underground to stay away from downtown? It's going to be dangerous tonight." I didn't want tons of collateral damage or more prisoners.

"Consider it done, boss. Anything else?" Shorty would have made a great soldier.

"Check in with me tomorrow. Take a count of how many people you have starting out, and again at the end. We want to make sure nobody else is taken."

"Ten-four."

By the time I turned to looked at him, he was gone. Shorty had blended in with the crowd like a chameleon.

I was alone again, and I wasn't sure what else do to. The minister was still speaking, and the crowd was moved with each one of his words. The space had no boundaries, no walls, no sacred art or crucifix anywhere, but you could feel the Lord in its midst. I closed my eyes, and I could feel energy rolling over me in every direction. Unlike the crazy witches' energy, this was soft and warm. It felt like soft silk caressing my face, or warm waves. I found myself swaying to an invisible force I wanted so badly to touch.

I opened my eyes, and the band had started playing again. The crowd was moving to the same beat. It was captivating. I started to look around. There were smiling faces everywhere. The church had set up tables on the far side for what appeared to be breakfast. The food was not what caught my eye. A guy who looked just like Eric was carrying boxes. I didn't want to yell his name, in case it wasn't him. Instead, I walked carefully in his direction.

"Do you guys need some help?" I had learned early in my military career that the easiest way to get people to like you was to volunteer. It was the same way in most places.

A lady in her fifties, or maybe sixties, smiled at me. She looked as if she'd had work done on herself. She had age spots on her hands, but her face looked really good.

"Of course, sweetie. We could always use more hands. Do you mind helping unload the truck?" Her voice was very musical. It had the same quality as the preacher's. I wondered if the two of them were related.

I made my way toward the truck. The guy was definitely Eric. He was facing the bed, pulling crates closer to the front. He was wearing shorts and a long-sleeve shirt. He had a baseball cap on, and he looked younger.

"Aren't you supposed to be in bed?"

He almost jumped at the sound of my voice. "Isis, what are you doing here? Please don't blow up anything here." Eric had a horrible perception of me. Scary.

"It wasn't on my list, but thank you for the reminder. I'd better be going." I turned around and started to walk away. I really didn't need that from him today.

"Isis, I'm sorry. Please wait." Eric was holding my arm.

My first instinct was to knock his hand off me. I controlled myself and turned to face him. "Yes? What other insults are you getting ready to throw at me?" It sucked to be like a mayhem commercial. For some strange reason, he wanted to blame all the insane crap in this town on me. As if the witches weren't doing anything here.

"I'm sorry about that. I'm tired and maybe a bit edgy. What are you doing here? I thought you were Catholic." How did he know my religion? I guessed that part really didn't matter.

"I am, but I still enjoy a good service. Even the pope promotes better relations with other faiths."

"So, that's the only reason you're here?" Eric really should have become an investigator. He asked plenty of questions.

"I had a meeting with one of my sources." I looked around at the church. I was not going to admit to Eric that Shorty was my only source. "Maybe we should talk and move. I think they're waiting for those things."

"Oh, crap. You're right." Eric looked back to the truck.

"Let me help you."

Eric looked around almost reluctantly. Finally, he handed me a couple of boxes. They were full of rolls and apples.

We walked back to the breakfast table together. We handed the volunteers the boxes and went back for more.

"The ladies normally have more help, but for some strange reason, five of their regulars didn't show up today."

"Probably because they're getting ready for genocide." I beat Eric to the truck.

"What?" A sleep-deprived Eric was really slow.

"I'm pretty sure the witches were volunteering here. They've been working in most of the shelters and nonprofit organizations to find victims and get their trust. After tonight, for one reason or another, they won't be coming back." I prayed it would be because we'd found a way to stop them. "Why are you here?"

He looked a little shy. "This is one of my favorite events in town. Everyone here truly wants to be here, and they care for one another." We carried the last of the supplies to the table. Eric headed back to the truck. "Can you feel it?"

"I can feel something. I don't know what it is." I looked around the place again. The fellowship was incredible.

"Do you trust me?"

That was a very odd question coming from him. I knew Constantine trusted him, but did I? The man drove me nuts at times, but, somehow, I did trust him. I nodded.

"OK. I don't recommend you doing this around town. Open your sight."

I looked at him in pure horror. Was he trying to scare me to death? With all these people here, I had no idea what I would find.

Eric stepped closer and held my hand. "It's going to be OK. Try it."

I took a deep breath, closed my eyes, and opened my sight. I was bracing myself for demons, monsters, and maybe even hell. Instead, I was surrounded by golden light. The place was illuminated by a soft, warm brilliance, and a canopy of light covered the crowd. The Church under the Bridge was a Church of Light and Warmth. Everyone around me was glowing, even Eric. He looked like an avenging angel.

To my left a lady sat on the ground, crying. Two children sat on either side of her, holding her hands and soothing her. As I looked, their wings expanded, and, by God, they were cherubs. They smiled at the lady and wiped her tears. My heart exploded with emotions, and I had tears running down my face. I couldn't stop them. The church was the most beautiful thing I had ever seen. I couldn't see the people, just their souls. At this very moment, those souls were pure and full of love, and they radiated that. Eric came closer to me. I cried on his shoulder.

"You should close your sight now, before you pass out."

I didn't want to. I was in awe, but I forced myself to do it.

"Eric, is she OK?" The head volunteer lady was by our side when I finally opened my eyes. Eric was gentle, as I had never seen him before. He slowly let me go. The lady handed me some tissues.

"She's had a very long week."

"Oh, sweetie, you poor thing. You're among friends now. Come, join us." It wasn't a question but a statement. She took my hand, and I let her lead me toward the food table. Eric was right behind us. Texarkana had a way of surprising me every day. Jesus's recruitment techniques were not as flashy as Jake's, but they were just as powerful.

Chapter Thirty-Three

I made it to Reapers after noon. Unlike Catholic Masses, which lasted only an hour, this was at least two. After the service, I helped the volunteers clean up. I wasn't sure how, but the underground community knew who I was. Their expressions were mixed at first. Some stayed away, as if I had the plague. With the number of people disappearing around me, I didn't blame them. The other half was very welcoming.

The energy or magic in that place was so intoxicating. I agreed to go back the following week to help. That was crazy. I didn't make it to my own Mass every week, but I was picking up a second church. I was losing my mind. It was odd to start thinking of war after that service. For some reason, I wanted to find those witches and pray with them. Maybe talk reason into them. By the time I opened the door to the loft at Reapers, reality hit. The boys had pictures of dead bodies all over the kitchen island and table.

"Wow. Where did you find all these?" They looked almost like dried-up mummies. I couldn't guess the age of any, but their clothes were fairly modern.

"Evidence file from New York. The victims." Constantine jumped from the table to the kitchen counter. That quickly, peace-talk ideas were gone. The war was back on.

"Constantine, if we don't stop them, they're just going to keep doing this." My stomach was turning as I looked at those poor people.

"Pretty much. They'll probably go away for a while. They have enough years accumulated, but they will do it again. Who knows what part of the world next?" Constantine was going over the pictures as well.

"Those poor souls are gone." My voice came out a whisper.

Even Constantine felt sorry for the dead. He wouldn't meet my eyes. "Yeah. They will never go home." Oh yeah, the war was on. "Where have you been?"

"Are you sure you're not my dad?" I tried glaring at Constantine. But have you ever won a staring contest with a cat?

"Why do you think they call me the guardian? That's my job description."

"Good point. I totally forgot. I still don't have to like it." I was not winning that argument. It wasn't as if I ever won any arguments with Constantine.

"You don't have to like it. Just conform to it."

"Constantine, did you ever advise any generals in the military? 'Cause you have an evil side to you." He had a very dictatorial personality.

"Just Patton, at least directly. I had others I mentored from afar."

"Oh, wow. Only General Patton." I took a moment to process that. "I'm not even surprised."

"Where do you think he got his style from?"

"Lead me, follow me, or just get the hell out of my way. I always wondered why he was so angry. Now it makes sense."

"That was one of my best quotes. Now, girl, stop stalling and talk." Typical cat. They were easily distracted, but once they were done, they were right back on their target. Constantine did not forget a thing.

"I met Shorty at the Church under the Bridge." I had too much energy, so I started pacing the room.

Bartholomew was quiet by the computer area. "Great place. People forget their problems there. Pure magic. I love it." He looked entranced with his thoughts. Too bad those didn't last long. "Anything new?"

"The witches need to move the people by six p.m. That doesn't give us much time to find them."

"We're probably too late to find them. We need to figure out where they're going. Either stop them en route or go after them."

I looked at Constantine carefully. "Our plan is to break into purgatory, find the people, and bring them back. Simple, straightforward. I like. How are we breaking into purgatory?" I didn't know any magic to break supernatural barriers.

"Simple. We use the door the witches create. They have to keep it open long enough to get out and dump the bodies. It would take them too much power to blast two doors in one day." He was watching me carefully.

"Why doesn't purgatory have guardians on the other side?" I was so confused.

"You don't need to guard souls whose next destination is heaven. What could they possibly do?" Constantine had a point. "Unfortunately, we took for granted the ambitions of your species and the things you're willing to do to achieve things. Humans can be truly evil."

"Thanks, Constantine. Now tell me how you really feel. Are you sure you don't need a nap?"

Constantine was looking vicious now.

"He's hungry. We skipped breakfast," Bartholomew said from the computer room, almost giggling. "Maybe he needs a Snickers Bar."

"Oh, you've got jokes now." Constantine was working himself all up. He was looking like a small, vicious tiger.

I walked over to the pantry and pulled out a couple of cans of tuna. Constantine was pacing around, ready to unleash hell on Bartholomew and me. Bartholomew stayed really far away. I preheated the oven. While the oven was heating up, I opened a can of tuna. Constantine stopped in mid-pounce in Bartholomew's direction. He made a quick U-turn and headed my way. I placed the tuna in a bowl and the bowl in front of Constantine.

"Here you go, Mr. Lion King." I could have sworn he growled at me. I stepped away from the angry beast.

While Constantine ate his meal in silence, I prepared Bartholomew an open-faced tuna sandwich with asparagus and cheese. It took less than five minutes to toast the bread, add mayo to the tuna, and then layer the sandwich. Toast went on the bottom, followed by the asparagus, the tuna, and then the cheese. A few minutes under the broiler, and the sandwich was done. With the new gluten-free bread we had bought, I didn't feel bad making him a sandwich.

"OK, Bart, come and eat now. I don't need you transforming into the Hulk over there." I didn't have to tell Bartholomew twice.

Food was the only thing that would separate that boy from the computer area. He brought a stack of papers with him.

"Here you go." He handed me the papers.

"What's this?" I opened up the sheets.

"Obviously, maps. I tried to break them down by area." Bartholomew had been busy. By the looks of it, they had gotten up as soon as I'd left.

"Maybe if I looked at things before asking, I could save myself the smart replies." I glared at Bartholomew over the maps. He smiled back brightly. Boy geniuses were a menace to themselves. "According to the priest and the ghosts, we're looking for a location where the walls to purgatory are weak. What can cause that?"

"Ley lines are the most common," Constantine said between tuna bites. Thank God, he was coming back to normal. I liked nice, useful Constantine so much better.

"Does Texarkana have any ley lines? Whatever those things are."

"Ley lines are—"

"Constantine, not now. You can explain the concept later. Do we have any?"

Constantine wasn't even mad. Which meant the tuna was doing its magic.

"Not any strong enough to break the barriers," Bartholomew said between bites. We needed to work on manners with these two. "I checked earlier. Sorry."

"No ley lines. What else, then?" This was not my specialty.

"Crossroads and intersections have power. They allow the flow of energy and at times redirect it," Constantine said.

"Is that why feng shui discourages people from building houses in front of the end of a street?"

Constantine stopped chewing and looked at me, surprised.

"Oh, don't give me that look. Feng shui is fairly common now."

"You're right, but most people don't make the connection. Every major religion has understood the power of energy and magic." At least the lecture hadn't lasted long this time. Constantine was back at his tuna.

"That's not good." Constantine and I turned to look at Bartholomew as he spoke. "If crossroads are that big a deal, State

Line is a giant magnet. Not only is a major street, but it's a highway, and it separates two states."

"Oh God, that's what they meant by loving the twin cities. But we need something that connects State Line to downtown." I opened Bartholomew's maps on the counter. I found the downtown map and traced State Line down. Bartholomew and Constantine were both looking over my shoulder.

"Holy cow," Bartholomew whispered.

"You've got to be kidding me." I was in shock.

"Can you humans make things any more complicated?" This time, I completely agreed with Constantine. "Why would anyone in their right mind put a post office in the middle of State Line? That stupid building is sitting in two states." Constantine was staring at the map in pure anger.

"That is the second-most photographed post office in the country. Not to mention the FYI—the Texas Marshals and the correctional officers have offices there. This is a giant nightmare." I thought I had issues with dead people.

"That's a federal building. We can't bust in there." Bartholomew looked at the map as he chewed.

"We? Where you think you're going?" I sounded like my godmother, but I didn't care. I was not letting Bartholomew get hurt on my watch.

"With you. Isis, you can't do this on your own. Besides, Constantine can't enter purgatory." Bartholomew was looking directly at me. There was no fear in his eyes, and he was not backing down.

"You can't enter purgatory? Why?" How come nobody had ever explained that before?

"Purgatory is a human creation for souls. I'm a magical cat, but even I have limitations. In the end, only humans can enter—not even Death." Now that explained why he was so upset about the whole purgatory thing. It meant he couldn't help. "Bartholomew is right, Isis. You're going to need help. I don't like it any more than you do."

"Bart, this is dangerous. If something goes wrong, I might not make it out of there."

"Exactly why you need me. I thought we were all a team. I want to be part of this." For an eleven-year-old boy, Bartholomew was really brave—or naïve. "Isis, please. I'm tired of being left behind. Besides, I could just follow you anyway."

I wasn't sure which part scared me the most. I knew the feeling of being left behind all too well. I took a deep breath. "Fine. But you follow my orders and do exactly what I tell you."

"Deal." Bartholomew was the only one who was excited about that. Constantine and I just glared at the kid.

"Constantine, can you call your contacts and get us another vehicle, please? We need to blend in in Texarkana. The witches will be expecting Bumblebee." Getting downtown was important.

"Too easy. It'll be ready by five p.m." I really believed Constantine was the head of the mafia.

"Bartholomew, can you disable the cameras at the post office? Make sure there's no trace of us there." The last thing we needed was to get caught on camera driving like maniacs.

"Simple enough. I'll bring my laptop so I can monitor things as we get closer. I'll double-check all the police frequencies and scanners." Bartholomew was going over his list of things to destroy. Yeah, that child was dangerous.

"The post office is a huge building. It'll take us forever to search it all." I had no idea how that would happen.

"Maybe not, Isis." I stopped to look at Constantine. "Think about it. The building is on top of State Line. They really don't need to access the inside to get the most benefits. The outside of it would do. Besides, it's Saturday. They would draw too much attention walking into a federal building."

"That's good news, right? We drive around till we find the door." I was trying to sound optimistic.

"Something like that." Constantine needed to work on his optimism.

"OK, boys, we need to be rolling by five p.m. That gives us less than four hours. I'll get the gear ready. You both know what to do. We have a war to plan; let's go."

Both Bartholomew and Constantine nodded at me. While the boys took care of transportation, surveillance, and police issues, I was going to prep the firepower. For the first time, I prayed that Constantine had ordered every weapon he could imagine.

Chapter Thirty-Four

Why was I surprised that we were late leaving Reapers? It was 5:24 p.m. by the time we headed downtown. Granted, it wasn't a very long drive, but I was going at least three miles below the speed limit. This job was making me a real law-biding citizen when it came to traffic laws. We carried too much firepower. Not to mention Bartholomew and I were dressed for war. It wasn't hunting season, I was told, so we couldn't even use that as an excuse. Constantine had come through on the ride, as usual. We had an F-150, white, with dual cab and extended bed. Constantine wanted to make sure we could transport a large group of people.

By the time we made it downtown, my adrenaline was pumping. We needed to do something soon, before I had a heart attack. Bartholomew was busy working his magic with his laptop. I couldn't explain what he was doing; all I got was that the cameras would be disabled and perimeter secure. I was sure those words did not have the same meaning for him as they had for me.

"Done. Downtown is secure." Bartholomew had a huge smile on his face. I was really worried.

"Why are you all smiles?" He did look suspicious.

"When we blow up the post office, nobody will be able to blame us."

"We're not planning to blow up anything."

"Of course not. But just in case, we're covered."

As much as I was hoping we could avoid mass destruction, I didn't want to take any chances. I let Bartholomew finish his final checks.

Shorty had done his part. Downtown was deserted. Not a soul was walking around anywhere. Even the businesses that were normally open late on Saturday were shut down tight. That at least made me feel better. The fewer pedestrians around, the better. We drove around the post office several times and saw nothing. Had we made a mistake? Where could they possible be?

"Constantine, are you seeing anything?" Constantine was manning the drone, which was really scary on its own. It wasn't just any drone; it was military issue, with high-power cameras, heat sensors, and a few machine guns. His idea of watching the fort was dealing death from above. I was sure Constantine was part of the Eighty-Second Airborne—similar philosophy.

"The skies are clear, and not a soul on the ground. What did you tell Shorty to do, kill them all? He really cleared the town." Constantine was coming through the headpiece extremely clear.

"I was wondering the same thing myself. There isn't a soul in town. Anything on the scanners?" Constantine was also in charge of monitoring all the police scanners as well as the supernatural world. We were running out of time.

"Strange—they got an anonymous call reporting strange people with guns at Union Station. The caller mentioned seeing one of the missing people being dragged into the building."

Bartholomew looked at me, and I shook my head.

"That sounds too convenient. What do you think, Constantine?" I was sure the witches were not at Union Station. That place was abandoned. It was a train station owned by a civilian, one of the few in the country, and it wasn't in use. This could be another trap.

"We're running out of time. The cops are on the scene, and the place has been locked down. It doesn't feel right." At least we were all on the same page. "Eric is on the scene now. Swing by and see if you can talk to him. Just be careful with the MRAP."

"MRAP? Like the mine-resistant ambush-protected vehicle? That MRAP?" Was Constantine high?

"Yes, that one. Did I stutter? Why are you spelling things out for me?" Constantine had no problem going from happy to pissy in under two seconds. I was blaming his feline nature.

"Why would Texarkana have an MRAP?" What mine or ambush were they expecting in the middle of town?

"It's part of their SWAT. Try not to get kill or arrested down there. Keep me posted. I'm going to do another round with the drone. Constantine out."

"Is Constantine talking about himself in the third person?" I looked at Bartholomew.

"Are you surprised about that?" OK, he did have a good point.

I was on Seventh Street, and I took a right on State Line to head to Union Square. "That's weird."

"What?"

"I thought I saw two people playing chess in there."

He was still looking at the Vietnam memorial.

"Should we turn around?" I asked Bartholomew, confused. I didn't want to miss anything.

"Let's go find Eric first." I looked in the rearview mirror but kept on driving. I trusted Bartholomew's judgment here.

Union Station, or the Texarkana Train Station, was another one of those beautiful buildings that was neglected and falling apart. All the new buildings and businesses were going west on 30. I was a sucker for classic architecture.

I wasn't sure how far I was going to get. The station was behind the correctional facility on Front Street, right next to the police station. Either the witches were insane, or they didn't think they could get caught.

Bartholomew and I made it to the intersection of Pine and Front Streets. Constantine was right. SWAT was on the scene, and the place looked like a hostage negation right out of a movie. Police officers were everywhere. They even had snipers on the roofs. I was pretty sure the witches were not there.

"Impressive, but probably overkill." Bartholomew was looking out his window.

"You're getting the same vibe." I was making a mental note. Texarkana's rapid-response team was impressive.

"There's no way they're going to blast a door to another dimension in the middle of a firefight."

Bartholomew was right. Before I could put the truck in reverse, someone knocked on my window. I almost jumped out of my seat. I lowered my window slowly.

"What are you two doing here?" Why didn't Eric ever smile when he was on duty?

"Constantine sent us to find you," Bartholomew said from his side. "Are they here?" Bartholomew had a way of calming people down.

Eric didn't seem to mind answering Bartholomew, unlike me. "There are people inside. The snipers have seen several people with guns and hostages." He glanced over his shoulder.

"Constantine said you had an anonymous call. How do you know it was reliable?" I had no idea why that was bothering me. I didn't believe in coincidences, and this job was making me question everything.

"Abuelita called me to ask for advice. She made a tracking spell for Angelito, and it led to the station. She wanted to come and find him, but you told her the witches were after her. I told her to call 911 and leave the message." Eric looked worried. It probably didn't help that he hadn't slept in a couple of days.

"Why not have her leave her name?" Bartholomew asked.

"Very hard to explain to the cops that she used a spell to track him here. Nobody would ever take her seriously again. Besides, they wouldn't come," I said. I knew it in my heart, because up to a week ago, I didn't believe in any of this stuff.

"Oh yeah, I forgot. Police don't believe in magic." Bartholomew looked so young.

"The average person doesn't believe in magic. Remember that. You two better get out of here." Eric was scanning the area. He noticed one of the other cops looking in our direction.

"Let us know if you find Angelito, please." I was praying that Abuelita was all right.

"I will. Be careful. We're going to be busy here for a while. If they're not here, you're going to have your hands full." Eric started walking away.

"Thank you, Eric."

He nodded at us and kept on walking.

I looked at Bartholomew. "They're not there. This is a distraction."

"I was thinking the same thing. It's clever. They have the whole area blocked off, and nobody is looking for them. I think Angelito is in there." Bartholomew was looking at the building as he spoke.

"I do, too. I also have a horrible feeling that he's well-guarded." Bartholomew and I looked at each other.

"Isis, there's no time. If we try to help, we'll probably get arrested instead. Besides, if they left magical traps, Eric can handle it. We need to find them."

Bartholomew was right. There wasn't much we could do there.

"I know, but I feel bad. They're going in there blind." I took a deep breath before putting the truck in gear.

"Blind? Isis, please. Those guys live for this kind of thing. Snipers on the roof, MRAP blocking the way. This is training paradise. If they actually get to shoot somebody and rescue the hostage, that would be one hell of a story. We're in the way." He looked at me and smiled. He was a genius for a reason.

"When you put it that way, why ruin their life's mission?" I made a U-turn and headed back to State Line.

"Thank you. I'm glad you see it my way." He touched his earpiece to get ahold of Constantine. "Constantine, hostages in the building, but we're pretty sure no witches. What do you have?"

"I got a couple of thugs hanging out by a fountain. They look heavily armed, so be careful."

"Got it. We're on our way."

I nodded at Bartholomew and headed toward the post office.

"The fountain is on the back side. We'll need to park on the side and walk the rest of the way. Constantine, can you see anyone else?" I was hoping for a little more information or details.

"That's the weird part, Isis. It's just two of them. No car near them or anyone else wandering around. They're too big and wearing weather-heavy jackets to look natural there."

"OK, so how do we find this stupid doorway?" I had no idea what I was looking for.

"It's magic, Isis. Unfortunately, you're going to need to use your sight."

"Darn," Bartholomew said. I totally agreed.

"OK, we're on our way. Will keep you posted." I did the sign of the cross. If any time in my life I needed divine protection, this was it. I said a quick prayer for Bartholomew and myself.

Chapter Thirty-Five

We parked across the street from the post office on Woods Street. Bartholomew did one last check of the cameras and surveillance on his laptop.

"We've got sixty minutes on the loop before anyone notices something." He was typing something on his computer as he spoke.

"That's great, because we've got twenty minutes till sunset, so plenty of time." I was starting to freak out.

Bartholomew put his computer away. He grabbed a police baton from his backpack. I pulled my M16 from the backseat and attached the machete to my side. I had been wondering why we needed the extended cab. Now I understood—it was easier to grab weapons from. For a cat, Constantine had a great understanding of human needs and logistics. It explained how he had managed to survive all this time. Bartholomew and I grabbed a few more handguns and plenty of ammo. We were ready for war.

We made our way toward the front of the post office. It was weird the way the place was designed. It felt as if the front of the building should be facing State Line and not the back. We stayed close to the building and made our way to the front. I didn't know why I was surprised when the thugs came around the corner. They were expecting us. Constantine wasn't kidding—these two were the biggest men I had ever seen in my life. One of the Incredible Hulks grabbed Bartholomew by the shirt and lifted him at least four feet off the ground.

"Let go of me, you punk." Bartholomew was swinging his legs, but it made no difference. He looked like a baby suspended in the air.

I tried to help by rushing in. That didn't last long. I was backhanded at least six feet back. What did these guys eat? My face was on fire. Thankfully, my M16 was still strapped to my neck, or it would have blown off. I wasn't sure if I could take a clear shot. They had Bartholomew hanging like a sack of potatoes. I pulled one of the recorders from my pocket. I wished I'd had time to test it, but Bartholomew was starting to turn purple. I said a quick prayer and turned the thing on.

I was amazed. Two grown men dropped to the ground. They literally fell on the ground as if somebody had knocked them out. The lullaby was soothing, and I felt all the emotions I had poured into it while I was playing it. Bartholomew fell on his butt when the guy dropped him. I had not had time to warn him.

"Sorry about that, Bart. Are you OK?" I rushed over and helped him up.

"Why didn't you do that at the beginning?" Bartholomew was looking at the thugs in shock.

"I had no idea if it was actually going to work. Here are some earplugs, just in case it starts affecting you. Come on, help me move these two off the street. They'll draw attention." Bartholomew plugged his ears and helped me drag the big guys next to the fountain. We sat them on the curb and tried to make them looked as natural as possible. If you believed it was just two drunk guys, it would work.

"Now what?" Bartholomew was looking around the fountain.

"It's not going to pop up on us. Close your eyes and open your sight. We need to get in."

I did the same thing I had just told Bartholomew to do. I opened my sight slowly. I wasn't sure what was waiting for us. Thank God nothing and no one was there except for a huge split in the fountain. It was probably eight feet tall by ten feet wide. It wasn't like a garage door with clean, even lines. This was jagged, like when you cut the corners off bread and missed pieces.

"No wonder they needed the equinox. That thing is huge." Bartholomew was standing next to me, also staring at the huge hole.

"You're right. I was expecting a hole like a window or a door, not an underpass." These nuts were not extravagant. "Are you ready? You can always stay here and guard the hallway here."

"Right, and let you get killed. No way, Isis. I'm going with you."

I smiled at the little guy. He had guts.

"In that case, let's cause some mayhem. Constantine, we're going in. If we're not back in thirty, give Death the bad news and close this door up." I placed the recording next to our sleeping beauties as a safety precaution.

"That is definitely a last resort. Make sure to get out of there, with or without the hostages. Those witches won't leave here alive." Constantine's voice was venomous.

Bartholomew swallowed and looked at me. My eyes were wide with fear. Mental note: do not make Constantine mad.

"Going in. Safeties off; shoot first; ask questions later."

Bartholomew took the safety off his 9mm. I did the same with the M16. We nodded at each other and walked through the tunnel.

I was nervous about entering purgatory. The place was so bright, my mind was in pain. I felt as if I were choking to death in a furnace.

Bartholomew screamed next to me, "Close your sight! Hurry!"

It took me some effort to close the sight. The burning sensation stopped, and I could breathe again. I slowly opened my eyes. "Are you OK?"

Bartholomew was on his knees breathing heavily, but he nodded. I gave him a moment to recover. With my normal eyes, I took a look at purgatory. It was a version of Texarkana. Not like the real one; this one was cleaner, as if everything had been power-washed. The colors were brighter, more intense. At home we were getting ready to start fall, and the trees were changing color. The trees here were in full bloom, almost springlike. The weather was cool, and a breeze smelling of fruit filled the air. Even the air smelled cleaner. It was so weird—a permanent spring.

"I guess if I needed to wait for permission to go home, this would not be a bad place to wait," Bartholomew whispered.

"I wouldn't mind having weather like this all year long. I just wouldn't want to get stuck here for eternity."

"I agree. But where are all the people?"

"If purgatory is only a Catholic belief, I guess you'll only have the Catholic souls who were living in Texarkana here." It was an empty town, with no cars or people anywhere—except that stupid black van parked by the Vietnam memorial. "I've figured out why they needed the tunnel-size entrance." I pointed at the van.

We made our way through the empty street. The whole thing looked spooky. Bartholomew and I kept looking over our shoulders, but nobody was around. We reached the memorial. Bartholomew took the right side, and I took the left. The memorial was technically for the Korean and Vietnam Wars. The place was in the shape of a semicircle, with a couple of benches in the middle. The trees around the park were so thick and full, it gave the area the appearance of having a roof. From the road you had the impression the place was more enclosed.

Inside the parklike area, the hostages were lying on the ground. I reached the hostages first. There were at least seven people lying on the brick floor. I reached the hostage closest to me and bent over. It was the woman from the Granary. She looked thinner than I remembered. She had bags under her eyes. I took her pulse. She was still warm. Her pulse was weak, but she was alive. My celebration was short-lived. From the back of the memorial, Angelito's dear girlfriend, Lily, appeared.

"You really don't give up, do you?"

I guessed these witches didn't need any wands like in the movies. She was holding a ball of fire in her hands. I was still holding the M16, and I went for the trigger.

"Do you really want to test who's faster?" she said.

From my right side, another one of those oversize thugs came out carrying Bartholomew. He had Bartholomew's gun in one hand and was holding Bartholomew's wrist in the other. Bartholomew looked pissed.

"Shoot her, Isis. They're not planning to let anyone live, anyway." Nobody would ever deny that Bartholomew had spunk.

"Oh, look. You brought us one with lots of years in him. Two for the price of one. I love it." The crazy witch had the most mocking smile on her face. She was definitely demented. "Too bad your boss won't be here to take you home." Demented, and she thought she was funny. Great.

"Aren't you kind? Drop the ball, and we can do this one-on-one." I just wanted to knock her teeth out.

"Child, please. After fifty years, I don't believe in fighting fair. Law-abiding and listening to the order—what did it get us? A dead brother. We were told we can't go against nature. Bullshit! Those arrogant, self-righteous pigs got rich and happy, and my family died." Lily was demented, with a revenge motive and lots of years of experience. I was truly out of my league. "What? No witty comeback?"

"Nope. I got nothing for that one. You are demented." What I needed was a plan to get us out of there. We were facing a psycho witch with lots of power.

"Oh, that's a shame. Angelito said you were really funny." She was playing with the ball of fire and looking more evil by the minute.

"Obviously, Angelito is not a good source of information. He fell for your crazy ass." She actually laughed at that. "So, do we just stand here and wait, or do you kill me now? I'm ready for a fight."

"You are a feisty little intern. No, child. We lost a few specimens setting that little diversion. We're going to make great use of you. Tie him up and then get her," she ordered the thug holding Bartholomew.

I looked around the group and realized neither Angelito nor Ana were there. That was a blessing.

Lily glanced at the thug. It was barely a second, but it was long enough for the person on the ground to kick her. The witch lost her balance, and I opened fire and marched at her. We were less than twenty feet apart, and I was gaining ground. I wasn't sure what damage I would inflict. I didn't care. Unfortunately, I wasn't quick enough. She raised a shield, and the bullets just got stuck in it. But magic required focus and energy. I had plenty of bullets, and she would get tired. She backed away from me, and I kept pace. I emptied a thirty-round magazine on her.

Lily got ready to attack back, but, unfortunately for the pretty little thing, she had to drop her shield. I ran at her and butt struck her to the head with the M16. She wasn't expecting actual contact. Did I mention I was tired of getting beaten up? The witch went down like a sack of potatoes, and I kicked her in the ribs just for good measure. I heard a loud grunt from behind me, and I turned, M16 ready and reloaded.

"I didn't take all those lessons to get beaten up by a giant." The thug holding Bartholomew doubled over with his hands at his groin. Bartholomew managed to elbow him in the face on his way down.

"Nice job, Bart." The little man was full of surprises.

"Isis, what are you doing here?"

I turned back to the witch to find my mysterious helper. Thank my lucky stars it was the famous no-last-name Bob.

"Oh, thank the Lord, Bob, you're alive." I walked over and helped him up. He was also thinner—but alive. He was also very conscious, unlike the rest of the people.

"You're the famous Bob. Hi, I'm Bartholomew. How are you awake and everyone else is not?" Bartholomew was talking from his side of the memorial.

"Famous?" He looked at me, confused.

"Yeah, long story. Let's get these two tied up before they wake up." I pulled out industrial-size zip ties. Bartholomew did the same.

"Zip ties, Isis? Are you serious? That bitch can do magic." Bob looked very skeptical.

"Reinforced zip ties, my dear Bob. Cuts off their magic source. The only thing she'll be able to do with these is get plastic burns. Come on, now. Grab her feet."

Bob bent over and started helping. "Isis, what's going on here? Where are we? This is not Texarkana—not exactly."

I felt bad for Bob. He looked so lost. "No, it's not. It's purgatory." I finished her arms and legs and pulled out duct tape to cover her mouth.

"Isis, I'm not Catholic. Does that mean I'm dead? Are you dead?" He looked as if he was about to lose his mind.

"No, we're not dead, but we will be if we don't get out of here soon," Bartholomew said. "Come help me with this one."

I moved over to help Bartholomew. The big guy started moving a bit. Bartholomew knocked him out by hitting him over the head with his gun. The boy had a lot of anger. Bob grabbed Bartholomew's giant.

"Short version: Witches have been kidnapping people in Texarkana to steal their souls and lives. I'm now one of Death's interns, and my job is to stop them. Simple enough?"

"Oh, wow. I'm not crazy, and this is really happening?" He was looking between Bartholomew and me.

"Mr. Bob, you are not crazy. The world is a lot more complicated than you imagine. The monsters are real. Can you handle that?" Bartholomew was dead serious.

"Everything I saw in the war was real. I'm not crazy." Bob was talking to himself, almost spaced out. I was afraid he was losing it.

"I have no idea what you saw in the war, but it was probably real. The question is, what are you going to do about it?" Bartholomew looked at Bob patiently.

Bob looked around. "What do you need me to do?"

Bartholomew smiled and handed Bob one of his guns. "Welcome to the team." Bartholomew had no issues making friends.

"Do you still remember how to use that?" I asked him, a little wary. I didn't want to get shot by friendly fire.

Bob dropped the magazine, checked the chamber, and put the gun back together. "It's like riding a bike."

I smiled. Bob was ready.

"OK, so where are the rest?" I looked around, waiting for more witches to pop out of the air. We had less than five minutes before sunset.

"They went to set up something inside the post office. They were running late, so that one was supposed to prep us or something." The three of us looked at Lily while Bob talked. "To answer your question, Bartholomew, I stopped eating the food they gave us. Once I realized it knocked us out, I stopped eating. Nobody else listened." Bob looked around, distraught.

"Comatose people are going to make traveling a lot harder than I expected." This was not part of the plan. Why couldn't our plans just go smoothly?

"How about the van? We can take them out the same way they brought them in." Bartholomew was looking at us expectantly.

"Bart, you're a genius. OK, let's get them in. We need to be out of here now." I was so happy to have Bartholomew there.

Bob, Bartholomew, and I piled bodies in the van. For the first time, I was happy the van was around. It had no seats, so we just laid the poor people on top of one another. There was no way of making them comfortable. At this point, I didn't care. We got the last person in the van.

"Oh, Isis, we got company." Bartholomew was looking at the post office. The remainder of the coven was heading our way. Bob and I stuck our heads out of the van.

"You again! Where is my sister?"

Oh, great. Evil Angry Rose was back, leading her psycho coven. "Kill them."

I grabbed Bartholomew by his gear and pulled him inside. "Get in here, Bart. Time to go. Bob, drive. Guess we're not going the same way we came."

Bob climbed into the driver seat.

I got in the passenger seat.

"Isis, where to?" Bob was searching for the keys.

I opened fire on the witches from the passenger window. They were not expecting that. Luckily, two went down. That, unfortunately, made the others mad, and they started throwing spells. They cracked the windshield. Bob found the keys in the cup holder. I guess they weren't expecting their van to get stolen. Bob started the van, and I kicked the windshield out. We couldn't see anything anyways.

"Saint Edward's. There's a gate there."

Bob didn't need directions. I opened fire on the group.

Bob made a U-turn on the street and peeled out. Traffic laws and regulations were nonexistent there, so he gunned it. Bartholomew opened the van door and started throwing grenades. That really made them jump.

Chapter Thirty-Six

The speed limit in Texarkana, for the most part, was forty miles per hour. In purgatory Bob was going at least eighty. Saint Edward's was less than half a mile from the post office. We took Seventh Street toward Saint Edward's as fast as the van could handle it. Bob slowed down to take the right onto Beech Street. We were still going too fast for that turn. The van was on two wheels, and I was afraid we were going to flip.

"Too fast. Wow. Is everyone OK?" Bob was not slowing down as he spoke. I was grateful Bartholomew had closed the back door.

"Still here," Bartholomew said from the back. When I looked his way, he had fallen on his butt from the turn. I was holding on to the door handle for dear life.

"We got company." The witches were making their way to the church from Fifth Street. "They don't look happy," I told the boys.

There were three of them riding Harleys, and they at least had wands pointed at us. With the windshield gone, I used the edge of the window frame to hold my M16 for stability. With Bob driving like a madman, I didn't want to accidentally shoot us instead. I laid down suppressive fire. Those bikes were fast, and all three scattered.

"Isis, where is that gate? I don't see anything."

I looked at the church grounds and couldn't see it either. I was praying I wouldn't have to use the sight there as well.

"Head toward the grounds. It's somewhere on the campus."

Bob nodded and decided to go through Beech Street Church's parking lot. The witches were coming from both sides.

"Everyone, hold on tight." That was the only warning Bob gave us. He used the van as a battering ram and slammed into the witch on our right. Mental note: bike against van, the bike will always lose. Not a pretty sight.

"Ouch. She's going to feel that. I felt it." Bartholomew was a great backseat driver. I just shook my head.

We made it across the street as one of the witches blasted a spell at us. It hit the side of the van behind the driver seat. We now had a large hole.

"Bart, are you OK?" That was way too close to him for my taste.

"I'm good back here. Now I have an opening." Before I could tell him to keep his head down, he opened fire.

I guessed his video games were really good training, because Bartholomew had pretty good aim. He kept the remaining two witches zigzagging and unable to fire back. Bob pulled into Saint Edward's parking lot. We were looking around frantically for the gate. The witches were getting closer. From the driveway behind the church, a woman appeared. It was the lady in the green dress from confession.

She rushed to my window. "Isis, hurry. You need to get out."

"We're trying, but we can't find the door."

"Around the building, the door on the side of the rectory. Hurry. Once you go through, we'll hold the door. We can keep them out at least for a few minutes to buy you some time. Hurry."

"Thank you. I'll pray for you." I reached over and grabbed her hands. They were freezing.

"I know you will." She squeezed my hand and winked.

I was surprised when I realized I meant it.

"Bob, hurry around the church, toward the priest's house." I pointed to the driveway.

Bob was a great soldier. He didn't need to be told twice. He took the van around the church. Bartholomew was still firing at the witches. I wasn't sure how many rounds he was carrying, but he kept shooting. We were on the other side of the church. The rectory, the house for the priest, was behind the church. Bob made his way around the driveway.

"Isis, please tell me you're kidding." Bob looked at me in horror.

"Oh God, there is nothing easy here. Bob, get us through that gate." I had no words of encouragement for Bob. If we stayed, we would die. The gate was the back door of the rectory. A faint light radiated around it.

"Hold on, everyone." Bob hit the gas, and Bartholomew and I screamed.

I've seen those videos where they tell drivers to relax during car crashes to minimize the impact. I've never met a person who followed that advice, unless they were drunks. Drunks were the only people who survived bad crashes. They were so limber, they were almost like Gumby. I did completely the opposite. My entire body tensed, and I closed my eyes. If we were going to die, I didn't want to see it coming. I felt the surge of energy when we crossed the threshold, as the three of us screamed.

"Oh, wow, that was amazing." I opened my eyes, and Bob was doing a happy dance next to me. We were in the middle of Beech Street, in front of the church facing Fifth Street.

"Isis. Bartholomew. Where are you?" We were back on earth, and Constantine was back on.

"Constantine, we're in front of Saint Ed's." I had no idea how we were on the street, but I didn't care.

"Finally. Everything was dead for almost thirty minutes, and then I heard you scream." Constantine was talking pretty fast.

"Thirty minutes? Are you sure? We were gone less than ten." That didn't make any sense.

"Time is an Earth concept. It doesn't work the same in other realms. Anyway, what are you doing over there? You need to get back to the post office. I got you backup." Constantine sounded way too proud of himself. I was praying he didn't have any more ninja cats waiting for us.

"Isis, who are you talking to?" Bob was eyeing me cautiously. I had forgotten he didn't have an earpiece.

"Sorry, Bob. Talking to our guardian. We need to head back to the post office, quickly." I was looking around for more angry witches.

"You have a guardian now?" At least he started the van as he spoke.

"We both do. His name is Constantine, and he's a five-thousand-year-old talking cat. Whatever you do, don't call him kitty. He'll poke your eyes out." Bartholomew had moved up to explain things to Bob.

"Of course, you have a talking cat that serves as your guardian," Bob said very matter-of-factly, without an ounce of sarcasm in his voice.

"Isis, either he's taking this really well, or he's having a mental breakdown," Bartholomew tried to whisper to me, not very well.

"Bart, you do know I can hear you. After everything I've seen this week, I'm ready to believe in aliens." Bob was glancing at Bartholomew as he drove down Fifth Street.

"Definitely breakdown. Too much to handle all at once." Bartholomew was looking at Bob, fairly concerned.

"Nobody is having a breakdown here. Not till we find a safe place for these people and lose those witches. Got it?" It was my turn to glare at the boys. They both nodded quietly. "Good. Now keep an eye out for those witches."

"Do you think they followed us?" Bob was looking around everywhere.

"We have their precious cargo. They're going to want them back. Not to mention they're running out of time." It was the magic hour, as photographers called it—when the sun had set but you still had enough light to give pictures a dreamlike quality.

The streets were still deserted, but it wouldn't last. We needed to hurry. Bob was making sure not to draw too much attention to us. Not sure why he bothered; we were missing the windshield and had a giant hole in the back. We were less than a block away when the first witch appeared in front of us on Walnut Street. I opened fire. Shoot first; ask questions later. She raised her arm, and a shield blocked the bullets. Bob didn't need any instructions. He took a quick right to avoid the witch.

"How did they beat us here?" Bob was looking around, confused.

"They couldn't get through Saint Ed's, so they probably went back to their door. Be careful, Bob. They could be anywhere." With our luck, we could be heading straight for them.

Bob made a quick left on Sixth Street. The post office was straight ahead. Bob took off at top speed. I was praying he was paying attention to any weird movement. We were expecting a frontal attack. We were taken by surprise when the back door of the van blew up. The hit lifted the van at least three feet in the air. Bob hit the brakes right in front of the stop sign across from the post office. Before he could take off again, a witch jumped inside the van.

"This ends now, children." Unlike all the other ones we had seen, this one looked as if she was in her forties and getting older by the minute. Her hair was turning white as she walked in the van. She raised her wand at us.

Bartholomew, a lot quicker than I was, threw his club at her. She dodged it but was not prepared for Bartholomew tackling her. For an eleven-year-old boy, he was pretty strong. They were out the back door and rolling on the street.

"Bob, get to Union Station. The cops are there. Find Officer Smith and tell him we need backup. We'll keep them off you." There was no way in hell I was leaving Bartholomew alone.

"Isis, I won't leave you guys." Bob looked conflicted.

"Bob, drop them off and then come back for us. But you need to get those people to safety. Now." Leaving the M16 with Bob, I jumped out of the van to the craziest scene of my life. Until recently, I had never been in a fight. Now I was shooting at people and getting my butt kicked at least once before bedtime. If today was my day, I was going to make it count. I prayed Death would explain things to my godmother if this went bad.

Chapter Thirty-Seven

Two witches were blocking Bob's path, and he opened fire. The witches jumped out of his way. Bob hit the gas. I saw him take State Line going at least fifty. I had no idea that van could move that fast. I was impressed; the old man was driving as if he had stolen that thing.

Two witches climbed on their bikes to chase Bob. I pulled out my 9mm Smith & Wesson Special and fired at the tires. The witches probably had shields, but I was betting their bikes didn't. I blew up the tires on one bike and accidentally blew up the gas tank on the other. That bike went up in flames like a Fourth of July fireworks display. If people hadn't known before that something was going on downtown, they did now. One witch was on the ground doing a poor imitation of the drop-and-roll drill. Her friend was trying to assist, but it looked as if she was making things worse.

By the time I reached Bartholomew, he had the witch in a headlock. Those lessons with Eric were really paying off. He was trying to cut her air supply and knock her out. She was way too big for him and was shaking around like a wild snake. I rushed to help and kicked her on the side. That slowed her down. Bartholomew managed to knock her out, but we were running out of time. The rest of her coven was back, and they looked as if they were ready for blood. Once they realized they had lost their hostage, Bartholomew and I were going to pay for it.

"Bart! Bart!"

He was too busy with the witch to pay attention to me.

"Bartholomew, we need to take cover. Now!" I had to pull him off the witch. "Let's go, Bart; she is not moving."

Bartholomew and I ran down Sixth Street toward the post office. The two witches who had been blocking Bob were nowhere to be seen. We passed the fountain, and it was in pieces and in flames. The thing looked as if it had gotten hit by a missile. All that was left was a large crater and burning bushes. Normally, I was the one responsible for huge disasters. I had had nothing to do with this one.

"Constantine, what happened to the fountain?" Bartholomew asked as we ran past it.

"Constantine, a.k.a. the Terminator, happened to it." War had a horrible effect on Constantine. He was losing his mind and was proud about it.

"Why?" I was confused. What had that poor fountain done to Constantine?

"Once those witches came out, I decided we needed to stop them from going back in. So, the fountain had to go."

I was speechless. Constantine was serious.

"Constantine, why didn't you just break the spell or something less drastic? You know that fountain was city property. Do we have to pay for that thing?" Honestly, my team really did not believe there was such a thing as overkill.

"Isis, how was I supposed to break the spell from here? Remember, all I have is a drone. Blowing up the fountain broke their circle. Mission accomplished, so bombs away. No fountain, no more portal. We have insurance. We're covered."

There was no hope for Constantine. I had a feeling we didn't have State Farm. Massive city destruction was probably not covered.

As Constantine recounted his victorious campaign, Bartholomew and I took cover behind a truck parked in front of the Firestone Tire Center. I prayed the owner was nowhere nearby. At the rate we were going, this baby was probably going up in flames as well. Our truck was behind the post office. There was no place to hide. This stupid intersection had so much empty space, it reminded me of the Wild West. All we needed was tumbleweeds to roll by, and we would have the perfect setting for a shootout.

"Isis, I have one magazine left." Bartholomew had taken inventory of his ammunition. He had a gash on his cheek and blood running down his arms. I grabbed his arm, trying to discern the level of damage. "Don't worry; it's not mine. I might be bruised, but nothing is broken."

"I'm glad. After everything we've been through, you can't die on me now." I smiled as I spoke. I checked my gear as well. "I have two magazines left. Constantine, where's the backup?"

"On its way. Don't worry. Are you two OK?"

I was going to strangle that cat if we made it through this. "For now. Can't guarantee we'll last long. So, you'd better hurry. Those witches want our heads on silver platters." I peeked around the corner of the truck, and the witches were gathered across the street. It really was an old-style shootout.

"Now, children, if you give up now, we will make your deaths quick." Rose was speaking. How bad do you have to be in order to be the head witch of a murderous coven?

"Yeah, right. We have a better plan. How about you ladies give up, and nobody else gets hurt? How about that?" Who said I couldn't be a negotiator? I had this bantering thing down.

Bart looked at me, surprised. I shrugged.

"Give up? To you two? Please. You are outnumbered, and even your friend abandoned you. Now, why would you drag this out any longer?" Rose looked overly confident in her own powers. "Nobody is here to help you."

"Boss, I want their eyes. Make them suffer."

That sounded awful. I leaned over to better see the discussions the witches were having. Dear Natalie, my favorite two-by-four-wielding psycho, was talking. She had two patches over her eyes, and she looked terrifying. Why was it OK for the bad guys to want us dead, but we couldn't shoot at them first? Double standards were killing me. We needed a new manual with better rules, or a less dangerous job.

"Hey, lady, I didn't gouge your eyes out. Maybe if you stopped pissing off the souls, they wouldn't hate you as much!" I yelled.

"Isis, why are you antagonizing them? It's not like we have that much ammunition left." Bartholomew was looking at me, very skeptical.

"Trying to buy Constantine's backup some time. Besides, I really don't like them. If we have to go down, we are not begging." I looked around at the witches, hoping a plan would appear. They were not looking any happier.

"In that case, I'm all in." Bartholomew looked at me with a wicked smile. He loaded his gun and was ready for a fight.

"Now, children, do you honestly think you made any difference tonight? You will die. It's up to you how much you suffer. Let's make this quick. We are now on a tight schedule."

Wow, life and death meant nothing to them. They really needed some serious therapy.

"Oh, please. Do us all a favor and shoot yourselves."

I looked at the witches one more time. Rose was in the middle of her coven. She had three to the left and three on the right, including Lily. The fire victim was being carried by one of the thugs to the corner. Another thug was carrying the one Bartholomew had knocked out. Seven witches, one with a grudge from here to Canada. Not great odds.

"Consider it a gift, especially after all the pain you've caused us. You've put us six months behind." How kind of Rose to offer death so freely. I liked the fact that she was blaming me for all of this.

"Aren't you kind? Too bad my boss doesn't believe in making deals. She doesn't like people interfering with her business. You are pretty screwed." Bartholomew was in the prone position, ready to start shooting.

"Your boss is a joke. She, as you called her, can't stop us." Rose was a bit too full of herself. "Enough games. Fire!"

Spells started flying over our heads. Bart returned fire.

"Constantine, any news?" I yelled.

"Your backup is right there." Constantine was like a kid in a candy store, busting with excitement.

"Who are we looking for, Constantine?" Bartholomew looked at me, confused. Neither one of us had a clue what Constantine was talking about.

"You're looking for us, silly boy."

Bartholomew and I were scared out of our minds. Jake was kneeling to one side of me, and Death was on the other side of Bartholomew. They had just appeared out of thin air.

Bartholomew didn't waste any time with pleasantries. "Oh, God. Where did you two come from?"

"Down the memorial. You two took your sweet time to get back here. Isis, I like the look. Sexy." Jake was playing with my hair as he spoke. I slapped his hand and tucked away the loose strands he was playing with.

"I told you I saw two people at the memorial. You were playing chess, right?" Bartholomew was not letting that go.

"Nice. I'm impressed. I figured those stupid trees were covering us." Jake was giving Bartholomew his best smile. He was in another fabulous outfit, this one with a red tie.

"Yes, I'm that good. So, who won?"

"Trust me, little man, never play against Death. You never win." Jake gave Death a wink, and she smiled back. I had no idea how they made kneeling look good. It wasn't fair.

"You two were playing chess while we were getting chased by witches." I gave them an incredulous look. The witches had stopped throwing spells and were quiet.

"You had things under control, Isis. Besides, what's the point of having an intern if I have to save you every five minutes?"

I wasn't sure whether that was supposed to be a compliment or an insult.

"Thanks. Why are you hanging out with the devil?"

Death smiled as if this were just another day at the park. Only Bartholomew and I looked worried about the situation.

"Jake is one of our biggest clients, remember? I figured I'd save him the delivery cost and have him collect his own packages." Death smiled kindly at Jake. "Besides, these girls enjoy a flare for the dramatic. It's about time they experience a taste of it. It's only fair." Death was looking at her nails as she spoke. She looked at me, and there was nothing but coldness and emptiness in her eyes. For the first time, I was truly terrified of Death.

"Isis, watch your head." Bartholomew pulled me closer to the ground. My mind had gone completely empty staring at Death. It was a blessing he did; the witches were back to throwing spells. One flew by my head and slammed against the building.

"Thanks, Bart."

"No problem. Are you two going to handle them? We're almost out of bullets."

"We got this, Bartholomew. Jake, would you like to go first?" Death was arching an eyebrow at the devil.

Jake gave her the most predatory smile I'd ever seen. "It will be my pleasure." In one smooth motion, he was up and straightening his suit.

Death followed close behind him. She was wearing a three-piece black suit. She looked immaculate; even her hair was perfectly combed, not a strand out of place.

"I would recommend you two stay back here." Death didn't have to tell us twice. We nodded in full understanding. I joined Bartholomew on the ground to watch the crazy scene.

"Who the hell are you?" Rose was eyeing Jake with hatred. "I recommend you leave while you still have time. This is not your fight."

"Tempting. Unfortunately, my friend over here made me a better offer."

Death walked over to Jake and placed her hand on his shoulder. "I heard you were looking for me."

By the looks on the witches' faces, I was pretty sure Death did not look to them like the fine-looking woman Bartholomew and I were seeing. Their faces were pale.

"Death." There was true fear in Rose's voice. "You won't take us. Ladies, now." The witches looked like synchronized dancers. They took aim at Death and Jake and fired. They were so quick; I didn't have time to scream.

To the surprise of the witches, Jake and Death didn't need any shields. Instead, Jake absorbed their spells into the palm of his hand. He closed his fingers over the spells and dissolved them into sand. The witches were staring at him in pure horror. I didn't blame them. I was terrified. I didn't know which one was doing it—either Death or Jake—but the temperature had dropped at least forty degrees. We were shivering.

"That was impressive. Scary as hell, and so impressive," Bartholomew whispered.

"This is not going to end well for them." I looked at Bartholomew, and he nodded.

"Cute. Not bad for amateurs. Too bad you went independent; you had potential. My turn." Jake was taunting them. He looked like a lion playing with his food. After everything they had done, I actually felt sorry for them. Jake pointed a finger at them. "Ready for real power?"

Death looked over her shoulder at us. "Isis, incoming." Her words were almost a whisper to me.

"Oh, crap." I dropped my gun, pulled Bartholomew toward me, and covered his face. "Bart, close your eyes."

I didn't have enough time to think. I closed my eyes and tried to get us as low to the ground as I could, covering Bart with my body. Whatever Jake let loose was almost like a nuclear bomb. I heard the screams of the witches. The air smelled of burned hair and meat. The truck in front of us took a major hit and was lifted over us. Bartholomew and I screamed. The force of the blast was so strong, we were slammed against the building. Everything went dark very quickly.

Chapter Thirty-Eight

Ouch! Everything hurt, including my spirit. I opened my eyes to a dark room. By the smell of the sheets, I realized I was in my bed. I didn't have to guess this time. Instead, I just spoke.

"Hi, Death."

She snapped her fingers, and my night light came on. Who needed the Clapper when Death was around?

"We need to stop meeting like this."

As usual, she just smiled. "At least you haven't lost your sense of humor." Once again, I was wearing PJs, and Death had on what appeared to be a ball gown. Who dressed her? "How do you feel?"

"Like roadkill." The fogginess that had covered my brain was slowly lifting. "Where's Bartholomew?" I tried to get up. "Oh God, this hurts."

Death was by my side in the blink of an eye. "He's fine. You took the majority of the blast. Try to relax now." She arranged my pillows again and sat on the bed. She was spending a lot of time tucking me in. At this rate, she was going to surpass my godmother.

"What happened?" At least I didn't have to struggle to look at her now.

"The usual. Jake needed to show off. He doesn't take it very well when humans try to outdo him. Especially arrogant ones who fail to recognized him." There was no judgment in her voice—just facts.

"How are we going to explain a nuclear blast in the middle of downtown Texarkana? And all those bodies?" Was it part of my job to come up with cover stories? I was really bad at that. I was starting to panic.

"Isis, breathe. Constantine took care of it. The news will be reporting a propane gas truck lost control and crashed into two vehicles in front of the post office. Horrible tragedy. Nine women dead, and a few men injured." Death winked at me and brushed my hair off my face.

"Are people going to believe that?" That was one hell of a cover story.

"A couple of eyewitnesses on the scene will corroborate it, and the story will hit the front page. A very horrible accident, nobody is going to think too hard on it. Humans don't want to hear about the supernatural world; simple works every time."

"Who did he get to be an eyewitness to that mess?" Last time I'd checked, all the witnesses were dead or beaten the hell up.

"It seems your friend Shorty was just around the corner when he saw the truck speeding down State Line. Imagine that." Death looked pretty innocent as she spoke.

"Yeah, imagine that." I didn't want to know how Shorty had gotten there and where Constantine had found a propane gas truck in Texarkana.

"You need rest, Isis. But, unfortunately, Constantine won't let you sleep till you eat something. He's been trying to give you an IV since you arrived. I recommend food instead."

"Does every intern have this much fun?"

"Some don't have nearly this much excitement in a lifetime, dear. Not bad for your first week. Not bad at all, Isis." She smiled kindly. Death truly cared about her interns. I don't know how she did it, having to see so many leave her so soon. "I can help with the pain, but you'll have one hell of a sunburn for a few days. Your hair will need some treatment as well."

"I'll take all the help I can get."

Death kissed my forehead, and, like magic, the pain eased from my body.

"Thank you." I was so relieved, I wanted to cry.

"Anytime, dear. Go check in with Constantine before he sends in the National Guard. I'll see you soon." She patted my cheeks and headed out the door.

I was not a hairy person, but even the few hairs I had on my arms were gone. Bad sunburn was an understatement. I was radiating. I didn't believe it was possible for a brown girl to burn, but I was proved wrong. I was making mental notes to avoid the devil at all costs. I was planning to spend a lot more time in church and out of the club.

I walked into the kitchen, and Constantine was pacing back and forth on the kitchen island. He was giving orders to somebody. I was afraid poor Bartholomew was up already. Nobody was in the kitchen. Constantine was talking into one of the walkie-talkies we had in the house.

"Isis, it's about time you were up. How do you feel? Never mind that. You look like hell. That's probably how you feel." That was definitely a first—Constantine was asking and answering his own questions all at once.

"Hi to you, too, Terminator. Who are you yelling at?" I opened the fridge and grabbed some milk. I felt parched.

"Hi, Isis." I turned around to find Bob entering the loft with two large bags.

"Bob!" I put the milk on the counter and shuffled over to Bob. I gave him a huge hug. He was careful not to hurt me.

"Death said to be careful with you and Bart till you're completely healed. You don't look so bad for surviving a giant blast." Bob was looking at me very carefully.

"Bob is right. You don't look half-bad. Of course, you're going to peel. Abuelita sent you some ointments, and she said you need to start using them now. She also wanted to thank you for watching over that crazy grandson of hers." Bob was pulling bottles from the bag as Constantine explained. "Eric also made you and Bartholomew more shakes. He said they'll help with healing and raise your immune system."

"Abuelita and Eric were here?" I was looking at the stack of bottles Bob had pulled out.

"Of course not. In your condition, we're not taking any visitors. We also canceled practice till next week so you can heal properly." Constantine had canceled practice. I was in worse shape than I had imagined. "I also told Abuelita you won't be going in for another week. We don't need any rumors of your condition linking you to downtown."

"So, we quarantine Reapers. How are we going to get food?" I really didn't want to starve to death.

"What do you think Bob has been doing? Girl, please. We're not new at this. Well, at least I'm not."

Constantine was still rambling when things finally clicked for me. "Bob, are you staying?"

Bob had a huge smile on his face. This was the best news I'd had in weeks. "The boss here talked to Death, and she agreed to hire me. I have the rooms by the entrance. They're fully furnished. I'll be in charge of security and even maintenance of the vehicles."

"Bob takes better care of the cars than you do. You're a menace on wheels." Constantine was cleaning his face with his paw as he spoke.

"I hope you don't mind..." Bob was looking worriedly at me.

"Mind? Of course not. Bob, this is awesome news. I'm so happy you're joining us. Are you sure you want to work with us?" This was a crazy life. I wanted to make sure Bob was OK with it.

"Isis, this is the best job I've had since leaving the army. For the first time, the nightmares make sense. I have a purpose again."

"In that case, welcome to the family." I grabbed the milk again.

"Stop. First the shake, and then the milk. We need to start your healing. You're not going to be lying around here doing nothing forever." I knew Constantine's caring demeanor was not going to last long.

Thank God Eric's shakes were good. They all had peanut butter for some strange reason. I grabbed a bottle and headed to the kitchen table. I looked out the glass window and saw a new car next to Bumblebee. The thing was covered with a tarp, but the shape was very familiar.

"What's that?" I pointed toward the garage.

"Your new car just arrived." Bob looked very excited as he moved toward the window.

"My new car? When did I get a new car?" What had I missed? I got up and moved next to Bob.

"You were not expecting to drive Bumblebee forever. That's our ride. You might blow it up." Constantine was standing near Bob. When had those two bonded so well?

"Can I go on the record and clarify that I did not blow up the Whale? That was not my fault."

"Isis, car, vans, and even trucks tend to explode when you're near them. So, to be on the safe side, we got you a Mini Cooper.

Low to the ground, fast, and a lot more stylish than that van of yours."

I was staring dumbfounded at Constantine. He had bought me a new car. And not just a new car—I had a Mini Cooper. Yes!

"What color?" I was ready to run downstairs and check it out.

"Midnight blue, of course. Are you doubting my taste in vehicles?" Constantine was giving me the evil eye.

"Constantine, I could hug you. You are amazing."

Before I even tried, he raised his paw. "Child, sit your butt down. Which part of 'injure' do you think I was kidding about?" He was trying to be serious, but he couldn't hold the glare. "Oh, come over here and let me pet you."

I jumped out of my chair and hugged Constantine. I scratched him behind his ears and rubbed his head. He purred loudly. Every once in a while, Constantine behaved like a normal cat.

"OK, enough now. You're messing up the fur." He was still purring as he spoke. "Remember, shake and then bed. You need rest."

"What are you two going to do?"

Bob was already heading toward the door, and Constantine was following him.

"We got a shipment in that we need to inventory. Bob has some ideas about remodeling downstairs that we are going to discuss. In other words, business as usual. Rest, Isis. You've had a busy week."

"Good night, Isis. See you tomorrow," Bob said. He was smiling from ear to ear.

"Good night, Bob. Don't work him too hard, Constantine."

"Yeah, yeah. It didn't take him three days to decide he wanted the job. So, I'm pretty sure Bob is fine. Rest now." Bob was holding the door for his evil dictator. "By the way, Isis, nice job." They were both out the door.

I took my shake to the couch and dropped down. I couldn't believe it had only been a week. I had been beaten up, blown up, and nearly executed several times, and, somehow, I had made it and saved the hostages. Not only that—I now had a family. Not your traditional family, but who needed traditional when you worked for Death? Not a bad week for a girl who had no idea what she was doing.

I finished the shake and curled up on the couch. I could see Bob and Constantine roaming the shop downstairs. Not a bad week at all. I closed my eyes and smiled to myself, wondering what tomorrow would bring.

Are you ready for the next installment of the Intern Diaries?

Even after eight months on the job, Isis is still surprised about the madness of the supernatural world. This time she has to face the walking dead. Continue the adventure in <u>PLAGUE UNLEASHED</u>.

Acknowledgments

Dear Reader,

Sometimes, thank you is not enough to truly express our gratitude and love for you. You are the reason we create these world and stories. If you reached this letter, I hope that means you enjoy Isis's adventures and the world of the Intern Diaries. Thank you so much for joining this journey with me.

Isis and the crew are very dear to me, but their adventures are just getting started. We just explored a small glimpse of the supernatural world, and the madness that is about to unfold in Texarkana. If you are in the Texarkana area, do take a ride around Isis's home turf.

If you enjoy the story, please consider leaving a rating and possibly a short review. Your reviews help others find the books you love.

With love,
D. C.

About Author

D. C. Gomez was born in the Dominican Republic, but grew up in Salem, Massachusetts. She studied film and television at New York University. After college, she joined the US Army, and proudly served for four years.

Those experiences shaped her quirky, and sometimes morbid, sense of humor. D.C. has a love for those who served and the families that support them. She currently lives in the quaint city of Wake Village, Texas, with her furry roommate, Chincha.

To learn more about D.C. and all her projects, check out her website at www.dcgomez-author.com.

Also By D. C. Gomez

In The Reapers' Universe- Urban Fantasy Books
The Intern Diaries Series
Death's Intern- Book 1
Plague Unleashed- Book 2
Forbidden War- Book 3
Unstoppable Famine- Book 4
Judgement Day- Book 5
The Origins of Constantine- Novella
From Eugene with Love- Novella
Rise of the Reapers- Novella

The Order's Assassin Series
The Hitman- Book 1
The Traitor- Book 2

The Elisha & Elijah Chronicles (UF and Post-Apocalyptic)
Recruited- Book 1
Betrayed- Book 2 (coming 2023)

Humorous Fiction
The Cat Lady Special – Book 1
A Desperate Cat Lady – Book 2

Young Adult
Another World

Children's Books
Charlie, What's Your Talent? – Book 1

Charlie, Dare to Dream – Book 2

Devotional Books
Dare to Believe
Dare to Forgive
Dare to Love